THE GALACT

Kirk was about to stop her when Chekov interrupted—he hadn't even finished sitting down. *"There isn't time,"* he said flatly. And the expression on his face was one of near terror. As heads swiveled in his direction, he said, "That ship—the *Wanderer*—in thirteen months, it will be beyond all help."

"Eh?"

"They're headed for Ellison's star—a catastrophic variable—in fact, it's the largest catastrophic variable in this spiral arm of the galaxy."

"But that's almost two light years away—surely we can do something to keep them from hitting the star—"

Chekov shook his head. "It's not quite that simple. What is going to happen is that the star will exert just enough pull on them to make an alteration in their course—a significant alteration. They're going to be pulled into a new course a hundred and eleven degrees off their previous heading. And that new course will put them headed straight toward—" Chekov paused, and Kirk could see the beads of sweat on his forehead, "—straight for the *galactic whirlpool."*

Be sure to ask your bookseller for the Bantam Spectra Star Trek titles you have missed:

SPOCK MUST DIE! by James Blish
THE GALACTIC WHIRLPOOL by David Gerrold
THE FATE OF THE PHOENIX
 by Sondra Marshak and Myrna Culbreath
STAR TREK: THE NEW VOYAGES edited by
 Sondra Marshak and Myrna Culbreath
STAR TREK: THE NEW VOYAGES 2 edited by
 Sondra Marshak and Myrna Culbreath
TREK TO MADWORLD by Stephen Goldin

THE GALACTIC WHIRLPOOL

A Star Trek™ Novel

by David Gerrold

BANTAM BOOKS
NEW YORK • TORONTO • LONDON • SYDNEY • AUCKLAND

THE GALACTIC WHIRLPOOL
A Bantam Spectra Book / October 1980
2nd printing ...... March 1981 *4th printing .... July 1984*
3rd printing ..... October 1981 *5th printing ... December 1985*
6th printing . . . August 1989

Published Under Exclusive License from Paramount Pictures Corporation, the Trademark Owner.
Star Trek is a Trademark of Paramount Pictures Corporation. Registered in the United States Patent and Trademark Office.

ISBN 0-553-24170-2

Published simultaneously in the United States and Canada

Bantam Books are published by Bantam Books, a division of Bantam Doubleday Dell Publishing Group, Inc. Its trademark, consisting of the words "Bantam Books" and the portrayal of a rooster, is Registered in U.S. Patent and Trademark Office and in other countries. Marca Registrada. Bantam Books, 666 Fifth Avenue, New York, New York 10103.

PRINTED IN THE UNITED STATES OF AMERICA

KR 15 14 13 12 11 10 9 8 7 6

For Jon and Molly
and Matthew and Cindy

Introduction

My first exposure to David Gerrold's writing drew this comment in a memo to Gene L. Coon in regard to the submitted story outline for what would become "The Trouble With Tribbles": "I think this is a whimsical idea, and certainly better than a couple assignments we already have in work. Suggest we buy the story and get an experienced writer to do the script. . . ."

As I looked up the notes on this opening paragraph, I realized I have known David thirteen years. Not only that, but he is still a close and dear friend. I must like this man. And I do—but it took a while. When we first met, he was a young man just out of college and inclined to be brash, especially about his writing; and I had already established myself as a writer and story editor in the television industry. I had fought my way up through the ranks, which then, as now, were not especially welcoming to young writers; and I firmly expected him to do the same.

He did—but that took a while too. I watched from a slight distance as David learned his lessons the hard way—the way all writers must—by writing. First a few scripts, then short stories and his first novel, editing an anthology of science fiction, collaborating with Larry Niven on another novel. We actually became good friends in that interim between the end of the STAR TREK series in early 1969 and the beginning of the animated series in 1973—when we found ourselves together on panels and giving talks at TREK conventions all over the country. David has since worked for me (on STAR TREK ANIMATED, FANTASTIC JOURNEY, and LOGAN'S RUN); I have worked for him (on LAND OF THE LOST and an early version of BUCK ROGERS); we both know each other's excuses for why the story is late. (It always is.) David has earned his credentials as a writer, as four Nebula and three Hugo nominations attest—as the winning of the E.E. Smith Memorial Award for Imaginative Fiction also attest. You hold in your hands his eighteenth book, STAR TREK literature which is a very long way from "a whimsical idea" that just might be worth risking some story money on.

It is said writers are revealed in their work, and it is true all writers put pieces of themselves and their experience (sometimes their fears and their dreams) on their pages. If you've seen David at conventions—emceeing a costume competition or competing in one, smoothly chairing a panel, dramatically reading sections of his work, delivering a talk on the state of science fiction or of "the art" in general—you may have developed an idea of who he is and how he is. But you wouldn't really know him.

If you've read other Gerrold books, you may feel you know a great deal about him, but you won't. (After all, David does appear in most of his own books, even if only as a young, skinny ensign assigned to some routine spaceship duty.)

David is many complex pieces, sometimes never seen by the reading or convention-going public. Here are some of them:

There is the David who served conscientiously at a convention, which included his sitting for three hours while difficult and uncomfortable PLANET OF THE APES makeup was applied so he could appear for his master of ceremony chores as "Cornelius." After a long and tiring day, he wended his way up to the bar —still in APES makeup and costume—and asked for a banana daiquiri. The bartender looked him over and replied, "We don't serve gorillas in here." Whereupon David straightened up with great dignity and snapped, "Racist. I'm a *chimpanzee*!"

There is the David whose immediate response, upon hearing that a friend or a project is in some kind of difficulty, is, "Sure. What can I do to help?"

There is the David who was deeply affected when Dog, the companion of his early, struggling writing days died. Later he haunted the pound until a shaggy white female pup appeared, and he paid one hundred thirty-two dollars for her, fiercely outbidding everyone else, because the pup was the image of Dog. David always said he was strictly a canine person, but on his way out of the pound with the new member of the household, David saw a thin, big-eyed tortoiseshell cat and her single orange kitten sitting forlornly in a cage. "Them too," he told the manager—and the Gerrold ménage acquired its first two feline residents.

There is the David who encouraged, taught, gave constructive criticism and challenges to a number of young writers, among them Kathleen Sky and Diane Duane. And he negotiated their first contracts for them as well.

There is the David who asked me to come with him and take a mutual writer friend out to dinner one night—because that particular gentleman was one who always picked up the check for everyone else, and no one had once thought to pick up one for him. Except David.

As I said, there are many aspects to David. In this latest adventure of the USS *Enterprise* and her crew, you will encounter the sensitivity, the sparkling sense of humor, the intelligence, and the surprises of this incisive storyteller. Sit back and enjoy your journey with him.

D. C. Fontana

THE GALACTIC WHIRLPOOL

1

Space. The final frontier.

A void as empty as death.

A billion times a billion stars gleam like motes of sorrow, whirling to the stately gavotte of time—like distant particles of dust caught and illuminated by a silver moonbeam, they are tiny beacons, each one a home for hope, no longer quite as distant or unreachable. No longer quite so infinite.

But still—*so very far away . . .*

The mind cannot comprehend the vastness. The *emptiness.* The silence . . .

Here, even the dust of space is measured in the number of atoms per cubic kilometer.

And in this emptiness, *something* moves . . .

A tiny metal speck. Almost insignificant.

So alone.

So far from home . . .

So far away from anything—

—From a closer perspective, the speck is a mighty vessel. A ship of metal and dreams, surrounded by stars too far and emptiness too deep.

And inside—four hundred and thirty souls share a dream: to boldly go where none have gone before. To seek out new life. New worlds.

So much of the universe is unknown. *So much of it is beyond the knowing. . . .*

And yet humanity goes, humanity searches.

The United Starship *Enterprise.*

NCC 1701.

She is the pride of Starfleet, the pride of humanity.

But most of all, she is the pride of her captain, one

James Tiberius Kirk, a man of singular determination and ability. If he is not the finest commander in the fleet, then he is certainly way ahead of whoever is in second place.

Years before at the Academy this particular ensign, James T. Kirk, had so excelled in one particular debate on the virtues of a republic that he was christened by his classmates, "The Last of the Claudians," a reference to the family that had produced the first six emperors of ancient Rome—Caesar (*aka* Julius), Augustus, Tiberius, Caligula, Claudius and Nero.

The nickname lasted about three minutes before a senior officer, an Englishman named Graves whose responsibility was the historical instruction of cadets, remarked, "The Last of the Claudians? Not bloody likely. A Claudian yes, but more probably one of the earlier ones—say Tiberius, perhaps."

The instructor had been needling James about the one fault he had that might possibly interfere someday with his judgment as a captain: his impatience. Sometimes it was such an overwhelming drive in the young student that it completely swamped whatever feelings of compassion he might otherwise have expressed.

Kirk used it as a reminder. When he found himself growing angry or frustrated, he would repeat it to himself as a mantra, a calming exercise of mind, "James Tiberius Kirk . . . James *Tiberius* Kirk."

It was the Tiberius that did it.

It made him stop. And think.

It was an unpleasant association and the memory of why it had been applied to him was doubly unpleasant. The name had once belonged to a man of *no* compassion, a man who had betrayed the responsibility to govern wisely over the lives that had been entrusted to his rule. Whatever other mistakes James T. Kirk might make in his life and in his command, he would not make that *same* mistake—he would not give anyone reason to compare him to his namesake. Instead, he would act in as rational and intelligent and *humane* a manner as he could, and that meant—*required*—that he always act in the most positive of ways. It produced in him a sense of *deliberate* compassion.

By the time James Kirk had assumed command of

the *Enterprise,* the process had become a conditioned reflex in his mind. He would think, "James Tiberius Kirk . . ." and the name—*his* name—would remind him of his hard-won standard of justice and morality, the one set of standards he held higher than any other code of behavior, even higher than the Starfleet Code of Ethics. The actions of one James Tiberius Kirk would be—*must* be—as admirable and unimpeachable as were humanly possible for him to maintain, regardless of external and arbitrary demands and conditions.

Often, he found himself standing by the side of his command seat, absent-mindedly drumming his fingers sharply once or twice on the arm or back of it. By instinct, he was a man of action, a problem-solver, a *doer* of deeds. He had an aptitude for making decisions, and that was what made him so valuable to Starfleet. There were better navigators in the fleet, Ensign Chekov, for one; and better, more logical brains as well—Mr. Spock, for another. But there was no one in Starfleet who was more *apt* to make the *right* decision in a moment of crisis.

It was his compassion; because it was so much an act of control, so much a conscious part of his decision-making process, there was no way he could ever lose it in an acid-bath of anger. There was always that extra moment of deliberation. When he drummed his fingers twice, impatiently, on the arm of his chair, it was not impatience at his decision, but impatience at himself for having to be consciously and deliberately humane instead of instinctively. He wished that it were a feeling of the heart instead of just a purpose of his mind.

But in the long run, it made little difference where the compassion came from—as long as it was there in the actions. And in James Kirk's case, Starfleet's judgment was correct. If he'd left his decisions to mere human instinct, he would have had more tendency to lash out at the things that made him angry and frustrated.

Like now, for instance.

A Klingon battle cruiser had been reported in this sector on three separate occasions, slipping in and out of the deep-space sensory nets like some elusive ghost.

No one was sure if it was really here or not, and Starfleet's most elaborate computers could give only probability estimates no better than hunches.

There was no particular threat . . . yet. But there were mining colonies on Mordred and Guinevere, two of the moons of the gas giant Arthur, (and a scientific station on the third moon, Lancelot, which followed in the Trojan position*), that were under Federation protection and the *Enterprise* had been dispatched abruptly to this otherwise unimportant quadrant to investigate the reports. This was a mission of true cold-war diplomacy, a show of colors to demonstrate that the Federation stood ready and willing to defend its rightful sphere of influence and maintain the rights of its citizens.

The Klingons were probably only "sharking"—testing the defenses, so to speak—but even those elusive feints had to be responded to. If the strategic policy-makers of the Klingon Empire sensed weakness in the Federation, they would move to exploit it.

Kirk had been carefully instructed on this mission: "Seek out unknown vessel or vessels in the quadrant and investigate. If said vessels are of a neutral or allied sphere of influence, offer them whatever assistance they may need, and do so with the full support of Starfleet and the Federation. If said vessel or vessels are of unknown nature, you are to use established procedures to initiate peaceful and friendly relationships. If, however, said vessel or vessels are of a hostile nature, your duty is to meet and withstand whatever threat may be posed to the safety of the Federation and its citizenry. You are empowered to take whatever steps you and your advising officers regard as necessary in such case, *up to and including the capture and/or destruction of said hostile vessels.*"

At the bottom of those orders, Admiral La Forge had added, "May you act with the spirit of humanity."

---

*If the Earth and the moon are thought of as the two points of an equilateral triangle, then the third point is the Trojan position. There are two Trojan positions, one traveling ahead of the Earth in its orbit, and one trailing. An object placed in the Trojan position will continue orbiting in a triangle with the host bodies. The Trojan position is a good place to station a space habitat.

Kirk had smiled when he saw that. The admiral was an old friend of his; the La Forge family had been breeding fine officers for Starfleet since Admiral George La Forge had commissioned the light cruiser U.S.S. *Detroit,* two hundred and seventy Earth-years previously. The current Admiral La Forge had been the one to recommend James T. Kirk to his appointment at the Academy so many years before. It was a trust that Kirk intended to honor through his service to the fleet.

He was willing to do whatever his oath to Starfleet demanded of him.

It was the *not* doing that was driving him crazy.

They had been *searching* the quadrant for twelve days now in an ever-widening spiral with its center at the last known high-probability nexus, but if there were a Klingon warship—or even any *other* kind of vessel—in the quadrant, they hadn't found it yet. Not even the remote-sensing, deep-space buoys reported any contacts. Or even probabilities.

It was *maddening.*

And in his impatience, Kirk even questioned Starfleet's wisdom in ordering the mission. If they dispatched a cruiser-class starship every time the Klingons feinted at the borders, they would be pulling men and matériel away from areas where they were badly needed. The Klingons could weaken both the defenses *and* economy of Starfleet just by a constant process of distraction.

But Starfleet knew best. Most of the time.

Kirk sighed aloud, a gentle exhaling of his breath.

"Sir—?" It was Lieutenant Uhura. "I beg your pardon?"

"Lieutenant?"

"I thought you said something."

"No—no, Lieutenant. I was just thinking, that's all." He turned his attention back to the big forward viewscreen. On it was displayed a computer-generated schematic of their search-vectors superimposed over a variety of probability wedges, colored according to their priorities. It could have been a routine training exercise in the simulator at the Academy, and with results every bit as insubstantial.

Kirk realized he was drumming on the chair arm again and forced himself to stop. He stepped across the bridge to the science station. Mr. Spock looked up from his hooded viewer with impassive eyes at the sound of Kirk's approach.

"Spock . . . ?" Kirk's look was hopeful. "Anything?"

"Negative, Captain—"

Kirk nodded in annoyance. "Somewhere there's a Klingon battle cruiser with a very self-satisfied captain. This feels like another one of Koloth's little maneuvers. He's probably laughing himself silly over the left-handed-quark hunt he's sent us on."

Spock replied with his usual careful indifference. "It is a well-known fact, Captain, that Klingons are easily amused."

Kirk had started to turn away—he turned back. "Mr. Spock, that sounded suspiciously like a joke."

Spock deliberately raised one eyebrow and *coldly* returned the Captain's stare.

"Sorry, Spock. I forgot myself." It was a gentle game that Kirk played with his half-Vulcan Science Officer. Chiding Spock was his way of trying to reach the *human* part of his soul. Kirk had never had reason to consider whether or not Spock appreciated the transactions. He took Spock's annoyance at face value. If he'd thought about the relationship at all, then it was the implied denial of Spock's human half that Kirk found—not grating—but somehow *illogical*. If such a word could be applied to Spock.

Spock lowered his voice thoughtfully. "Captain, while you're here, there is one . . . *anomaly* that one of the deep-space buoys recorded—but the readings are not clear. The anomaly was on the very fringes of the sensory net some time ago—and it was a sublight reading. All we have are probability factors on it."

"Could it be our Klingon friends?"

"It's unlikely. Not with these readings. A Klingon vessel at that distance wouldn't have registered. This is something either very large or with a very high sublight velocity. Or both. Whatever it is, the fluction of its singularity-envelope registers as the expression of a very large *realized-mass* with a specific vector quality."

Kirk eyed his First Officer with tempered amusement—Vulcans did love their jargon, didn't they? Never mind, he had the more immediate problem to consider. "But, it's *not* a Klingon . . . ?"

"No, not a Klingon," Spock confirmed.

"I don't suppose you have any . . . ah, thoughts on what the object *might* be, do you, Mr. Spock?"

"The *anomaly* could be an artifact. . . ."

"But—?"

"But it would be illogical to speculate without more information."

"Right." That was one answer Kirk already knew. Usually if Spock had any thoughts on a matter he included them with his report of the data; it was part of the personal efficiency which his Vulcan heritage demanded—but there was an equally compulsive quirk in Kirk's *psyche* that also demanded *personal* verification; he had to ask anyway. Kirk had always had the vague inner feeling that Vulcans were perhaps a little *too* deliberate in their logic, and that part of that deliberation somehow mitigated *against* the volunteering of information, even though his long experience with Mr. Spock had shown that such was not the case. At least, not with Mr. Spock.

Kirk began thinking aloud. "We *could* go check it out, couldn't we?" He placed his hands casually behind his back and rocked gently on his heels.

Just as casually, Mr. Spock took up a matching pose next to Kirk—but without the heel rocking. "It would not be illogical to investigate."

"And we have been searching this quadrant for twelve days without any evidence of a Klingon warship . . . and we ought not to go home *completely* empty-handed."

Spock nodded in agreement. "Starfleet would want the anomaly investigated in any case—we might as well save them the effort while we're out here. . . ."

"We haven't found anything else in this quadrant—and we have searched a very large area. . . ." And we are getting bored and frustrated; it would be a diversion. It would be good for morale. But he didn't say this last part aloud.

At the helm, both Chekov and Sulu were looking

up, bemusement gradually giving way to interest. Lieutenant Uhura also glanced up from her communications console.

"—but on the other hand," Kirk continued, now arguing the other side of the question, "—it is definitely *not* our Klingon phantom, is it?"

"It is extremely unlikely," suggested Spock.

"So—it could be considered a—," Kirk chose his words with care, "—a dereliction of our mission to break off the search and go see what this—this *anomaly* is, don't you think?"

"Undoubtedly."

"Even so—," James T. Kirk continued, pursuing the thought like a Socratic scholar worrying at a bone of contention. "Even so—what if this—this anomaly is something . . . " he brought his hands up before him, gesturing as if to enclose the thought, ". . . something beyond the experience of the sensory buoys . . . ? Some new Klingon tactic perhaps?"

Spock gave a sidewise nod of consideration. "That thought had occurred to me. It would not be the first time that a Klingon warship has tried evasive maneuvers specifically to confuse the deep-space sensory nets. I considered that perhaps the anomaly might be the sensory 'ghost' of a shielded vessel. . . . "

Kirk seized upon the thought. "Could you give me some odds on that possibility, Mr. Spock?" But he didn't want to seem *eager*. He continued to rock back and forth, staring ahead at the viewscreen.

Spock also gazed at the huge panel, as if in deep consideration. "There were none of the usual telltales that betray a shielded cruiser—I would hypothesize there's . . . maybe one chance in a thousand that it could have been a Klingon battle cruiser."

"One chance in a thousand . . . " Kirk mused deliberately. "One chance in a thousand. Even so, even if there *were only*—what was that, *one* chance in a *thousand*—shouldn't we investigate?"

Sulu and Chekov exchanged a glance. Chekov began setting up the problem on his astrogation computer. Sulu prepared to set up the new course instructions.

Spock suggested quietly, "There's probably not one chance in *ten* thousand . . . "

"One chance in *ten* thousand—," Kirk considered that.

"Perhaps not one chance in a *hundred* thousand . . . or even a million—," Spock continued.

Kirk turned his head and looked at him. "You're not helping with *that,* Mr. Spock."

"Sorry, Captain."

There was a smile in Kirk's expression now. "Yet wouldn't you agree, Mr. Spock, that no matter what the odds—whether it's a Klingon vessel or not—if we don't go, we don't find out what it is at all, do we?"

"There is that," Spock admitted.

"And our mission *is* . . . to seek out new life. . . . "

". . . *And* new worlds," Spock added.

"Then it's agreed." Kirk turned to the helm. "Mr. Chekov—"

"Already plotted and ready to go, *Keptin!*" Chekov said with delight.

Kirk was not surprised. "Mr. Sulu?"

"Locked in, *sir!*"

Kirk looked at Spock. Spock looked at Kirk with half-raised eyebrow. It was a shared moment of mutual understanding.

Captain James Tiberius Kirk of the United Starship *Enterprise* turned back to his helmsman and said, "All right, Mr. Sulu—let's go see what it is."

Sulu returned his Captain's grin and punched the button marked *Initiate.*

2

As a matter of fact, Spock had been brooding about the anomaly for some time before mentioning it to his Captain. It was one of those vaguenesses that carried just too much opportunity for error, and Spock wanted to be certain that there was something there before he reported it; unfortunately, the statistical likelihood of the presence of such an indicated artifact was so low as to preclude even the smallest level of certainty.

The *thing*—whatever it was—was definitely *not* the Klingon vessel they were hunting, of that much he could be sure; but what the measurements *did* indicate was an artifact so unlikely that his first impulse was to double-check the reliability of the reporting sensory probe to verify that this was more than just a hiccup of probability. The problem was that the singularity envelope of the anomaly registered so close to the sensitivity threshold of the probe's scanning equipment that there was legitimate reason to doubt the existence of the anomaly. There was no way to tell if it were an actual perceptivity fluction or merely just a momentary squiggle of residual instrument noise.

What finally decided the matter for Spock was a thorough check of the deep-space buoy's scanning equipment. The overall, cross-referenced sensitivity of the buoy was rated at —151 db, ± .2 db. The probability envelope of the anomaly registered only .85 above this threshold, but system analysis of the probe's instrumentation and computational capabilities indicated that a sudden deviation of reliability of even that small amount would also register on the verification circuits as a measureable deviation of the equipment's own reference levels. And of course, such a deviation would have triggered a corresponding downgrading of the reliability of the information by the logic circuits of the probe's own probability monitors. That such a downgrading had not been registered in the memories was a pretty clear statement to Spock that the probe, at least, was not in error.

The only *logical* conclusion was that there was a *stimulus* present. That much he was willing to validate. There was *something* there, very far away from the probe and only very faintly perceived, but still large enough and/or fast enough to effect a perceptible ripple in the sublight stress field, a ripple large enough to register on the equipment of a deep-space scanning buoy at a distance of several *trillion* kilometers.

Incredible!

It would have to be very large—the size of a small asteroid perhaps—and/or moving at a very large sublight velocity—perhaps as much as one-half the speed of light.

Simply incredible!

There were times when the maintenance of composure as mandated by his Vulcan heritage was a very difficult responsibility indeed. That he would have to wait some hours for additional information about the anomaly was almost enough to tempt him into a momentary flash of impatience. Not that he would ever display such a feeling, of course, but the mere internal existence of it in itself was enough to produce a qualm of conscience and possibly even self-annoyance. Spock took a half-second to note the existence of the thoughts, then filed them in that section of his memory reserved for such, along with a resolution to reexamine his regimen of disciplines. Perhaps he might schedule for himself the performance of an additional series of meditational exercises of emotional control; he must not allow the human influences around him to dilute his senses of analysis by weakening his internal control.

This entire process of analysis and resolution had taken him less than three seconds, and already he was wondering if perhaps he had taken too long to come to the appropriate conclusions—and wondered also if that were additional evidence of the human influences both within himself and without. However, Spock resolved not to pursue that train of thought any further —too much self-analysis was counter-productive in that it used up valuable on-time without producing worthwhile results. The Vulcan satirist, T'Pshaw, had summed it up thus: "Over-emphasis on the examination of one's rationality is a good indication that one ought to have one's rationality examined." The Terran philosopher, Solomon Short, had phrased it: "This neurotic pursuit of sanity is driving us all crazy." An unorthodox phrasing perhaps, but the thought was valid.

Having put a coda on that train of thought, Spock turned back to his science station and began preparing specific analysis programs for the anomaly when they finally closed on it. Its origins would be particularly interesting.

Behind him, Captain Kirk had returned to his command seat and was dictating a private note: "Captain's

Log, Stardate 4496.1. We have broken off our search to investigate the presence of . . . of a sensory anomaly. First Officer Spock notes the extreme unlikelihood that the anomaly is related to the object of our patrol; however, the anomaly is so unusual that investigation seems . . . worthwhile." He hesitated, frowning. What else was there to say? Nothing, he decided, and clicked off. "Lieutenant Uhura," he said. "What's the projected subspace radius at the anomaly . . . ?"

"One hundred and sixty-three hours, plus or minus twenty minutes, Captain." She turned in her seat to face him, one hand reflexively reaching for the Feinberger device in her left ear.

Kirk nodded unhappily. He didn't like being that far out of communication with Starfleet. It would take nearly seven days for a subspace radio message to reach the nearest starbase, fourteen days before they would have a reply. He grumphed quietly, then said, "Send a coded advisory of the situation. The *Enterprise* is assuming on-site jurisdiction for the investigation. We're invoking the Local Responsibility section of the Starfleet Code."

"Aye, aye, Captain." She turned back to her console, already encoding his instructions.

The Local Responsibility section of the Code not only granted the authority, but *required* a ship's captain to assume control of any situation within the Federation's sphere of influence and Starfleet's jurisdiction, but beyond the immediate control or advisory presence of a mandated starbase. A subspace radius of 36 hours or more automatically required the ship's captain to invoke the Local Responsibility section. It was a piece of busywork perhaps, but a necessary one.

When Lieutenant Uhura finished sending off the subspace message, she returned to her previous responsibility, the preparation of a set of contact signals should the anomaly turn out to be a functioning artifact.

Not only were the standard hailing messages required, a multiplex of signals that meant "friendly vessel," or its equivalent, to all presently known space-traveling species, but also a set of primary contact signals should the vessel be manned by members of an unknown race. While there were specific formulae to be followed, a communications officer was also required to make local adaptations as necessary. For example, the fact that this anomaly was traveling at a velocity that could be anywhere from one-fourth to one-half the speed of light indicated that faster-than-light travel was probably unknown to the builders of it, a fact which suggested that subspace radio capability was also unlikely. If so, then perhaps even multi-digital standards of transmission (which had not been developed by human beings until *after* the development of subspace radio) were probably also unlikely, and this would require additional modifications in the nature of the signals to be transmitted. There were too many different ways of sending and receiving information and one could assume nothing. If there were inhabitants within the artifact, which wasn't certain yet, then the *Enterprise* had to be prepared to transmit signals that they could not only receive, but translate as well. For instance, it would do no good to transmit an FM signal at 100 megahertz if the artifact were only capable of receiving AM signals at 100 kilohertz. And regardless of AM or FM, what if the information were digitally encoded? How many bits? And what sampling rate? How many channels per bandwidth? The problem became even more complicated when one considered the problems of broadcasting a video signal. What spectrum of colors are we referencing to? How many frames per second? How many lines to the scan? Or are we even scanning lines at all? Is it possibly a spiral scan? Clockwise or counter-clockwise? And so on . . .

Chekov's problem was no easier. It was his responsibility to determine the probable position of the anomaly, extrapolate its trajectory and plot a course of interception. He had only the single bit of information from the deep-space probe to work with, the vector quality of the object, nothing more—he had no precise measurement of its velocity. As a result, he was working with a four-dimensional (time-variable) vector wedge. The object's course probabilities were a cone-shaped fan of possible positions that widened astronomically as one traveled further and further from the original point of reference: the scanning fix of the deep-space probe.

He had begun by giving Sulu a course that angled away from the reporting probe's sphere of scanning and in the general direction of the bogey's one charted position; they could start from there. It would take a while to close that distance, and meanwhile he could use the time to develop a more accurate trajectory for the bogey. Assuming that the projected vector wedge was an accurate locus, they at least knew the limits of their search area. If they could come within five trillion kilometers of the object, they would be able to detect it. And as they came in closer, they would be able to correct their intercept course as necessary.

The problem was that lacking more precise information about the object's original velocity, Chekov had just too *large* an area of possibilities to consider. The deep-space probe's first bogey report was almost a month old and the object could be almost anywhere within a cone 45 light-days long and twice that distance across at its leading surface, a circular-boundaried area that expanded at the rate of one light-minute per minute. Even Earth's own solar system was only 14 L-hours in diameter. The *Enterprise* could very well end up hunting *this* object for twelve days too—or more—and with the same results as they had achieved on their Klingon pursuit. There was an old Russian proverb that was applicable here, Chekov mused unhappily; something about a "wild moose chase."

He sighed and finally decided to use what some navigators called "The Moscow Solution." He aimed straight for the center of the target, closed his eyes and prayed.

Actually, he used a *modified* Moscow Solution—he plotted an expanding spiral up through the center of the probability cone—but the principle was the same. You close your eyes and pray. And trust your luck.

Even so, Chekov was rather pleased with himself when he finally locked the program into sequence and called it up on the board for Mr. Sulu.

Sulu grinned at Chekov and began setting it up.

3

In all probability, there wasn't any object.

The odds were against its existence.

And if there *were* an object, then the odds were even more against its discovery.

By *any* system of logic, the chances of discovery were so miniscule as to border on the fantastic. The Notorious Murphy Coincidence would look inevitable by comparison.

But then . . . this was the U.S.S. *Enterprise* that was searching.

So they found it in 39:14 hours. And twenty-three seconds.

That was the initial contact. It would take another hour and thirty-two minutes to close with the object.

On the bridge, Captain Kirk was very pleased. "I knew they were good," he said to himself. "I just didn't realize they were *this* good."

The object was huge. Even from this distance, the instruments confirmed that it massed many megatons.

And it was fast. For a sublight object, that is. It was traveling at nearly one-third light-speed. In fact, the *Enterprise's* problem in rendezvousing with the object was not so much locating it, but *catching up* to it.

The paradox here was that most modern starships were built to travel either very fast or very slow. (On a cosmic scale, that is.) It's the speeds within those two extremes that are difficult to achieve. There is little need for a starship to travel at one-third the speed of light when it already has the capability of achieving realized-velocities many times the speed of light with its warp drive. And impulse power is more than sufficient for maneuvering within a star system, where higher immediate velocities would be wasteful and redundant. Impulse drive was efficient, to be sure, but like the ion-drive technology it was based on, it had its limitations. The use of it to push a starship up to one-third light-speed would take many days of acceleration.

The alternative was to brake down from warp speed, which was actually a much steeper gradient, but at least in this case, the *Enterprise* would be on the downhill side of the equation. It could be done by neutralizing the starship's warp fields with a carefully calculated discrepancy. The energy of that discrepancy, instead of being funneled back into the matter-antimatter units, would impart itself instead directly to the mass of the *Enterprise* and her occupants. If they had figured correctly, the energy would manifest itself as velocity, and they would have the one-third light-speed velocity they needed to match trajectories with the object. If they had erred, the energy would manifest itself instead as heat and the starship and her crew would be incinerated into raw plasma before their nerve endings would have time to register the fact.

The technique was tricky.

But then . . . this was the *Enterprise*. Kirk wasn't worried.

At the helm, Sulu had already begun scanning ahead with the visual sensors, even though they would have to be within a thousand kilometers for any kind of detailed image. He peered ahead eagerly. Beside him, Chekov was already preparing his deliberately unbalanced neutralization of the ship's warp drive.

"Fifteen hundred kilometers," Chekov said. "And closing." He touched buttons. "Warp-down procedures initiated. All systems green."

It was a tense moment. Kirk moved up beside his navigator and laid a hand lightly on his shoulder. "You're doing fine, Mr. Chekov."

"There it is—," said Sulu suddenly. A dark spot in the center of the screen, almost invisible. He touched a button and changed the scanning spectrum. The object glowed dimly red with radiated heat. But that was all it was radiating.

"Five seconds to warp-down," said Chekov. "Mark, and four . . . and three . . . and two . . . and one . . . and . . . " The overhead lights dimmed momentarily, then came back up to full strength. Readout screens flickered to indicate the sudden change in ship's velocity.

"—and we're still here," said Kirk quietly.

Chekov looked up at him. "Was there ever any doubt? I remember one time, at Gagarin Station, we had a simulation where—"

"Later, Mr. Chekov." Kirk pointed to a monitor. "You still have some fine-tuning to do. Use the impulse drive to make course corrections. Approach to 100 kilometers and hold position. Lieutenant Uhura, initiate contact procedures."

Kirk glanced up at Spock's overhead screens. The information there was neutral. The object gave no indication of awareness of the *Enterprise* at all. No radar, no subspace detectors, no scanners of any kind. At least none that registered on any energy spectra the *Enterprise* was equipped to detect.

Even so . . .

"Come to full alert," Kirk ordered. "All positions, stand by."

In one sense, at least, the order was redundant. The entire ship's crew was already alert. There were four hundred and thirty individuals in this ship, all possessed with an intense curiosity, a need to *know*. The view on the forward screen was being piped throughout the *Enterprise*.

As they came in closer, Sulu touched buttons thoughtfully. As he brought the image on the screen up to full magnification, there was an audible gasp of surprise among the crew members on the bridge. Even Spock appeared startled. Startled for a Vulcan, that is.

It was dark. And it was huge. It blotted out the stars behind.

And it was an artifact. A creation. Someone had *built* it.

But there were no lights on the object, no beacons to illuminate its many-faceted surfaces. No glittering windows or transparent domes. All was still and empty, almost bleak against the background of velvet and jewels. Here, this far from anything, lost in the deep between the stars, there was barely enough light to glint off an occasional metallic surface. There was no sense of scale—but even so the sheer bulk of it was ominous and over-powering. It was an undeniable presence.

It was a city in space. Huge and shrouded. A black island. A majestic wheel of silence and mystery, turning slowly in the night.

For a long moment, the silence of the dark was echoed on the bridge of the *Enterprise*. The men and women of the starship stood quietly, held by their own awe, caught in a rapture of contemplation. The experience was a familiar one to some of them. It was repeated every time they came into the presence of another facet of the universe's will toward life. An artifact, a ship, an alien being—even a message—it was the implication of the evidence that would make them stop and *wonder* at the marvelous variety, the infinite diversity of the cosmos.

There was a saying; Solomon Short, the Terran Philosopher was reputed to have said it, "There are no atheists on starships." But because he had lived and died before there were any starships, it was not until a century afterward that humanity began to understand just what he really meant. And by then, the truth of it was so obvious to all who had traveled through interstellar space that the statement was a cliché—except at moments like now, of course. Representatives of humanity stood once again on the threshold of discovery, and the truth of the cliché, the gut-wrenching reason why it was so, reasserted itself as a wave of joyous emotion, a bursting of feelings that surged up in the hearts and souls of all who stood before a screen and gazed in quiet amazement, smiling, grinning, even laughing and applauding.

Except Spock, of course. He prided himself on having the good taste not to display his internal processes; most emotions tended to be so *visceral* anyway. He would have made an expression of distaste, except that too would have been a show of emotion. He raised one eyebrow thoughtfully, noted that the object was "remarkable" in its own way, and turned back to his hooded viewer. To Spock, the joy was not in the wonder of the discovery, but in the knowledge to be gained from it. It was not the mystery that excited him, but the solution.

Kirk finally broke the moment of rapture; but even so, his voice was quieter than normal. "Mr. Sulu, throw some light on that object. Lieutenant Uhura?" He glanced back over his shoulder.

"Negative response, Captain."

"Keep trying. Mr. Chekov, approach to twenty-five kilometers. Then launch three probes. Mr. Spock, send a subspace squirt to Starbase. Update every fifteen minutes." He stepped to the command seat and touched the controls on the arm. "Mr. Scott, Dr. McCoy to the bridge please." He tapped quietly on the chair arm with his forefinger.

The first of Sulu's spotlights came on then, illuminating the *thing* before them and turning it from a hulking black shape into a fantastic concatenation of wheels within wheels, a spindle of ice and metal with graceful towers for spokes. A circular suspension bridge, wrapped around a cylinder, studded with industries. The eye could not resolve the wealth of detail, the turning shapes—new spotlights came on, sending new patterns of shadow across the artifact. And the remote-probes added their spotlights too, slanting their rays sideways across the many surfaces.

And in this bath of light the object was transformed into a ghostly vision. It came ablaze with reflected light. Metal and glass and mylar, plastic and ceramic surfaces glittered as brightly as the day they were first fabricated. The wheel was a city, the city was an island, the island was a civilization, rotating majestically in the dark valleys of the night. Spires and towers and minarets, bridges and turrets and platforms. And all was done in shades of pearlescent luminosity: pastel and glimmering colors, rose and coral and turquoise, a gray that was pink, veined with white and yellow. Shadows of purple swept across plains of pale sherbet. Diamond facets caught the light and arced it back; deep blue metal gleamed. The object filled the screen and kept expanding as they approached; its details swept around and around, rushing past the eyes of the *Enterprise* as if on some mad caucus race of their own; too quick to be perceived clearly, they blurred into the illusion of towns and villages, it seemed, airfields and highways, refineries, harbors—the eyes played tricks on the mind; or was it the other way around? The surface shapes of this—this *thing*—were too confusing. The mind translated them into familiar concepts for lack of referents.

Kirk had to force himself to turn away from the screen. The image was hypnotic. "Sulu, mute that." His expression tightened imperceptibly. "Tiberius . . ." he whispered. "Tiberius . . ." There was something about that thing—something that struck chords. History . . . there was something. . . .

The door behind him whooshed open. He turned to see Scotty and Bones entering together. "Scotty? What do you make of it?"

Chief Engineer Montgomery Scott was noncommittal. "Aye, it's big. That's for sure."

"I'd like to meet the designer," said Bones. "I'd like to shake his hand . . . or claw . . . or paw . . . or tentacle. . . ."

"I'd much rather meet the contractors," said Scotty. "Those are the geniuses for you. The fellows who made it work."

Kirk turned to face Spock, who was already regarding the three of them with the impassiveness of Vulcan impatience. "The real question, Commander Scott, is *why* it was built. *Who* built it and why is it *here?*"

All three of them looked expectantly back at him. "You have a speculation on the matter?" asked Kirk.

"Vulcans never speculate," Spock said. "The facts are this: it travels at one-third the speed of light. This fact suggests that the builders did not have warp drive. Neither is there evidence of impulse engines. The technology appears to be primitive—by our standards. The object's size is its compensation for lack of faster-than-light capability. It is a ship. An interstellar vessel, obviously, for we have found it in the deep between the stars. Its builders, perhaps recognizing that such a journey would take centuries perhaps, built not a ship, but a world. A civilization, if you will. They have been traveling on their journey for centuries and they have centuries of travel left to go." He paused and added,

"The engineering solutions to some of their long-term problems must be fascinating . . . . "

"Why aren't there any lights on the ship?" asked Scotty.

"Who would see them, Commander? They are light-years away from the nearest life."

"But what about communications?" Uhura broke in. "I've been hailing them since we first came in range, and there's no response of any kind."

"Perhaps they do not expect anyone to be calling them out here. They obviously don't have subspace capability."

"What about tight-beam laser to their base? Centauri colony and Earth used tight-beam laser-relays for almost a century before subspace was developed. Despite the four and a third year time delay, it was still better than no communication at all."

"Perhaps . . . " suggested Spock, "they left no one behind to talk to."

"Or perhaps—," interrupted Kirk, "—that ship is a derelict. Maybe its builders are long-since dead."

"That possibility occurred to me too, Captain; but it is the more hostile possibilities that are the immediate concern. The object radiates heat. That is evidence that life-sustaining conditions may still exist inside it. And that implies that something inside is maintaining those conditions. Something intelligent."

"It could be the ship's computer," noted Scotty.

Kirk asked, "Mr. Spock, what are its interior readings?"

"Confused, Captain. The outer skin is fairly well shielded." He looked embarrassed and turned back to his hooded viewer. Spock did not like having his limitations demonstrated.

Kirk turned to Scotty. "Can you transport a crew inside?"

Scotty shook his head. "I would*na* want to try it. If the outside is shielded enough to confuse sensor readings, I doubt I could get an accurate fix on a target site. And the fact that the beastie is rotating makes it almost impossible to insure field stability during reconstruction. You might slide into a wall before you'd finished arriving. Sir."

Kirk sighed. "I was afraid of that. All right—begin preparations for a manual entry. Just in case." He touched the button on the chair arm. "Executive staff to the briefing room please."

4

The briefing room of a starship has been popularly characterized as an austere chamber, an empty space between bulkhead and corridor, populated only by table and chairs.

The image is correct, but misleading.

The briefing room is actually a secondary information tank, the primary information tank being the bridge of the starship. The seemingly blank walls of the briefing room are in fact full-sized screens that can call up images from every computer bank in the ship.

What is not fully understood by the lay public is that this secondary information tank is also the singularly most important tool on the ship, even more important than the bridge; every other tool exists to amplify the power of a sense or muscle, but the information tank exists to specifically amplify the power of the brain.

It is here that a captain comes to consider the critical decisions of command, particularly the difficult choices that will test not only his crew and his ship, but his own strength, wisdom and compassion as well. These are the problems that are too large for one man alone and cannot be fully assessed in the privacy of his own mind, but demand the confidence of the ship's trusted executive staff—which is why briefing room sessions are *not* to be taken lightly. There is a Starfleet motto which is grilled into every new cadet from the very first day at the Academy: "All of your problems are solved first in the briefing room."

It is the captain's responsibility to make decisions. It is the advising officers' responsibilities to present all the information pertinent to that decision. Including their misgivings. *Especially* their misgivings. A captain needs information not only to support his operating thesis, but more importantly information that *tests* it, information that disagrees with it, and so forces the consideration of the problem from as many different perspectives as can be perceived. This is a Starfleet tradition, and few individuals have ever risen to the rank of captain without having developed a healthy respect for the wisdom of it. *The Worry of the Headstrong Captain* is more than just a bawdy back-room ballad: " . . . He has a doubt and dare not show it; he might be wrong, but never know it!"

In James T. Kirk, the respect for the Starfleet tradition of free discussion expressed itself in no expression at all; instead, he wore a carefully calculated mask of neutrality, one of deliberate blankness. He sat back in his chair with folded arms and let his various officers discuss the matter among themselves. He would enter the discussion only to guide it toward a consensus of understanding and eventual resolution (and there were courses in discussion-leadership that a captain had to have taken too). Usually, by the time a consensus was achieved, the correct decision had already made itself obvious and did not have to be arbitrarily made. It was amazing, sometimes, how events could work themselves out properly, if left free from the good intentions of a strong leader. And there was a Starfleet motto applicable here too: "The quality of a captain can best be measured by how well his ship runs without him." Responsibility, well-delegated, makes a crew responsive.

Spock was elucidating the options: "We can—and will—continue trying to establish radio contact on all frequencies. But we do have a probability estimate of better than 73.42% that if we do not receive a reply in three days, then there is no sentient life left aboard the vessel.

"Should we receive a response, of course, we will automatically shift into First Contact Mode and proceed according to the standard program until such time as deviation is mandated by circumstance. Failing to receive a response, we have two options. First, we can report its position via subspace squirt and return to our original mission—the search for the Klingon vessel reported in this quadrant. That option, of course, passes the decision on how to proceed here back to Starfleet, and in this case, such a course of action need not necessarily be considered a failure to take decisive action. This vessel has been in space a long time. A few weeks or months longer before we establish contact with them while we sort the situation out would not be crucial. We are not operating under a time deadline. Furthermore, the ethical boundaries of involvement—"

Kirk momentarily tuned Spock out. Something in the back of his head had *twanged* at a phrase in the Science Officer's monologue: ". . . passes the decision . . . back to Starfleet . . ." Now, *where*—? Oh, yes; now Kirk remembered. Truman. The buck stops here. No, Kirk decided privately; that would be equal to admitting that this was a situation that the *Enterprise* could not handle, and that would be equal to saying that James T. Kirk was unworthy of his captaincy of a Starfleet vessel. Therefore, it was not a viable option. But he didn't expect to have to say so aloud. After all, this was the *Enterprise*. If they couldn't handle it, who could?

"—Therefore, if we do assume the task ourselves," Spock was saying, "then we have to examine this situation not only from our point of view, but from the point of view of the inhabitants of the other vessel. If there are no inhabitants, that is no problem, of course; but, if there are inhabitants, then in all but the most improbable of circumstances, we are going to be *alien* to their experience—and to their world-view."

"And some of us—," interrupted Dr. McCoy with a wry sideways smile, "—are more alien than others."

"Dr. McCoy," Spock said drily, "humor is occasionally the highest expression of human intelligence; more often it is the last refuge of the incompetent." He raised his eyebrow at him. McCoy raised his own eyebrow right back. Spock, visibly annoyed—for a Vulcan, that is—said, "It would be appreciated by all if you would keep your responses pertinent to the problem. . . ."

Kirk smiled inwardly. "Go on, Spock," he prompted. Discussion was sometimes a misnomer here. Arguments in the briefing room could also be vicious, tedious and emotional. Spock and McCoy, for example, rarely missed opportunities to snipe at each other's philosophical positions, that being the only way they could express their affection for each other.

"That we are alien to their experience," continued Spock, "would seem obvious by the fact that their vessel is not capable of faster-than-light travel. A civilization aware of FTL drives would not invest so much energy into building a multi-generation ship. Therefore, it is not unreasonable to postulate that whatever we do in the process of contacting them may result in severe culture shock."

Kirk accepted Spock's hypothesis thoughtfully. "But it has been shown, Spock, that most spacefaring cultures, *regardless* of FTL capability, are usually already aware of the *possibility* of life alien to their own, even before first contacts are made—you can't travel to other worlds without first wondering what you're going to find there—and that awareness should significantly lessen the culture shock of first contact."

Spock nodded in agreement. "But the possibility remains. What we have here is a civilization isolated as no other civilization has ever been isolated. Furthermore, it is a civilization that has had time enough to become set in its structures; a kind of cultural petrification, if you will. It seems logical from the vessel's size and construction that the inhabitants of this ship had no knowledge of suspended animation or other hibernation techniques. Instead, they had to build a complete world to sustain themselves on their journey. That also implies that their lifespans are limited and that this must be a multi-generation ship. And if so, then it also follows that many generations have passed since its launching; we are light-years from any possible homeworld. Therefore, we are long-since removed from the original launching generation. They have never known any world but this one; this is the world that has shaped their psychological view of the universe. They probably imagine themselves to be fragile, alone—and somehow special in the eyes of creation. They do not even have the psychological influence of a primary star as a cultural stabilizing focus. To the people within, whatever they are, this world exists as a fact alone in the universe, separate and unique. They cannot help but have a distorted perception of their own relationship to the universe. The mere fact of their insulation from anything in its natural state would produce such an ignorance of the concept of nature—"

"Wait a minute, Mr. Spock—" That was Chekov. "That's all very well and good, but they would have books and tapes—"

"Mr. Chekov, you have books and tapes of your own. Do you believe a witch's hut could get up and walk on chicken legs?"

Chekov looked startled. "Of course it couldn't—that's just an old fairy story."

"But you have some very convincing holo-tapes of that story."

"But I still know that it's just a story."

"Not if you lived on Baba Yaga, an island off the coast of the southwestern continent of the planet Mussourgsky. During the wet season, different parts of the island tend to submerge and it is often necessary to relocate dwelling places in a hurry; that's why there are no permanent structures. Instead, most buildings are mounted on walkers. To the children who live there, *The Hut of Baba Yaga* is history, a true story, and that's how they know it. If you had grown up there, so would you." Spock paused and said in a more generalized tone, "The point is that the inhabitants of this particular vessel just a few kilometers beyond that bulkhead, may very well consider the stories of their own origin to be myth, despite whatever corroborating evidence may be in the memory banks, because as individuals they lack the personal experience that such things are possible just as Mr. Chekov lacks the personal experience of walking houses. These people have no way to tell—except by faith—which of their tapes are true and which are fables; if they are at all rational, they will tend to discard the outrageous stories as fable, and to these people, stories of planets will be outrageous. Whatever their *conscious* knowledge, it is the unconscious world-view that will determine their—if you'll pardon the expression—gut-level responses." Spock looked around the table at all of the other officers. "That is why I am suggesting extreme caution here. The kind of environment that they have built for themselves will generate severe psychological accommodations, and we are going to be testing most of those accommodations."

"Accommodations—?" asked Kirk.

"For instance, while they would certainly be aware of the requirements of their artificial ecology and the technology necessary to maintain it, that might be the outside limit of their view of all ecological science. The rest, of course, would be only theory, simulations in a computer; they would have little real knowledge of a state of existence not rigidly controlled and maintained. The concepts of 'wilderness' and 'freedom' might be meaningless to them. In such a world, dogma would be absolute because it would *have* to be. In such a world, there would be no change because change might be dangerous to the society's continued stability. Certainly, they would have outlets such as changing styles and sports contests and various sorts of competitions, but these would all be sublimations. The intensity of the culture's interest in any given outlet is a good example of how strong and necessary a sublimation it is. The essential fact of such a culture would be its resistance to major challenges aimed at its basic operating thesis; in this case, their uniqueness. We represent more than just an alien species to this culture; we represent an alien way of thinking. We might be so totally beyond their experience that they would not be able to perceive us in rational terms."

There was silence while the various officers around the table considered this concept and tried to deal with its implications.

"So . . . what you are suggesting," asked Kirk, "is that our presence might be startling enough to drive these people mad . . . ?"

Spock looked impassive. "Madness is not the term I would have chosen, as it carries strongly negative connotations, but the thought is correct. 'Irrational behavior' is a more applicable description, and a very likely result. If I may quote one of your Terran philosophers, 'Sometimes the only rational response to an irrational situation is irrational behavior.' We will be shattering their conception of the nature of the universe, and their feeling of their own uniqueness. Certainly, the fact that there has been no response to our attempts at hailing them speaks loudly as to the degree of their isolation. They obviously aren't listening for others because they don't believe there are any others." Spock concluded thoughtfully, "Of course, all of this is based on the unlikely chance—less than 27%—that there are sentient inhabitants of the vessel."

"Why is it so unlikely?" McCoy put in. "Someone had to build it. If they were smart enough to build it, why wouldn't they be smart enough to maintain it and keep themselves alive?"

Spock deliberately shifted his gaze away from the doctor and continued on as if he hadn't spoken at all. "Machines break down. Especially machines that are constructed by the lowest bidder. The chances of a failure on board any vessel increase with the passage of time. After enough time, a failure of some kind is inevitable. Given a long enough time, the cumulative impact of all the individual failures will make the survival of the ship's inhabitants problematic. Twenty-seven percent is a generous estimate."

McCoy spoke up in a deceptive drawl, "If that's how you feel, what are you doing about the *Enterprise?*"

Spock turned his head slowly and studied the doctor distastefully, "Dr. McCoy, the *Enterprise* was partially designed by Vulcans . . . and that should speak for itself."

Kirk allowed his smile to show. "Let's get back to the immediate issue here, shall we? We have a vessel. They don't respond to our attempts to communicate. We can't beam in, so either we find a door, or we break in. If we break in, there is every likelihood that the inhabitants—if any—will view such action as hostile. An invasion, perhaps. We must be prepared for the possibility of . . . military response. Scotty?" Kirk turned to his Chief Engineer. "What kind of weaponry would they be most likely to have?"

"Aye, Captain, it'd be a primitive sort. Faster-than-light's the key to a lot of advanced technology. Not having it, they'd not have phasers, nor any antimatter weapons, and probably not even magnetic disruptors.

There aren't any telltales on that vessel's hull. They could have paralyzers—but that would be a threat to us only if we're based on the same DNA vibratory frequencies as they are. They do have the capability of explosive-projectile weapons, but I would*na* want such weapons aboard *my* spaceship. I'd wager they'll be using electrical charge weapons instead. Stunguns or ballafires, most likely, but dart-projectors are possible too. They might also have various gas and chemical devices, but those are rarely instantaneous and possibly dangerous to the vessel's life-support and ecology systems; the same with biologicals, so I'd say that specific vector weapons are unlikely here too. Unless these people have had prior experience with humans, and if that's the case, then there's no tellin' what they'd throw against us."

Kirk accepted the report. One fact was becoming clear. He looked around the table at their serious faces. "It is obvious that we do not have enough information about that ship and the people who built it to make a full assessment of what we're dealing with. And it seems as if we are not going to get very much more information without boarding her. It is not a course of action that I want to take. But we are in a situation where we cannot decide whether we should board her unless we first board her to find out if we must. I don't like it."

There was silence around the table. None of the advising officers liked it either. But regardless of that, there was still the one rule sacrosanct in Starfleet, beyond all others: Article One of the Starfleet Charter, in which the essential mission of all who take the Oath of Service is clearly stated: ". . . to explore strange new worlds, to seek out new life and new civilization, to boldly go where none have gone before. . . ."

And that, after everything else was said and done, was the final authority on every decision, even outranking that of the captain.

But of course, there was no one who ever questioned Article One. You didn't join Starfleet unless you were already possessed of a hunger beyond curiosity, a need to *know*. The officers of Starfleet did their jobs not because they had to, but because they *wanted* to.

"All right," said Kirk, pushing his chair back from the briefing-room table. "Let's get on with it."

5

On the forward screen of the bridge, Mr. Scott had synthesized an image of the giant vessel, which wheeled almost as majestically as the vessel itself just a few kilometers away.

"What we have," Scotty was explaining, "basically, is a cylinder, ten kilometers in diameter, almost twenty-five kilometers in length. There are three fusion plants at each end. One of them may still be working. The thermal radiation indicates a low level of operation—either that or it's been shut down only recently—but I believe it's workin' because there's an ingenious heat-exchanging system still at work; they're using water to circulate the residual heat throughout the skin of the ship." Scotty's voice was tinged with admiration for the centuries-dead designers. On the screen, the synthesized image glowed red to indicate the location of the working fusion reactor and the lines of the ship's circulatory system which extended to the mid-point of the cylinder. "But only one half the vessel is heated that way, as you can see," Scotty said. "The other half, where none of the plants at all are workin', is cold. Whatever heat there may be in the after part of that ship is whatever seeps through from the forward section, the heated part."

Kirk nodded thoughtfully. Spock took a step forward and said, "Obviously, this is not the method of operation the vessel's designers had in mind."

"Aye, no," said Scotty. "The vessel is propelled by a set of ion-drivers. You see those twenty-four columns that run the length of the cylinder? Those are the magnetic tubes. They can be used in either direction, depending on the timing programs; very clever too, the vessel has the equivalent of twenty-four primary thrusters at each end. They can accelerate and decelerate on a trajectory without having to flip-over at mid-point." Again, Scotty grinned with admiration. "It's my guess that it takes two fusion plants to power those engines, and at least one more reactor to provide power for the vessel's life-support functions. That's the reactor that's workin' now. The propulsion plants are down, of course, have probably been down for some time because the whole system is cold. I mean *cold*, Captain. There's almost no detectable residual heat. They've obviously been adrift for a long time. Based on the most likely rate of heat radiation, those engines have been off for over a century."

"Over a century!!" That was Chekov, turning around to stare at Scotty, a startled expression on his face.

"Aye," nodded the Chief Engineeer.

Kirk raised one hand slightly to interrupt. "I appreciate your . . . ah, concern, Mr. Chekov, but as navigator, your talents will be better put to use tracking the course of that ship backward, looking for a planet of origin. Knowing that they've been adrift for at least a hundred years should give you an idea of where they were when they lost their power. Backtracking from there should give you some probabilities."

"The problem is not so simple, Captain Kirk," Chekov said in his heavily accented English. "The more systems they have visited since their launching, the harder the problem becomes—but I will solve it!" He added hastily, "If it can be solved."

Kirk covered his amusement by turning back to Mr. Scott, "Go on, Scotty."

"Aye, as you can see by the comparison of the diagram with the actual ship, there are a lot of things that have been added to the basic cylinder, that huge collar around the waist that makes it look like a wheel, for instance. That looks suspiciously like the collar for a hydrogen ramjet. And if that's so, then they only used their ion-drivers to reach ramjet speed, and then they'd switch over. But if that *is* the collar for a ramjet frame, what happened to the frame?"

Kirk rubbed his chin as he thought. No answer was obvious however. "What about entrances, Scotty?"

"Aye, there are some—but Mr. Spock had a thought about that."

Kirk swiveled in his chair, "Mr. Spock?"

The half-Vulcan Science Officer acknowledged his Captain with a slight nod. "If you will recall, Captain, I hypothesized the fragility of the inhabitants' world-view and the dogmatic buttresses that such a world-view would require, and the potential this creates for possible hostilities. It's my suggestion that we avoid immediate contact with whoever or *what*ever may still be living in the forward part of the vessel by entering through the rear. That will give us some opportunity to assess the situation *before* we have to assume a course of action."

"Sort of . . . case the neighborhood before we knock on any doors?"

"Eh?" Spock looked puzzled, then quickly sorted the remark as a colloquialism. "I believe that's what I said, Captain."

Kirk was too preoccupied to enjoy Spock's bemusement; he was studying the image on the viewscreen again. He realized that he was absent-mindedly biting at the knuckle of his right fist and forced himself to lower his hand. It began drumming on the chair arm instead. The problem was, he told himself, deliberate caution at every step—it made the whole process seem so plodding and so frustrating. Even when events moved at breakneck pace, which was almost always, it was the constant process of decision making—and the necessary process of deliberation that each decision demanded—that made the job so challenging.

But there were times—frightening little moments—when the answer to a question was *not* obvious, at least not to *him,* and yet an immediate decision still was required. It was in those moments—when he could see the validity of both sides of the question, but the preferability of neither—that he most had to depend on the wisdom and experience of his advisors. *Now* was one of those moments. Nothing would happen until he made the decision, and he, Captain James T. Kirk of the starship *Enterprise,* had to abrogate part of his responsibility to the perceptions of another.

Fortunately that other person was Commander

Spock, whose perceptions were generally extraordinary, but even that tiniest bit of surrender of control was enough to unnerve Kirk.

He realized abruptly that everyone on the bridge was waiting for him to speak. He looked around carefully, then said, "Yes, I agree. Let's proceed to the next step of that option. Put a crew down, Mr. Scott."

"Aye, Captain—we'll be puttin' 'em on the tail. And I'll be sending the first two over by shuttlecraft to anchor a TCP unit to the site. I'll not be having transporter problems if I put down a coordinating platform first."

"Right." Kirk touched the arm of his seat. "Ensign Susan Kelly report to shuttlecraft bay." He thought a moment, then added, "Navigation trainee Mante N'Komo to the shuttlecraft bay."

Scotty nodded and stepped back up to his own station on the bridge to order the shuttlecraft made ready, also a Transporter Coordinating Platform.

The shuttlecraft approached the giant vessel slowly; one more example of Kirk's deliberate caution. Ensign Kelly was piloting; trainee N'Komo was assisting. Kirk was still on the bridge of the *Enterprise,* watching from his command and control seat. The rendezvous was a simple task; Kirk had assigned his two junior officers to see how well they could handle the responsibility. He nodded with approval as Ensign Kelly brought the shuttlecraft into position directly behind the giant vessel, on the same axis of rotation, and imparted a spin to it that exactly matched the bigger ship's rotation. The great wheel-belted cylinder and the tiny shuttlecraft spun together as if they were on a giant spindle, but they were not connected and there was nothing at all between them; indeed, it was some of the purest nothing available in this or any other universe.

"Aye," said Scotty. "She's got an eye, that one." He turned back to his console. "Release the probe."

A small hatch opened in the nose of the shuttlecraft. A device that looked like a spider floated out, trailing a silver cord behind it. It moved steadily forward, toward the tail of the giant vessel, straight for the center of its rotation, the south pole axis. The probe touched, seemed to hesitate a moment, then anchored itself. The end of the cord remained attached to the giant vessel, but the spider began climbing back toward the shuttle-craft.

"Aye, good . . ." breathed Scotty. He turned to Kirk. "Contact crew has already beamed over to the shuttlecraft, Captain."

Kirk nodded in acknowledgment. "You may proceed, Scotty."

A few moments later, the spider began to travel down the cord again toward the alien ship. This time, there were two spacesuited figures and a TCP unit anchored to it: crewmember Second Class Micah Omara and crewmember First Class Ussef Stokely. The TCP unit was called George.

The men remained anchored to the grappling cord when they touched the hull of the alien ship. They secured the TCP unit immediately, and activated it. On the bridge, Scotty noted a bank of green ready-lights on his console and turned to Kirk. "We've got the transporter now, Captain."

"Good. Have the rest of the exploration team suit up and stand ready." He touched the communicator button on the chair arm. "Mr. Stokely, Mr. Omara, good job. You may initiate a preliminary survey of the vessel's exterior hull."

"Aye aye, sir." Both of them switched on their helmet cameras then, and anchored their suit-ropes to the grapple; then they released their safety loops from the cord. Because the grapple was at the center of rotation, they were weightless here; "down" was any direction away from the center. And the farther one traveled, the more "down" it became. Stokely and Omara were two human flies on a disk of metal under a rotating night; as they worked their way outward from the center, the perception that they were on a vast wall gradually increased. They were like two mountain climbers working their way down a steadily steepening slope—with the sense of gravity increasing every step.

"Don't look down," cautioned Stokely. "That bottom step's a dilly."

They were working their way toward one of the three huge containment domes that Scotty had identified as fusion plants. They were spaced in an equilateral triangle around the ship's stern.

Directly "above" them, a glimmer of light piled up on the transporter coordinating platform and two more spacesuited figures appeared, grabbing immediately for the platform's railing as soon as they finished materializing. They anchored their suit-ropes, as Stokely and Omara had done and began working their way outward and downward toward another of the fusion domes. Two more figures began to materialize almost immediately.

On the bridge of the *Enterprise,* auxiliary screens began to display the pictures relayed back from the individual helmet cameras. The metallic surface of the alien vessel gleamed only with the light of the beams from the various probes and the *Enterprise* itself.

Mr. Spock looked up suddenly from his science station. "Captain?"

Kirk looked over to him. "Spock?"

"The second team has attached microphones to the hull of the vessel. I think you should hear this." He touched a button on his console and the sounds were amplified throughout the bridge, sounds of machinery, and other sounds mixed with them: a mechanical whirring prevailed, something high and whining, overlayed with the soft susurrus of air in motion, and a sound like water falling, and another lower sound, a deep bass rumble, and something gurgling, and something that sounded like an old-fashioned motor chugging—and very far away, very faint and distant, a sound like . . . voices? A distant chorus of confusion.

"It seems as if somebody *is* home after all. . . ." Kirk swiveled around to look at Uhura. "Lieutenant Uhura, anything?"

She shook her head, one hand touching the Feinberger device in her ear. "Sorry, Captain. Still no response. I'll keep trying."

"Captain—" That was Scotty. "We've found something on the hull—"

On the screen ahead, the image unsteady—it was being transmitted from a helmet camera—was a deep circle set into the hull of the vessel. A porthole. The image swelled as the unseen wearer moved his face as close to the glass as possible. A line of print at the bottom of the screen identified the wearer as crewmember Stokely. He was shining his beam directly into the porthole, angling it this way and that, trying to pick out details on the other side of the glass. The beam disappeared into murkiness—

—then, abruptly and with terrifying suddenness, there was something at the window staring out at them! A face, grotesque and distorted through the glass—upside down, its expression almost unreadable —eyes wide with amazement or horror, swiveling back and forth to stare from one suited figure to the other, mouth agape with shock—the creature's skin was dark, wrinkled and fringed with matted hair.

Then, just as suddenly, the face was gone, and they were staring at an empty porthole.

On the bridge of the *Enterprise,* Kirk had come half out of his chair; now he lowered himself back into it. "Scotty," he said quietly, "beam over a cutting laser and a portable airlock. We're going in. Lieutenant Uhura, replay that tape."

Once more the porthole filled the screen. Once more, the terrifying face appeared in it.

"There, freeze it," ordered Kirk. "Now rotate the image till that face is right-side-up."

On the huge forward screen, the enigmatic face was frozen in an attitude of startled shock—but the expression was mirrored by those of the men and women on the bridge of the *Enterprise*. The inhabitants of that strange alien vessel were human—undeniably, incredibly human!

6

A portable airlock is standard procedure for boarding an unknown vessel, when use of the transporter is inadvisable for one reason or another. It is considered a breach of space etiquette to board a ship without direct invitation, but in those cases where a

Starfleet captain must take that step, it is an even greater breach of etiquette to breach the integrity of the other ship's hull, opening it up to deep space in the process of boarding it. In fact, such action has even been considered an act of hostility by some cultures, and is therefore specifically *not* recommended. The portable airlock is the most suitable answer for such situations.

The unit itself is a large inflatable plastic bag, a wide mouth at one end, an airtight door at the other. The mouth of the bubble-to-be is sealed fast to the hull of a ship. When the hull is opened inside this bag, the ship's interior atmosphere will fill the portable airlock; this, of course, will create a small pressure drop within the entered ship, but that is preferable to letting the air bleed off into vacuum. The larger the ship, the less noticeable is the pressure drop; in fact, for anything larger than a pleasure yacht, the overall change in PSI is negligible.

The portable airlock provides immediate access to the entered ship's atmosphere. Once the mix of gases, trace elements, temperature, ionization, humidity and pressure has been determined—and matched—a direct access tube can be connected. In the meantime, the most immediate step after the inflation of the airlock is the installation of an airtight door in the hole that has just been cut in the hull of the entered vessel; one more safety measure mandated by common sense as well as Starfleet safe-contact procedures. Once this is effected, the airlock can begin to function as an airlock, and individuals can enter the bubble through its outer door and from there, enter the ship itself. In this particular contact routine, Starfleet procedures mandated the connection of the access tube before entry was effected.

Kirk was almost too impatient to wait for the access tube to be connected from the shuttlecraft to the portable airlock. Once connected, the rest of the contact crew could beam directly to the shuttlecraft and then use the access tube to enter the alien derelict(?) directly without the necessity of suiting up first. But that face at the window—that made him hesitate.

It was definitely an example of "the bug-spot event."

At Starfleet Academy, Lunar Station, new cadets are instructed to put on a spacesuit and take a landrover fifty kilometers south to the moisture-extraction station, and then return. Ostensibly, this is a test of the cadet's ability to safely conduct a solo mission. In actuality, it is a test of his ability to cope with the unexpected. On the downhill side of the inner slope of perpetually-shadowed Gernsback Crater, just a few kilometers from the station, the cadet will quickly begin to notice the formation of what appear to be bug-spots on the faceplate of his helmet. Most cadets don't notice the flecks on their helmet until after they've tried to wipe them off two or three times; then they start to wonder, "Bug-spots?!! On the moon?!!" Of course, the answer is obvious. The wheels of the landrover are throwing up tiny dots of lunar dust that have clotted around precipitation from the moisture plant. But of course, anyone who isn't prepared to conceive of the specific and peculiar set of conditions under which "precipitation" can occur on a lunar landscape will never be able to understand the bug-spots on the faceplate of his helmet as he wipes and wipes and fruitlessly tries to clean them off.

There are several possible reactions for a cadet under these circumstances: he can turn around and return to base, he can continue onward to the moisture plant, ignoring the continuing buildup of bug-spots, or he can stop and report in. This latter response is ungently referred to as "calling for help." Cadet James T. Kirk had simply stopped the landrover, gotten out, looked at the wheels for a moment, walked around to the back of the rover, took two sheets of plasti-flex and a staple gun, and installed makeshift fenders above the rover's wheels. Then, before getting back aboard, he walked around the rover once more, just looking at it. Satisfied that he had not overlooked anything, he climbed back in and proceeded onward to the station—but just a little slower than before. The cadet evaluation team that had been watching him through the moisture station's high-power telescope gave him high marks for comprehension and adaptability in the face of unknown circumstances.

Nobody who fails this test will ever be promoted to the command of a starship. There are other positions in Starfleet for them; the captaincy of a Starfleet vessel belongs to the kind of man who can cope with the sudden unknown. Those who have taken the test are sworn to confidentiality; the "bug-spot event" is a familiar term to upperclassmen, referring to the unexpected occurrence that cannot reasonably be predicted and totally destroys all previous hypotheses about the nature of the problem. The "bug-spot event" demands an immediate reassessment of all possible courses of action, including the possibility that one may or may not have experienced a discontinuity of rationality. The "bug-spot event" is also sometimes called "a surprise."

Irrationally, one thought was chasing itself around in Kirk's mind. Whatever happened from this moment on, whatever explanation there might be for this derelict's existence, this singular moment—the face at the window—would be one of the ones most written about; not only in history books for the lay public, but also and especially in textbooks intended for cadets at the Academy. How he and the crew of the *Enterprise* handled themselves in the moments and days to come, and the decisions they made, would be scrutinized by unnumbered generations of space students. It was an unnerving realization.

Nothing makes a decision seem so formidable as history looking over one's shoulder.

Logically, he wanted to stop and assess the situation —but logically, he already knew that there was no logical assessment. His long association with Mr. Spock had taught him a little bit about logic and its relation to decision-making. This was one of those decisions where the worst course of action might be to hesitate. Whatever intelligence there was inside that vessel, they dared not give it time to prepare a hostile response. On the other hand, a mad rush to break into the alien ship might equally guarantee hostility from its inhabitants. But on the third hand (as Lieutenant Arex might say) . . . the portable airlock was already in place and inflated, and the access tube was being sealed into place. In effect, his decision was already made.

James T. Kirk had a reputation for rushing in where Andorians fear to tread, and one day that weakness would probably kill him—but he reminded himself, as he headed for the transporter room, "I won't send any crewmember anywhere I won't go myself." That was his usual excuse for actively involving himself at the forefront of every new situation, sometimes even pre-empting the duties of the contact team.

As soon as the portable airlock was operational, a bottled sample of the alien vessel's air was passed back to the shuttlecraft to be beamed to the *Enterprise* for analysis. By the time the access tube was sealed to the airlock, the correct mix of gases, and trace elements would be known. It was the very real possibility of hostilities that mandated the necessity of providing the quick escape of the access tube.

In an emergency, of course, an access tube would be connected directly to a disabled vessel's hatch, or if no hatch were available, to a "doorwell marker" on the hull where an emergency exit could be reasonably cut. But this was not an emergency, and there were specific procedures for this circumstance, procedures which had been developed to allow a starship captain flexibility of response.

The access tube was a clear plastic hose, large enough for the average sentient being to walk through, and ribbed with a fiber spiral to give it strength and help it hold its shape under varying pressure conditions. It led from the nose of the spinning shuttlecraft to a spot nearly four and a half kilometers from the axis of rotation. The vessel itself was nearly ten kilometers in diameter and some twenty-four kilometers in length. The gingerbread spokes of the wheel around its waist extended ten more kilometers outward from the hull. And, if Scotty's surmise were correct, they were only the remains of a larger structure. Interestingly, Spock had computed that the internal simulation of gravity, produced by the effect of centrifugal force, as experienced by an individual standing on the inner side of the spinning hull, would approximate 1.75 gee. An Earth-normal gravity would be experienced somewhat closer to the center of the vessel's rotation. At the point they had attached the access tube, the perception of gravity was 1.33 gee. The access tube was attached to the vessel at a 45° angle, so that at the point of insertion it functioned as a staircase.

Kirk was the first one through the access tube, with Spock close behind. They pulled themselves hand over hand along the handrails, until the sensation of gravity became strong enough for them to "skip" down the stairs, taking them two or three at a time; finally the ever-increasing pull forced them to slow down and proceed at a more careful rate. The dangerous thing about falling down an access tube like this one is that as a body falls, the pull on it increases, making it fall faster and faster. People had been killed by a careless step; that's why there were safety webs every ten meters.

At the bottom, the three-member installation crew—still in the sealed airlock—were just performing their final safety checks on the new hatch. Behind them, in the receiving bay of the access tube, Stokely and Omara were preparing the contact team's equipment for themselves and for the two senior officers who had elected to accompany them. As Kirk and Spock stepped *carefully* out of the stairwell part of the access tube into the receiving bay—they were acclimatizing themselves to the one-third higher gravity—Stokely stepped forward to hand each of them a phaser and communicator; he handed Spock a science tricorder, already calibrated.

Kirk nodded, and turned to the installation crew, still working inside the airlock. "How long till we can open it?" he radioed.

Through the transparent wall, he could see the cadet with the monitoring tricorder. She shook her head. Kirk didn't recognize the woman; she must have been one of the new trainees. She radioed back, "We're waiting for analysis to match the atmosphere."

But even as she spoke, her communicator beeped; it was the Analysis Lab. "Are you sure that atmosphere sample came from that vessel?"

"I took it myself. Why?"

"Because it's air."

"Air?"

"That's right. Oxygen, nitrogen, and trace elements."

The cadet looked confused. Kirk and Spock exchanged a glance. Kirk felt he should have been surprised, but he wasn't. Not after that face at the window. Somehow . . . this particular little surprise seemed exactly *right*.

Analysis was saying, "—oh, there are some differences between it and Earth-normal atmosphere; the pressure is a little bit lower, a slightly different mix of trace elements, and so on; but the overall mix is well within the spectrum of acceptability and almost approaches the optimum Justman Curve—and that margin of difference could easily be a result of specific life-support accommodations—but you can breathe it all right. The only caution is that there's a slightly higher concentration of CO_2, so I'd suggest taking auxiliary O-packs along with E-rations; you'll have a tendency to tire faster in there—especially at that 1.33 gee. But, other than that, there's no reason why you can't just open the door and go on in."

Kirk and Spock looked at each other again. Kirk looked around the alcove, the portable airlock with its newly installed hatch at one end, the stairwell hatch at the other so the alcove could function as an emergency airlock too. He looked through the walls at the access tube itself, the distant shuttlecraft, the Transporter Coordinating Platform high on the wall above them—all the careful precautions they had taken to maintain the integrity of the vessel's atmosphere—and grimaced in reaction. Sometimes all the precautions in the universe—oh, never mind.

"Open it up," he said.

7

They stepped through into the airlock, and pressed the panel to open the hatch. Three green ready-lights flashed, and the three overlapping safety doors whooshed quietly open. The space beyond was dark. A slightly moist smell wafted from the opening.

Omara moved cautiously toward it with a wide-angle flashbeam; he leaned forward to sweep the gloom, revealing a room not much larger than the airlock they stood in. Its walls were featureless. There was a door in the opposite wall.

Kirk was frowning thoughtfully. "Look at the thickness of the hull, Spock."

"Obviously, the designers lacked knowledge of stressed-metal shielding, which would imply that they also lacked knowledge of stress-field screening as well. But we could have surmised that. If they had knowledge of stress-field physics, they would also have had a faster-than-light drive." He added thoughtfully, "This hull is probably only an outer shell. I would not be surprised to find at least one or more inner hulls."

Kirk acknowledged the comment with a nod. He had been thinking much the same thing. The construction of this vessel was proving to be a sophisticated set of refinements on what was basically a primitive design.

Stokely sniffed. "The air smells stale . . . musty."

"It's safe enough, Crewman." Kirk stepped through the open hatch, switching on his own flashbeam as he did so. The room was featureless and gray. Spock ducked through the hatch, already scanning with his tricorder, followed by Stokely and Omara; they had shed their spacesuits. Stokely was tall and fair; Omara was short and swarthy. Despite their disparate appearances, they were one of the best contact teams in Starfleet. They proved it now; as Omara circled the room quickly, scanning it with a professional eye, Stokely moved to the door in the opposite wall. There was no electronic switch for it. It was set in a metal rail and latched with a mechanical lock. Stokely reached for the lock and turned it clockwise; it resisted for a moment, then clicked open.

Stokely stopped and stared at the lock then, considering the implications of what he had just done. He had opened the door. A little too easily.

The lock had been at just the right level. And it had

opened clockwise, as most human-designed locks do. He had known how to open it as surely as if he had grown up with doors built exactly to the same specifications. He looked a little stunned at the realization.

Kirk and Spock exchanged a glance. It fit the pattern. Kirk was beginning to suspect something. . . .

"Go on," he said, unstrapping his phaser. "Open the door."

The door stuck for a moment, then squealed in protest and Stokely shoved it open. Omara stepped past him to sweep the room beyond with light.

The second room was larger than the first, but otherwise it was equally featureless and gray. At the opposite end was another sliding door, but this one was open. The space beyond was shadowed in gloom.

Cautiously, they moved toward it, Spock holding his tricorder before him like a shield. Stokely unclipped his own flashbeam, and now there were three light-sources exploring the dark.

Kirk raised one hand for silence. "Listen . . . "

They hesitated. Omara guessed, "Water . . . ?"

Indeed, the floor here was damp, and from the corridor came the steady sound of water dripping.

A sudden motion in the dark—

They whirled, phasers ready—"Hold your fire!"

It was a round ball of color, floating a meter off the floor.

A bright red balloon?!!

Stokely and Omara exchanged glances. "Someone's having a birthday party?"

"Not quite," said Kirk.

They looked at him with sudden interest and curiosity, even Spock. "You know what it is?"

"It's a drifter. That's what they're called—or sometimes hoboes, tramps, air-bums. They're helium-filled bubbles. In the early days of space travel, all spacecraft used to have them. Now, only certain Academy training vessels and historicals have them. They're used to locate slow leaks. If a ship starts losing air pressure in any one area—slower than can be detected by ordinary sensors—it will still have an effect on internal air-flow patterns; the hoboes move toward leaks. Look for the spot where they congregate. That's called a hobo-jungle; that's where the leak is."

Spock stepped forward and caught the hobo in one hand. He examined it thoughtfully, then let it go without comment. It hung almost motionless in the air, eddying only slightly. The atmosphere of this vessel would tend to move opposite the direction of spin; the hobo reflected that motion.

Omara stepped through the door, quickly turning to shine his beam in all directions. Stokely covered him with his phaser; Kirk and Spock followed. They were in a wide corridor, damp with condensation. Water was dripping off the walls and puddling on the floor.

The corridor was unlit. Their beams penetrated the gloom only a short way. In the distance, the floors curved upward into blackness. There were faint sounds—vibrations transmitted through the hull of the vessel. The sounds hinted at machinery and voices, but even with amplification and real-time logic applied, Spock's tricorder could not clarify what the source might be; perhaps the computers on the *Enterprise* would be able to make sense of the noise.

Kirk aimed his beam spinward and antispinward. Occasional hoboes could be seen hanging here and there in the tunnel, their colors faded and drab. Narrow trickles of water flowed past their boots in an antispinward direction.

In the center of the corridor were four metal tracks. Spock bent to examine them more closely. "For moving heavy machinery, probably." He straightened, then looked at his tricorder again. "Captain, there are heat-sources moving somewhere up that corridor." He pointed spinward.

Kirk accepted the information without expression. "Set phasers for stun," he instructed.

His communicator beeped. He shifted his weight to restrap his flashbeam to his left hip, then passed the phaser to his left hand to unstrap his communicator from the back of his right hip. He exchanged the communicator and the phaser between his two hands, caught his breath and flipped open the device. "Kirk here."

"Captain—" It was Uhura. She reported crisply, "Long-range sensors are picking up a ghost; it appears to be a Klingon war vessel, possibly a dragon-class cruiser. It's a very faint ghost, not even a solid tracing; we're running a probability scan on it now."

"What kind of course is it on?"

Uhura's answer was immediately disturbing. "It seems to be staying deliberately on the sensory fringes."

"Close enough for us to see, but too far away for us to see it clearly. . . . " Kirk said to himself. "It's an old trick—" He exhaled his annoyance, already resigned to the decision he had to make. Into the communicator, he said, "Thank you, Lieutenant. Have Lieutenant Riley report to the transporter room to join the contact team. And Crewmember Garcia too." He pressed the reset on his communicator. "Transporter room, two to beam up."

"Sir . . . ?" The transport ensign was hesitant, almost embarrassed. "Could you climb up the access tube and beam over from the shuttlecraft? We're having trouble with our monitron focus here—it's that hull—and we can't beam up anything until we recalibrate. And even then, if we're going to put anything aboard that vessel, it's going to require a coordinating module or a communicator for a focus."

Kirk started to say something, then looked at Spock's impassive face and said nothing instead. "Stand by, transporter room. Mr. Spock?" He stepped through the door and crossed to the open hatch, muttering something under his breath. Spock followed dutifully.

Stokely looked at Omara, "What'd he say?"

"Something about two guys named Murphy and Finagle. He wants them assigned to sewage maintenance."

"Yeah," agreed Stokely.

8

Lieutenant Kevin Riley had been extensively trained in Starfleet contact procedures; he had scored higher on the simulation problems than any other member of his class. But there had been that incident with a Capellan choir, and even though nothing specific had been said, there was still the feeling in some parts that Lieutenant Riley had been somehow instrumental in producing the resultant discord.

Riley had even gone to Kirk and asked for a transfer off the *Enterprise;* he did not say so specifically, but he felt he had disgraced his ship and that this perhaps was the only course of action left to him. It was a matter of honor. But Captain Kirk rejected his transfer application without comment. And there the matter had lain for nearly two weeks—until Lieutenant Riley had unexpectedly run into the Captain in the ship's gymnasium, and Kirk had asked him to work out with him in a hand-to-hand combat routine. Riley managed to pin the Captain twice, but the other seven rounds in the set went to the larger, more experienced Kirk. Afterward, Kirk gave him some pointers on technique and they went through three more practice rounds. Riley won two of them—but even though Kirk slapped himself meaningfully on the belly and grunted something about the extra kilos of mass creeping up on him, Riley still suspected that the Captain had thrown at least one of the rounds. It gave him the temerity to bring up the subject of his rejected transfer.

Kirk didn't answer immediately; he just grabbed a towel and went into the steamroom. Riley followed. Inside, Kirk was silent for a moment, then said, "If I let you transfer, Riley, that stain will follow you for your entire Starfleet career. It'll be an unspoken thing, there won't be anything written on any record—but you know how the rumor mill works. If I let you transfer it's the same as my saying I don't have any faith in you. Right now, the best thing I can do for you is to keep you aboard the *Enterprise* and make you demonstrate that you are a competent and dependable crewmember. The best thing you can do is not lose faith in your own abilities. Everybody makes mistakes, Riley—even captains—but it's the ones who pick themselves up and get on with the job, who are most valuable to Starfleet." He stopped then to give Riley a chance to think about what he had said. After a moment, he added quietly, "Kirk's law, Riley: once could be an accident, twice could be a coincidence—but the third time makes your Captain look like a fool too." He let the words sink in, then heaved himself off the redwood bench and left the steamroom, leaving Riley sitting there and sweating. And thinking.

Afterward, Riley realized something else. Captain Kirk almost never used the gymnasium during Alpha shift; that was when he was usually on the bridge.

He took the Captain's words to heart and reapplied for active duty on the *Enterprise* contact team; the duty was one of the touchiest tasks aboard a ship. The behavior of a contact team with a new species would affect the pattern of relations with that species for years, perhaps decades, thereafter. It was a crucial duty and Riley was determined not to fail his Captain again.

Riley stood in the corridor with Stokely, Omara and Garcia. All were armed; their phasers were set for stun. They wore their flashbeams strapped to their wrists to keep their hands free. Marilyn Garcia of the Analysis Lab was carrying the science tricorder.

"Let's keep close," said Riley. "And let's keep our behinds covered too."

"I wouldn't be so eager, Lieutenant." That was Omara. "You'll find things here a lot different than you're used to."

Riley looked at him coldly. "We'll see. Now, let's move out."

The others took up their positions silently. Mr. Spock had suggested that they explore the spinward direction of the corridor first and try to establish contact with the lifeforms they had previously detected.

The corridor was wide enough for a ground car, but the ceiling was only three meters high. They moved slowly through it, their beams stabbing through the gloom to disappear against the upward curve of the distant floor. They picked their way across the rivulets of water that had encrusted the metal tracks on the floor with a slick layer of greasy slime. Garcia stooped to take two samples, smearing them expertly onto slides and then dropping the slides into a case she wore on her side; she smiled once at Riley. "I'd guess it's some kind of algae, but there's no light here. Maybe it's an oil-eater, a tailored bacterium. They used to use them for industrial applications; they secrete an oil residue that retards rust. It's just a guess though."

"How about that," said Riley. He looked at the slime—and Crewmember Garcia—with new respect. But he wasn't going to let himself be distracted. Not this time. He waved them on.

There were doors on either side of the corridor. Some of them were closed. The open ones revealed rooms of varying sizes and as featureless as the one they had entered through. They did not try to open any of the closed doors. There were occasional wells with ladders climbing out of them and leading up through the ceiling. Riley peered up and down one of them, saw that the well was zigzagged with set-backs to prevent objects falling from the center of the ship to the outer hull and backed away. No, they wouldn't explore these—not just yet— anything that limited their lines of sight was not to be trusted. He directed Garcia to scan it with her tricorder; if nothing else, Scotty would want to see the pictures of it later. One of the first rules of contact exploration was that everything—no matter how small or negligible it might seem at the time—was important enough to record for analysis. Omara also had a tricorder and was scanning as they moved.

Abruptly, they came to a branching of the corridor. A passage opened up on their left; it pointed toward the forward part of the vessel. It was the same size as the corridor they were in and it too had a set of tracks running along its center. They aimed their beams down the tunnel, picking up a few hoboes floating here and there, but farther down the light was swallowed by the murk. The sound of water was louder here, and there were strange echoing noises. Like rats perhaps, only larger.

Riley flipped open his communicator. "Riley here. We're at a T-branching. The new corridor seems to go forward. What do you suggest, sir?"

Mr. Spock's voice came calmly back. "We have triangulation on your position, Lieutenant. You have moved ten degrees spinward. Hold your position for a moment." There was a pause—perhaps the Science Officer was conferring with the Captain—then Spock's voice returned, "Move slowly up the corridor, Lieutenant, but proceed with caution."

"Yes, sir. Riley out." He restrapped his communicator. He wondered what was happening on the bridge. Kirk had put the whole ship on full alert. Probably they were standing by and watching for the Klingon ghost to do something, even though they most likely knew it wouldn't approach at all—therefore, the full attention of the Captain was probably directed here, on Kevin Riley and his contact team. He wiped his forehead. He could almost feel the weight of the responsibility.

He swallowed, waved his team forward and they padded cautiously down the new passage. There was no water flowing down the center here; instead, it was puddled occasionally on the floor where it met the antispinward wall. On either side of the tracks were walkways that had once been carpeted. Now they were dull, hard mats. Whatever color they had originally been was undetectable. Now they were gray-brown.

Overhead, there were rows of luminescent panels, long since gone dead. There were occasional vents and utility boxes in the walls, some of them marked with unfamiliar symbols—unfamiliar, yet somehow . . . hovering just on the fringes of meaning.

Abruptly, the corridor widened—

It was an intersection, sort of. The corridor opened onto a wide circular shaft; the passageway became a circular balcony around it, then continued forward on the other side. Another spinward/antispinward passage intersected at right angles, and there were several smaller passages spaced between the openings for the wider ones. But it was the shaft itself that drew Riley's attention; even as he moved forward to the railing to peer up and down, he was directing Omara to record the scene.

Their beams revealed rails running up the shaft toward the center of the spin, and downward toward the outer hull. "Elevators?" Garcia asked.

"Maybe—look, that's where they could have stopped, over there." Stokely pointed.

Riley angled his beam around—they were in a vaulted chamber, with balconies and doors on all sides. He didn't like it, it was the perfect place for an ambush. But when he looked at Garcia, she shook her head. Her scanning tricorder showed no lifeforms within detectable range.

Riley opened his communicator again. "*Enterprise?* Are you getting all this?"

"Acknowledged, Lieutenant," came back Spock's emotionless reply.

Riley was going to ask Spock which direction he thought they should go, but his eye was caught by something in Stokely's beam—a staircase, spiraling up around the walls of the shaft. He followed it up and up and up. At the top, there was a faint yellow glow.

Riley said slowly, "We thought we'd climb the stairs . . . sir. . . ." He waved at Garcia to point her tricorder upward.

The communicator was silent a moment. Then Spock's voice returned, "You may proceed, Lieutenant."

Riley exhaled, relieved; then put on his best grin and pointed Stokely and Omara to go around to the right, while he and Garcia circled to the left. The access to the spiral staircase was almost directly opposite their position.

The stairs were proportioned for human beings.

All of them—the three men and the woman—stood before the rising steps and exchanged a look of . . . concern. Riley took the first step, then looked back at the others. "Well—? Are you coming?"

They climbed slowly, their beams continually sweeping up and down the shaft, exploring every nook and cranny —but finding only nooks and crannies. Occasionally, they passed doors and smaller passages, but Riley kept climbing toward the distant light. Garcia placed it as being only a third of the way toward the center of the vessel from where they were. They would still be within the outermost shell; if there was an inner hull, they hadn't found evidence of it yet.

There were places where the stairs were wet with water and streaked with more of the slime. Stokely almost slipped once, which garnered him some jibes from Omara. They climbed upward, once or twice being hit by small running streams that tumbled down the shaft and disappeared into the silence below.

The stairs climbed up to meet another intersection like the one they left below. Garcia and Omara scanned it, then Riley pointed them upward again. They passed two more of the intersections, then Riley let them stop to rest at a third. Omara gasped, still trying to catch his breath, "Gravity's lighter here."

"It's still more than Earth-normal. Why would anyone want to build a spaceship for high-gees?" Stokely complained.

"If it was a colony ship, as Mr. Spock thinks, then they wouldn't necessarily know what kind of planets might be waiting for them. Perhaps the higher gravity levels were so they could begin acclimatizing themselves to the higher gees as soon as they knew they would have to. It's just a guess," said Riley. He opened his communicator again, "Mr. Spock? We're at the third—or is it the fourth?— intersection. I think there are only three more before the top."

"It's the fourth intersection, Lieutenant. We're still getting strong signals from you, but please try to be more accurate in your counting. Have you scanned any more of the inhabitants of the vessel?"

Riley shook his head, then realized that the Science Officer couldn't see him. "Nothing, sir."

Spock's reply was impassive. "You are nearly three-quarters of a kilometer into that vessel, Lieutenant. Watchfulness is advisable."

"Aye, aye, sir—"

A sudden noise, something clattering across the floor

—Riley turned, his phaser pointing toward the source—

There was nothing—

—no, wait a minute, there!—

A crossbow?!! Lying on the deck—?

He stepped toward it and—

They hurtled out of the darkness, screaming like an explosion—Riley was almost too startled to fire, but Garcia's phaser arced past his shoulder, silhouetting seven lumbering shapes. They were dropping on ropes from above—and they had faces like a Klingon's nightmare—they wore scales and claws and fur and—

Riley found his wits then, his finger tightening on the trigger even before he was certain what he was firing at—the flares of the phasers were almost physical smashes of light in this great shadowed well—the shaft echoed with the electric screeches and the sudden dazzling flashes. Two of the huge attackers fell, another one screamed; something grunted and scrambled across the deck in full retreat—

And then it was over. And the attackers were gone. Three bodies lay on the deck. Riley looked at the other three members of the contact team. Not one of them had spoken yet. "Everybody all right?"

Stokely and Omara both nodded, but without interrupting their steady turning, sweeping the area with their beams and their suddenly hard expressions. They held their phasers ready, moving them in wide arcs—up and down as well as across. Garcia looked shaken, but she was turning with her tricorder, scanning again. "They're gone now," she said.

Riley acknowledged. They advanced slowly toward the three fallen bodies.

The communicator beeped. Riley realized he was still holding it open in his hand. He raised it toward his mouth. "We're all right here. Just a little, uh— misunderstanding."

"Lieutenant Riley, report!"

"Stand by, sir!" he snapped back. He shone his beam on one of the attackers. The thing—the creature —whatever it was—appeared to be a collection of all the worst parts of a dozen different kinds of nastiness.

Human-sized, it had long bearlike arms with huge metal claws, scaly armor and spines down its back, and a face that was all teeth and snarl.

He nudged its weapon with his foot—a machete.

Garcia moved up beside him, scanning with her tricorder.

"Stunned?" he asked.

"Dead," she reported. "This one has a broken neck." She looked upward. Riley followed her gaze to a rope still swinging back and forth. "The other two—," she said. "I don't know."

"Sure is ugly—" Riley started, then stopped.

Garcia had bent down to the creature and pulled off its face.

It was a mask. And the armor and the claws were part of the costume too. The other two creatures were also mere disguises.

Underneath, they were human. Garcia's tricorder said so.

Riley's face tightened in one brief flicker of pain, then he flipped open his communicator and began to report.

9

Captain James Tiberius Kirk of the starship *Enterprise* was very annoyed with a certain unnamed Klingon commander. As long as that war cruiser stayed in sensor range, he could not leave the bridge of his ship. Battle-readiness was one responsibility he could not delegate.

But neither could he abandon the exploration of this strange derelict to initiate pursuit and interception of the Klingon cruiser.

There had been a course at the Academy created with just this kind of circumstance in mind. It was one of the optional electives that upperclassmen taught for the benefit of lowerclassmen: an informal series aimed at promoting the art of creative cursing.

It had long since been proven that a certain amount of oath-taking was a healthy outlet, good for relieving the pressures of command and responsibility, and thereby reducing the strains a captain is subject to. Creative cursing was highly recommended as an ulcer-preventative, and several generations of overstressed cadets had raised the art to new highs of originality—in the process, also proving that geniuses tend to have senses of humor radically different than those of lesser mortals. "The Great Bird of the Galaxy" for instance, had been created in one memorable session, and a whole new category of curses and blessings had been born as a result.

Scatological, sexual and religious-based curses, of course, were regarded as the work of amateurs. To be worthy of respect, a curse should arouse simultaneous sensations of pain and laughter in the listeners; it should bring tears to the eyes; indeed, a truly inspired oath should create ripples in the stress field itself and make all listeners within three parsecs turn around and stare in shock and admiration. A mild Starfleet curse should curdle an egg in its shell; a strong one should do it before the egg has even been laid.

The bemused faculty at the Academy had tolerated the student-taught course for some years—until the battle of Donatu V, when a beseiged Star-Colonel, in response to a Klingon demand for surrender, had answered, "Mertz!" and created such confusion among the Klingon translators that reinforcements had time to arrive and save the day for the Federation. After that, participation in creative cursing was actively encouraged, and excellence at the art was regarded as evidence of a particular strain of inventiveness that had so far eluded identification and analysis.

But all that James Tiberius Kirk could think to say at this moment, was: "May his engine room become a test lab for the seventh corollary of Murphy's Law."

Spock raised an eyebrow at his Captain. Uhura turned to stare. Scotty looked up from his console. Chekov and Sulu exchanged concerned glances and turned around in their chairs to look at Kirk. If this was the best that their Captain could do, they were in serious trouble indeed. Obviously, James Tiberius Kirk was so annoyed, he couldn't even channel his energies for a proper oath.

—but Kirk wasn't annoyed so much as he was preoccupied with analyzing the situation.

He knew full well that the phantom cruiser would not approach, would not take any action at all, hostile or otherwise. Its sole purpose was to be seen by Starfleet vessels, distracting them from their other duties. It was a very insidious and carefully calculated maneuver designed solely to annoy and frustrate.

And it was succeeding.

Kirk realized he was drumming on the arm rest again. "I hope that Klingon has many ambitious sons," he said to himself, then realized that Spock was standing beside his chair, waiting. "Spock?"

If Spock had heard the remark, he gave no sign. "Captain, there is still the matter of Lieutenant Riley and his contact team. . . ."

"I haven't forgotten, Spock."

Indeed, the upper screens all around the bridge were continually replaying the images from Stokely's and Garcia's tricorders.

Ideally, Kirk would have beamed over for an on-site inspection, but that option was denied him by the presence of that *wasting* Klingon war cruiser, so that left him only two choices: either recall Riley's team or let them proceed.

Starfleet contact procedures were based on probabilities, and captains were instructed to consider their contact teams "expendable, if absolutely necessary." The question was the determination of circumstance so definable—and that, of course, was what had to be left up to the captain's judgment. It was Kirk's decision and there was no way he could fudge it.

Of course, sooner or later a contact team would have to proceed to the forward part of the ship to find the tenders of that one working fusion plant—so a withdrawal at this time would only postpone the necessary. And would also give the hostiles a chance to prepare greater defenses. Therefore, there was no reasonable argument in favor of withdrawal except perhaps to preserve the safety of the contact team—and the contact team *could* be considered expendable. If absolutely necessary.

But it wasn't a good idea to *waste* contact teams. For one thing, it tended to weaken a crew's faith in their captain, as well as their willingness to serve on contact teams.

He heaved himself out of his chair and crossed to an unmanned console on the port side of the bridge. Privately, he reran the tapes of the attack, then took a look at the computer's twenty-four-hour evaluation of the performance of each member of the contact team, but especially Riley's.

The question was one of competency—not so much how Riley had handled himself in the past as much as how would he handle himself in the future—but the only guide Kirk had to the future was Riley's past.

All of the stats, all of the graphs, all of the charts that the computer could generate for him could not answer the one question that Captain Kirk most needed answered—a question of human judgment. But then, that was the reason why Kirk was the captain and not the computer. Nor even Mr. Spock. It was a question of . . . something he couldn't quite pin down—

"Tiberius!" he said to himself—and suddenly he knew what the question was. It was a question of *compassion.*

And knowing that, he knew also what the answer was. He remembered a conversation in the ship's steamroom. It wasn't just that Riley had to prove his competency; it was Kirk who also had to prove his renewed faith in the Lieutenant. It's easy to have faith when there's no reason to question it. It's when one has reason to doubt that faith proves its value.

He turned around abruptly and said, "Lieutenant Uhura, tell Lieutenant Riley to proceed as originally directed."

"Aye aye, Captain." Uhura was beaming; she agreed with the decision. Around the bridge, Kirk could see that his other officers agreed as well; there were quiet smiles and a general relaxing of the tension. Good, he thought, they understood. If Kirk had called Riley back, it would have demonstrated that he didn't trust the junior officer without a leash. And it could very well have shattered the last of Riley's faith in himself. And it would also have proven Captain James T. Kirk a hypocrite.

But the real reason why Kirk had made the decision to let Riley proceed was based on something deeper.

There had been a certain Lieutenant James T. Kirk who had made a mistake once—and there had been a certain captain who had given him the chance to rectify that error and thereby prove himself. The circumstances were unimportant, but Kirk remembered the feeling that had possessed him then: that he would rather die in the effort to prove himself worthy of the trust of his Captain than live with the disgrace of his previous error. Of course, he had not died, and after he had successfully completed his mission, his Captain had summoned him privately to his cabin and told him that he had passed a valuable test. "Any idiot can die for his ship, James; what takes real genius is surviving! That's what we try to look for in our officers—not just problem-solving ability, but survival skills as well—so he can go on to solve the next problem and the next and the next. After all, what good is an officer who self-destructs? The only way we can ever find out if an officer has that survival skill is to put him in situations that will directly test it. Remember that when you become a captain yourself someday."

Kirk had remembered it.

In fact, he was already planning to have the same little talk with Lieutenant Kevin Riley when he returned to the *Enterprise*.

If he lived.

10

When the Captain's order came through, Riley's first reaction was amazement—then a slow grin spread across his boyish face. "Yeah . . . " he said, "let's do it. A piece of cake."

Omara scowled at him, "You think so? You'll change your tune soon enough, Lieutenant Riley."

Riley hesitated half a beat, then let the jibe roll off, deliberately not noticing it. He waved the group upward.

More cautious than ever, they resumed their climb toward the glow at the top. Omara shook his head in wonderment, then shifted the weight of his gear and followed after.

Stokely had put on a pair of infrared goggles to see heat-sources in the dark, but there were no further attacks and they reached the top without incident.

The stairs climbed to a final landing in a deserted plaza. The source of the light was still above them, still too high to be seen clearly.

"What's the gravity here?" Stokely asked. "It feels lighter."

"Point seven nine," Garcia answered. "We've come a long way."

The four team members moved away from the stair shaft and across the plaza warily. Their beams were almost unnecessary here; the glow from above bathed the area in eerie twilight. They kept them lit anyway, but Stokely did push the infrared goggles up onto his forehead.

Riley found himself thinking about those goggles—if Stokely had been wearing them before, they might not have been caught by surprise in the attack.

Stokely was looking back at him, a strange expression on his face; his hand was still frozen in the act of pushing the goggles up. He had realized the same thing.

But Riley said nothing. He could see that Stokely was already berating himself far more efficiently than he could ever do. Besides—Riley knew exactly what Stokely was feeling now—a burning shame at having let his fellow team members down. Riley thought of Kirk. And himself. And Stokely. He said, "Stokely, do you want to take the point?"

Stokely looked startled. "Uh—yeah, sure." He allowed himself a smile of relief. Riley grinned back.

The plaza fed into corridors on all sides—most of them shadowed in gloom. The contact team oriented themselves by the *Enterprise's* deep-scan triangulation, and then began moving forward again, toward the bow of this gigantic ship. The corridor was wide, but dark. Stokely lowered his infrared goggles again.

This corridor was unlike the others they had been in. It was wider and the ceiling was higher. And there were alcoves on either side that could have once been shops of a sort—but were merely bare openings now. Debris littered the floor, and there were even cobwebs hanging from bare struts.

The air was dry here—and musty-smelling.

"You know what this makes me think of—?" Omara whispered.

No one answered.

"The ruins at Old City. New York." His words died in silence. The air was heavy in their lungs.

A voice in Riley's head was saying something. He had to listen hard to make it out. Something he had been told once—"Ask the next question!"

He thought about it as they continued to shuffle warily down the corridor. Finally he asked, "Why?"

After a long moment, Omara yawned and said, "I think it's the proportions of everything . . . "

Riley considered that. He was yawning himself. He lifted a hand and said, "Stop. Shine your beams around."

They did so. "You're right, Omara, it does look like Old City, doesn't it." And something else—

He coughed once, trying to clear his throat—realized what was happening and managed to gasp, "There's something wrong with the air here! Put your O-masks on!" But even the effort of shouting left him reeling with dizziness. He was toppling even as he fumbled with the mask. Beside him, Garcia had already hit the floor and Omara was collapsing against one wall. Riley hit the floor hard—but he refused to let himself lose consciousness; he was dimly aware of the drilled-to-infinity breathing routine of the mask. He was taking slow shallow breaths. Counting with the breaths, he rolled over and realized he was next to Stokely—who was just fumbling his mask into place.

Stokely's eyes locked with his. Riley nodded toward Garcia; she was closer to Stokely. "I'll get Omara—"

And then he had to catch his breath again. He didn't wait to see if Stokely had understood; he started working his way over to the wall. Omara had passed out without ever hearing the warning about the air; his O-mask was still in the pocket of his survival suit. Working with fingers that felt thick as elephant legs, Riley could not get the mask out. But there was no time to waste—Omara looked comatose. Riley unsealed the mask from his face and placed it over Omara's nose and mouth. The nerve circuits in the mask took over the control of Omara's breathing. He began to gasp for air.

Riley returned his attention to Omara's O-mask—for some reason it wouldn't budge out of the pocket—something was catching and holding it back; it was the airtube! Riley pulled the mask free with a jerk and pushed it onto his face with both hands. He collapsed across Omara's chest, sucking eagerly at the fragile breath of life.

Behind him, there were sounds—he counted five breaths, then five more, then lifted himself on one arm to look. Stokely and Garcia were working their way toward them.

Riley pointed, and the four-member contact team, crawling on their hands and knees, began to work their way back the way they had come. They reached the mouth of the corridor and collapsed, still gasping for breath.

"It's a polarized O-field," panted Marilyn Garcia. "There's oxygen in the air—that's why the tricorder didn't beep a warning—but it isn't any kind of oxygen we can breathe—" She had to stop then and bury her face in her O-mask again.

"I'm familiar with the—the chemistry, Garcia." Riley managed to answer.

They lay there for a moment, the air rasping in their throats. Stokely turned himself around so he could watch the open area of the plaza; he held his phaser loosely before him. To Riley's inquiring stare, he said, "In case those—hostiles attack—again—"

"Good idea," said Riley. Omara and Garcia pulled into positions of alertness too.

"An O-field—," wondered Omara. "Wow . . . !"

"Somebody sure wants to stop somebody from going down that tunnel—," Garcia said.

"Probably—the hostiles—," Riley answered, and even as the words fell out of his mouth, he knew that was the answer. "Whoever's on the other end of that tunnel doesn't want visitors. And obviously, they have the technology to make it stick." He took another breath. "I guess we're going to have to pay them a visit."

"Huh—?"

"How?"

"What—?!!"

Riley pointed at Stokely. "The phasers, if we set them for scatter-beam, we'll ionize the air. Ionization disrupts an O-field. And if we use our O-masks off the tanks instead of extraction, we should be all right."

Omara's eyes narrowed darkly. "You'd better check that with the Captain, Riley."

"Sure," said Riley. "You don't trust my judgment, do you? All right." His grin was malicious. "Let's face the music—" He flipped open his communicator. "Riley here. We ran into an O-field. No problem though. We're going on. I'd guess the O-field is evidence of applied intelligence."

Spock's voice came softly back, "The whole vessel is evidence of that, Lieutenant. We are maintaining tricorder-monitoring, but we would appreciate renewed attention to your verbal reports. You may proceed."

"Aye aye, Mr. Spock." Riley closed his communicator. He looked at Omara. "Any questions?"

Omara's expression had been deliberately blank; now it spread into a grudging smile of respect. "I guess I had you figured all wrong, Lieutenant—I thought—never mind." He shrugged and grinned, "Can I have the next dance?"

Riley sighed—was he never going to live that down? He heaved himself to his feet and reached across to give Omara a hand up. "It'll be no treble at all," he noted.

11

O-masks firmly in place, the contact team proceeded down the dark corridor again, Omara and Riley side-by-side in the lead. Riley was counting cadence softly: "—and a one and a two and a three—" On "three" he would fire his phaser ahead, a wide blue cone of power that sparkled the air like lightning, "—and a four and a five and a six—" On "six" Omara would fire forward, his beam now disrupting the polarized O-field. And then Riley would begin the count again.

They moved cautiously forward, unconsciously keeping time with Riley's steady count. The continual dazzle-flash of their phasers lit up the corridor like a strobing beacon, but they were so close to the point-sources of illumination that they could not get clear glimpses of what lay hidden in the distant gloom ahead —or behind, for that matter.

Riley checked the power charge of his phaser. Fortunately it didn't take much energy to disrupt an O-field. Almost any electric charge would do it. Their weapons were set for the lowest value of Stun. A human being caught in the beam would have felt only a slight tingling sensation—a sensation familiar to anyone who had ever fired a high-powered phaser and felt the intense static charge of the air in the immediate vicinity of the beam. There was an old joke in Starfleet about the phaser being the one weapon that made your skin crawl no matter which end of it you were on.

Each flash of their phasers left the air filled with glittering pinpoints of light that shone for only an instant before flickering quickly out. The contact team moved through a fantasy of magic sparkles—under other circumstances, the sight would have been delightful.

It was when their phaser beams stopped making flickers in the air that they knew they were safely beyond the worst effects of the O-field.

Here, the tunnel was littered with debris and the walls were scorched as if by explosive weaponry—but the scars were old and dusty. Even so, they paused to let Garcia run her tricorder over one of the larger gouges in the floor.

"This looks like it could have been a residential area," said Stokely. "Apartments, courtyards—see, even little patios set away from the main street." He pointed up. "And even balconies—you have to use your imagination a little, but you can see what it could have been, can't you?"

Garcia studied the look of the architecture with a professional eye. She said softly, "It's a good guess—but we shouldn't assume anything yet."

Abruptly they were at the end of the tunnel. It just stopped in a sudden dead end. The wall was a blank face of metallic-looking patchwork.

They stood and stared at it, then looked at each other.

Riley shrugged. "We should have expected it." He flipped open his communicator. "Riley here. We've come to a dead end." He looked up and down the wall. "I'd guess it was not in the original design. Garcia, scan that for them, please. The metal looks like a crazy-quilt construction. Whatever they had available, they welded it in. The O-field, and now this wall, are probably their first lines of defense against the hostiles on this side." He hesitated, then let himself say it anyway. "We're going to have to cut through."

"Acknowledged, Lieutenant," replied Spock. "Please stand by."

The four members of the contact team stood and waited. Riley slid his O-mask off his face and sniffed the air. "Smells all right to me," he said.

Omara grinned at him, "I'll wait, if you don't mind, to see if you fall over or not."

"What do you think, Garcia? Can we cut through?"

She looked up from her tricorder—she had been scanning the patchwork wall at close range. "No problem, Mr. Riley. It's not metal at all, but pieces of foamed neoplast. Mostly, it's a construction material. It's strong, but if you put enough heat into it, it'll melt like butter."

"We've come this far," remarked Stokely. "It'd be a waste to turn back now."

"That's what I was thinking," said Riley. "And besides, we've already cut our way into their hull—cutting through one more wall won't make that much more difference, will it?"

Almost as if in answer, his communicator bleeped. He flipped it open and Kirk's voice came thinly through. "Riley," the Captain asked, "you think you can handle this?"

"Yes, sir! I'm sure I can." And then he realized he had answered just a little too quickly. He hoped he hadn't sounded like a fool.

But if Kirk had noticed, his voice showed no sign. "All right, Lieutenant. Go ahead. And Riley—"

"Sir?"

"Uh, never mind."

"Sir?"

"I was just going to tell you to be careful," Kirk admitted. "But under the circumstances, it seemed obvious that you had probably figured that part out already." And then he added, "Good luck."

Riley felt a quick rush of pride. "Thank you, sir." He was grinning as he signed off.

Omara and Stokely exchanged approving looks and reset their phasers. Omara unclipped a stylus from his kit and swiftly marked the outline of a door on the surface of the obstructing wall. By the time Riley had finished restrapping his communicator to his belt, the two of them were standing and waiting for his order. And grinning just as broadly as he was.

"Just say the word," Stokely prompted.

Riley nodded. "You may fire when ready, Grisly. I think that's the appropriate command, isn't it?"

Omara cautioned, "Better put your O-mask back on, sir. No telling what's in that wall. Some of these things give off toxic gases when they burn." He waited till Riley had done so and given him a thumbs-up signal and then turned to his partner with an "after you, Alphonse," gesture.

Stokely accepted it graciously, then pointed his phaser at the wall with deceptive nonchalance. A needle-thin beam of arcing blue brilliance sliced up one side, across, then down the other and back across the bottom. There was almost no smoke and only a thin trickle of smoldering black fluid at the bottom that sizzled into a quickly-hardening puddle.

Riley looked questioningly at Stokely and Omara. The beam had cut the wide outline of a door, but—

Omara held up one hand in a "just a moment" gesture. He crossed to the wall, lifted his O-mask, pursed his lips and gently blew at it with an air of deliberate finesse.

The perfectly cut outline of a door toppled slowly inward—and there was light! Brilliant and warm and dazzling—a familiar yellow glow that made them think for one sudden disorienting moment that they had found a door to an outside world—

—and there was the smell of flowers! And ferns! And other things not so easily identifiable, but every bit as delicious and confusing. Clover! Sage! Wild fennel! And strawberries?!! They were enveloped by a heady sense of magic. All kinds of growing things had permeated the air with their perfumes: a lush green scent, rich and woody and wondrous.

"It smells like summer. . . . " whispered Garcia.

And, as if summoned by her words, a single insect came buzzing out through the hole they had cut, exploring. They stared at it, astonished: it was a honeybee. A familiar black-and-yellow-striped honeybee.

It buzzed curiously around them for a moment, startling them with its boldness, then—not finding either flowers or scents that warranted closer investigation—it disappeared back through the door into . . . summer.

12

They moved into a corridor of light.

It was dazzling—they lowered goggles into place over their eyes, but still they squinted against the glare of colors and brilliance.

Above them, high in the distance, lights gleamed incandescantly like banks of tiny suns—on all sides, they were surrounded by greenery.

The crewmembers moved slowly—stunned—through a maze of chest-high tanks, each one laden with wide-leafed plants, the woody stalks reaching eagerly toward the light. They were huge vines, climbing the metal stanchions of the chamber, each one laden with gigantic tomatoes.

Riley, Stokely, Omara and Garcia stared in wonder, feeling suddenly small. The vines were pillars of green studding a compartmentalized landscape. The tanks went on forever; rank upon rank of green tanks and green stanchions stretched away from them, all to be lost in a distant glare of whiteness. To either side, they could see the rows curving gently upward, again to disappear in a line of blurry bright halo.

This was not merely a city hanging in space that the *Enterprise* had discovered; this was a whole nation! A continent! A world, with resources and ecology all its own! Their tricorders recorded it all silently.

Riley was the first to find his voice. "We've found the farm . . . " he whispered.

"One of them, anyway," said Garcia. "There are probably others."

Riley looked at her.

"This one is mostly tomatoes. And a few friendly companions, like basil—but mostly tomatoes. That means they've got to have other farms for other crops. Look how the plants here are taking advantage of the lower gravity on this level to climb the stanchions. That one must be at least ten meters high—and look at the size of the fruit on that vine! Like basketballs!"

"Low gravity does have its uses," said Riley.

Garcia shot him a look—maybe he hadn't thought that she would catch it, but she had—that particular statement was the punch line to one of the bawdiest stories in Starfleet (reputed to be an accurate account of an incident which had occurred between a certain libidinous chief engineer and the female delegate from one of the L5 nations, but just as possibly the tale was only apocryphal, there being no polite way to double-check the source . . . never mind). Riley was already looking in another direction.

"Boy," said Garcia. "Would I like to see their other farms! This is truly extraordinary. Just amazing."

"Oh, come on, Garcia," said Stokely. "You've seen farms before."

"Yes, but nothing so *primitive* as this on such a *large* scale. This is no museum display, Stokely. These people depend on this farm for their lives. That's why they've defended it as vigorously as they have from the savages. I'm surprised we got in as easily as we did. This is evidence of a very tangible kind. What we are dealing with is obviously a very capable—and *structured*—society. They are adaptable and able to make good use of the materials at hand." She pointed. "Look—this wasn't designed to be a farm. That's the bare superstructure of the ship there, those stanchions. Whatever was here before was completely dismantled so this farm could be installed—probably more shops and homes like those we passed."

The men exchanged a glance.

Omara voiced the question. "Then what happened to their primary farms, that they had to build these?"

"Maybe this is the only one," suggested Stokely. "Maybe it was built in *addition* to the others—to support a larger population perhaps?"

"I doubt that." Garcia shook her head. "It isn't consistent with what we've seen so far. I'd postulate that the shut-off section of the ship, the part we've already passed through, is evidence of some kind of—collapse; some physical disaster, or ecological, perhaps even a social discontinuity. The savages, for instance—what makes a people return to a primitive form of existence? This farm, though, is evidence that somebody is rebuilding a new life out of the ruins—"

She stopped herself abruptly, a surprised look on her face. "Do you realize what's happening?" She looked from one to the other.

"Huh?"

"When did we start calling the hostiles, 'savages'?"

Stokely, Omara and Riley looked at each other, shrugged in momentary confusion.

"Hostile, yes—," said Garcia, "—but we don't know for certain that they're savage. We've made an assumption here, possibly an unfair one. We're also allowing ourselves to identify with whoever built this farm because they have technology."

Riley grinned, "Now you sound like the Captain."

Garcia grinned right back at him. "I ought to. I studied under him at the Academy. As a junior officer, he taught the section on basic alien contact procedures. I found it fascinating. He used to say that it was dangerous to empathize with any situation—unless you were willing to empathize with *both* sides of it. He's one of the reasons why I decided to go into the contact service, and why I'm on the *Enterprise*."

"This isn't exactly . . . alien—" Omara gestured at the all-too recognizable tomatoes around them.

"That's why it's potentially even *more* dangerous—it encourages us to take the situation at face value—and maybe we *shouldn't*. The first rule of contact is to distrust all first impressions; they're usually wrong." Garcia realized that she was beginning to sound pedantic. The expressions on their faces were . . . tolerant and bemused.

"Right," she said. "Lesson's over. Let's go on."

"I want to report in first," said Riley, unstrapping his communicator. Despite the knowledge that their tricorders were continually monitoring and reporting their readings back to the *Enterprise*, there was no substitute for the on-scene observations of the contact team.

But before he could flip his communicator open, Omara said, "Hold it—" and pointed ahead. "Look—"

Way in the distance, at the very limits of visibility, something was moving.

It was only a flicker of darkness against the horizon of light, but it was moving toward them.

"Maybe they haven't seen us yet—" Riley gestured them back. "Get out of sight." The four of them moved back and split up, Riley and Garcia stepping into the left side of the cross-corridor, Stokely and Omara sliding into the opposite side.

Garcia was already peering at her tricorder readings. "It looks like it's one person only—about eighty-five percent probability."

"Shh," said Riley. He restrapped his communicator and unstrapped his phaser, double-checked that it was set for stun. Omara and Stokely saw what he had done and unstrapped their own weapons, but Riley waved them back. By now the figure was close enough that they could see him—no, *her*—clearly. Female. Definitely female. Wearing a brief kilt, sandals and a vest-top that was both halter and work-pack.

She looked to be no more than seventeen—but that could be a false impression. She could have been as young as twelve or as old as fifty. The likelihood of metabolic control of aging processes made it impossible to be certain.

She was speaking into a small hand-held communication device as she approached, "Is look-look break-through, allrah. Is not see demons yet." She stopped only a few meters from where they hid. Riley and Omara exchanged glances across the open corridor. The female was carrying a very deadly-looking high-powered dart gun.

She turned slowly, surveying the entire area. "Is best call quarantine. Entire sector. Look-look undamage. Is need security and cleanup."

"Staypuh," replied the device. "Hold pos. Go low."

"Check-check," she replied and restrapped the device to her belt. She sank down to one knee in a watchful position, her dart-gun held before her.

Riley sank back down behind the tank again. If the woman moved only a few meters forward, she would see them. He sucked in his lower lip thoughtfully. If he revealed himself to her, she would probably put a dart through his chest. The odds were good that it would have fatal results. The inhabitants of this part of the ship were obviously at war with the savages—no, make that *hostiles*.

He snuck another look.

Her hair was cut short. She wore no makeup. Her skin was a deep chocolate color—but whether it was natural or a prolonged tan from working regularly under these lights, he couldn't be sure. Her features were well-defined; her high cheekbones even lent her expression a slight air of arrogance. She turned toward him, and for one brief instant, Riley was almost certain that she could see him through the leaves—but when she didn't react, just kept scanning back and forth, he exhaled slowly. Her eyes had been the most piercing shade of blue he had ever seen.

He lowered himself back down to a kneeling position again and put a finger to his lips to indicate to the others that continued silence was still necessary. He shook his head grimly for emphasis.

He found himself wondering . . . could they disarm her? No, that might be risky.

He looked at the phaser in his hand. No, only as a last resort would he—

His communicator beeped.

The woman's eyes widened and—

—she whirled and—

—something whistled past Riley's right ear and—

—he rolled sideways across the open corridor, firing his phaser in a pattern of three quick flashes and—

—came up onto his feet, his phaser still held ready, but the woman was crumpled across her weapon.

"Farge!" he said.

Garcia was already moving. "She took all three shots—"

"Is she still alive?"

"Just barely—"

"Look—!" pointed Stokely. Far in the distance, a squad of black shapes was moving toward them. Running.

Riley flipped open his communicator. "Transporter room. Five to beam up. *Now!*"

"Hold it!" called Stokely, unclipping something from his belt. A remote coordinating module for the transporter so they or a subsequent contact team could beam back to the same spot. He stuck it to the underside of one of the tanks where it could not be easily seen.

"Hurry up," snapped Riley. He brought his phaser up again, but he didn't want to use it if he didn't have to; it would just make it that much harder to establish non-hostile contact later on.

But that security team, or whatever it was, was getting closer. They could hear their footsteps slapping on the deck. And they were heavily armed.

"Secured and operating," said Stokely, jumping to his feet.

"Transporter room, *energize!!*"

The air piled up in sparkles around them—

And a flurry of darts passed harmlessly through the space where they had been.

13

Dr. Leonard "Bones" McCoy studied the unconscious young woman on the table with a clinical eye. The readout screen at the head of the med-bed showed her life processes dangerously depressed.

"Will she be all right?" Riley asked. His expression showed his concern.

McCoy didn't look up from the hand-terminal he was studying. "I don't predict the future, Lieutenant. I only try to help it." Then, in a milder tone, "She has a fair chance. And she's young and strong. Now, go report to the Captain and leave me alone to work." To Nurse Chapel, he said, "Put her on a deo-five IV with two percent Adrenal-4."

Chapel looked at him with a question on her face.

"I know, I know—but it won't kill her and at least it'll give her strength. I'm not going to do anything more drastic to her metabolism until I'm certain it's an entirely human metabolism I'm dealing with. Take a scraping and run a full set of scans; particularly the amino acid series, the protein and enzyme analyses, and start a genetic chart if there's time. Have the lab start with chromosomes 6 and 7, and give me a count of the Hy-3 activators."

"Right," and Chapel was on her way.

Alone with his patient, McCoy sank slowly down into a chair by her bedside and studied the life-process readouts again. He didn't like it, not at all. Not one little bit. He patted the young woman's hand, but she didn't stir.

For the moment, there was nothing to do but wait.

But then, McCoy was used to waiting. A large part of medicine is the physician's ability to recognize when he should step back and think. And reassess. A good doctor doesn't heal the sick so much as he helps them to heal themselves, and the measure of a physician's capability can often be told by his patience.

He was still sitting there a few minutes later when Kirk came in. "Bones—," he said.

"I don't know," said McCoy, "so don't ask."

"How do you know what I was going to ask?"

"I read minds. You were going to ask how is she and how soon will she be able to talk. First, I'd like to be certain that she isn't going to die. She's awfully small and she took a very heavy charge. You might tell Riley that he needn't be so trigger-happy next time."

"He was scared, Bones. And who's to say that anyone else might not have done the same thing under the same circumstances?"

Bones didn't look convinced. Before he could reply, though, the intercom beeped. He stepped to it. "McCoy here."

A female voice: "This is the lab, sir. She's human. One hundred percent. Blood type, A-positive. The details will be coming up in memory as fast as they come out of the cooker."

"Thank you," said McCoy, switching off. He punched a series of graphs onto a screen and studied them for a moment, then turned back to Kirk. "We're going to be all right."

He loaded a pressure-hypo and set it. When he touched it to the young woman's bare forearm, it hissed softly. McCoy straightened to study the readout screen again. Two of the orange indicators had started to climb slightly. A third began to rise a little faster. "Good," he said. "She's still in shock, but she's coming around. This stuff will ease her into a gentle sleep."

"Can you wake her?"

McCoy turned to face him. "Physically, she can cope with it, Jim—but have you considered the mental shock she's about to receive?"

"Eh?"

"What if these people have been so isolated they no longer believe in the existence of anything but their own little universe? If that's the case, she's going to have one hell of a case of culture shock. At the very least."

Kirk exhaled louder than usual, not quite a sigh. "You're right, Bones, but we still need to debrief her."

"I know that," McCoy said testily, "—and what I'm trying to tell you is that she may not be able to stand an interrogation just yet."

"Debrief, Bones. The word is 'debrief.'"

"I'm a doctor, not a semanticist. I have a hard time telling the difference between debriefing and interrogation."

Kirk knew there was no arguing with McCoy. "All right, Bones. How long?"

McCoy made a grumpy sound. He juggled possibilities in his mind for half a second, then said, "I'd like to let her wake up by herself."

As if on cue, there was a noise from the med-bed.

The young woman had raised herself up on her elbows and was peering at them with curiosity and suspicion. "Who you?" she demanded, then as she began to notice the strangeness of her surroundings, her eyes began to widen. "Where this?"

McCoy moved to the side of her bed. "There's no need to worry, Miss. You're going to be all right and nobody here will harm you."

Kirk came up to the opposite side of the med-bed. "You're on the United Starship *Enterprise*, and I'm Captain James T. Kirk."

She studied him for a moment, her blue eyes narrowed sharply. "Is *one* Captain only!"

Kirk nodded gently. "And that's the way it should be. I am the Captain of *this* ship. Who is the Captain of *your* vessel and what is its name?"

"Is demon trick? Yes! You demons! Is not trusting tricksters! Enemies!"

McCoy looked across at Kirk. "Don't get her excited, Jim—" He reached for her shoulders to ease her gently back down on the bed, but she started to roll away from him, then came arcing back with a roundhouse punch that connected loudly with McCoy's right cheek and sent him staggering backward to slam against the opposite wall. He said, *"Oof—"* as the air was forced from his lungs by the impact, and began to sag.

The young woman kept on rolling, and rolled right off the med-bed to land sure-footed on the floor, facing Kirk with the bed between them. She crouched into a fighting position, her hands cocked stiff and menacing.

Kirk deliberately relaxed and held his hands high. "I'm not threatening you," he said. "You're our guest."

"You demons!" she hissed. "Is no dying unfighting."

"Is no dying at all," said Kirk. "You're in no danger here. That man you just knocked down is the doctor who saved your life—"

She started to look behind her, but flicked her eyes back to Kirk almost immediately. "Is trick! Yes," she insisted.

"No," said Kirk gently. "Is no trick."

"Is no believe."

"What can I do to convince you?"

She stopped to consider; a frown spread across her dark features. Behind her, McCoy groaned and began pulling himself to his feet. He palmed a utility hypo from the med-unit.

Kirk gave no sign that he saw. "We don't want to hurt you," he continued in a deliberately gentle voice. "I'm Captain James T. Kirk of the starship *Enterprise.* You are on the *Enterprise.* You are no longer on your own ship. We found your ship—your *world,* as it were—drifting like a derelict. Your ship is more than twenty light-years from the nearest human colony. You're lucky we found you when we did. Your ship is heading out of the galaxy. You're already well above the plane of the ecliptic—"

"Is no more talk-talk!" She cut him off. "Is gibberish. Child-talk. Fairy-story. Is—is—" She hesitated, flustered.

And McCoy stepped up behind her and pressed the hypo to her bare arm. It fizzed softly—

She whirled to stare at him, shocked, a betrayed expression on her face—

—then she crumpled slowly forward into his outstretched arms. McCoy caught her gently and held her like a father. He stroked her hair once. "You'll be all right, little girl, just as soon as you stop being scared." He looked over her shoulder at the Captain. "Maybe now you'll listen to your doctor's advice?"

14

There was a full complement of officers and section heads in the briefing room, waiting for the Captain and talking intensely among themselves. As Kirk strode in and took his seat at the head of the table, the background chatter faded to silence.

"All right," he began. "We've all seen the contact team's reports. They've done an exceptionally *good* job, considering the difficult circumstances under which they were working. Please note that I'm putting commendations into each of their records. Now then, I want some answers. We've already got plenty of questions." He looked around the table. "Mr. Chekov, have you back-traced that ship yet?"

Chekov looked embarrassed. "Uh . . . yes, *Keptin*, but it is so unlikely, we're running a second series of simulations."

"I grant the possibility that you may be wrong, Mr. Chekov; it's something we all have to deal with every day of our lives, but for the record, at least, what point of origin did your first simulation suggest?"

"Uh—you're going to find this hard to believe—I know, I had a lot of trouble with it myself—but, ah—"

"Just get to the point, please."

"—uh, Earth."

"Earth?"

"Well, the Earth system, at least. We, uh—found a fifty-three percent probability. They would have had to have visited several other star systems along the way, looping around the suns to come into a new trajectory for their next destination—but the courses match up almost perfectly with Mr. Spock's simulation of what a colony vessel would do—" He broke off and looked to the Vulcan Science Officer for help.

Spock nodded dispassionately. "If we make the assumption that this is a colony vessel—which it appears very much to be—then Mr. Chekov's simulation is also a history of several consecutive very bad decisions. If, as is suggested, they left the Earth system some one hundred and eighty-five years ago, they must have first aimed for Sirius-B. Finding no planet circling that star that they could have used without large-scale terraforming—which at that time would have been beyond their technological capabilities—they would have had no choice but to proceed onward to their next most likely destination, Wolf 359.

"Mr. Chekov's hypothesis, and I concur, is that the lack of suitable planets around these first two stars was so obvious that no final braking procedures were instituted at all. Rather the vessel was aimed to loop around the sun into a new trajectory, redirecting their momentum. With appropriately large sails, they could have also made use of the solar wind to add to their velocity. The object, of course, would be to shorten the travel time to the next star.

"If they did this several times in a row, as Mr. Chekov suggests, they could have built up considerable speed. This is where the bad planning comes in.

"We must assume," continued Spock, "that at some point or other, the inhabitants of the vessel, now into their third or fourth generation, began to get impatient. The model for generation ships of this type has always been that they would accelerate for half the journey, then decelerate for the other half. But this model has always presupposed that there was a habitable suitable planet waiting for you at the target star. With long-range scanning—even of the simplest and most basic types—it is possible to detect the suitability of a star system long before you enter it. That fact must have encouraged the colonists to postpone deceleration procedures until they were close enough to determine whether or not they should invest the energy resources in deceleration. Granted, this would mandate a more severe deceleration, but the odds against finding a planet would have been sufficiently high to warrant this kind of gamble. If a planet should look promising, you institute braking procedures, but not until then. You save your momentum. Should the system prove uninhabitable on any level, you still have your original velocity; you loop around the sun and you're on your way to your next destination already at your top speed—*and still accelerating*. To those within the ship, the chance of taking ten or fifteen years off the next leg of the journey—if worst came to worst and they had to continue onward in their search—must have seemed irresistible. To those faced with a choice between spending the rest of their lives knowing nothing but the ship around them or possibly, just possibly, walking on a planet—something they had never known in their whole lives, and never would know unless the chance were taken—it would have been the *only possible* course of action.

"Continually failing to find a planet, the cumulative result would be the accretion of such velocity that final deceleration becomes not just exceedingly difficult within the necessary time-frame, but for all practical purposes, impossible. Should a suitable planet be detected, it's too late to stop."

"Surely, they must have realized—" That was Uhura.

"At some point, yes. But consider two possibilities. Suppose they lost part of their drive system—a reactor goes down, for example, and there is no way to repair it. What then? They've lost part of their deceleration capability. From the evidence so far, it appears that they lost *several* of their reactors. A second possibility, and even more likely, considering the circumstances as well as the report of the contact team, is that there was some kind of social upheaval. A mutiny perhaps."

At the word, heads turned sharply in Spock's direction. Mutiny? Even Kirk looked concerned.

"Consider . . ." said Spock. "A planet is detected.

Hero's Star, for example. From a distance it looks to be habitable. Even at close ranges, the planet seems promising. But periodic flares of the primary bathe the planet in such intense hard radiation that life there is marginal, at best. But—if you had never walked on a planet in your whole life, and that planet was your only possible chance at a final home, how would you feel about a burst of radiation that comes only once in twenty-three years?" He looked around the table.

Some of the other officers were studying their hands or the tabletop. Others looked ashen, not having realized the enormity of the situation.

"Mr. Spock," Kirk said gently, "I had no idea you had so much . . . *compassion*. . . ."

"Compassion has nothing to do with logic, Captain. I am merely extrapolating a possible circumstance from the evidence at hand—*including* my own knowledge of human behavior." He returned Kirk's quizzical glance with a cool stare of his own. "May I continue?"

"Please."

"Given these assumptions—and they are only assumptions—I would postulate that the decision to stop at Hero's Star or pass it by and continue on to the next would very likely have sparked a civil war—which could have led to mutiny. Perhaps one side sought to disable the ship to keep it from proceeding on to the next star and that's why it's a derelict now. The war has never been resolved and the survivors are living at opposite ends of the vessel as farmers and . . . savages. Of course, this extrapolation is based only on the evidence we've seen so far, but the last system this vessel could possibly have passed through was in fact that of Hero's Star, and the trajectories and velocities that Mr. Chekov has calculated fit into this hypothesis extraordinarily well."

Kirk looked across the table at his First Officer. "Thank you, Mr. Spock. An excellent presentation. Are you . . . suggesting a probability rating for this . . . hypothesis?"

Spock looked off into space while he calculated. "Ninety percent, at least."

"Oh," said Kirk. "Then it's just a wild guess." There was a hint of a twinkle in his eye.

Spock said, "For a Vulcan, *yes.*"

Kirk let it pass. He was about to ask Mr. Chekov when his second simulation series would be complete when Mr. Scott spoke up. "Aye, that's a *vurry* pretty story, Mr. Spock, but it won't hold water. There's no record of a ship like that ever leavin' Earth at all. I know somethin' about shipbuildin' and I'd know if a ship like that'un had been built any time in the past three hundred years. That's an expenditure of not just mega-calories, but macro-calories, and you don't keep an expense like that secret, nor a construction project on that scale either."

"If you say so, Mr. Scott." Spock fixed the Chief Engineer with an expressionless gaze. "If you have no knowledge of the construction of that ship in Earth space, then you have no knowledge; but the ship is there, just a few kilometers away. And the young woman in Dr. McCoy's sick bay speaks a mutated, but still recognizable form of English. Therefore, it is more likely that your knowledge is in error than that ship's existence." He waited patiently for Mr. Scott's reply.

Scotty did not take it personally. But he folded his arms across his chest and returned Mr. Spock's look with one of his own. "Be tha' as it may, Mr. Spock, there never was a ship like that built in Earth space. And I know because I was the senior engineer at the San Francisco shipyards when the *Enterprise* and three of her sisters were built. That's the only shipyard with the capability of even *designing* such a vessel—and believe me, I've been through the records many times, lookin' to see how my predecessors dealt with their construction problems. Nay, Mr. Spock. That ship did-na' come from any shipyard I know of."

Kirk held up a hand before anyone else could speak. "Gentlemen," he said. "You may both be right. I suggest that our next most *logical* step is to adjourn to the *Enterprise's* historical section." He looked from one to the other questioningly. "Agreed?"

He didn't wait for their answers. He was already rising from his chair. They had no choice but to follow.

15

Despite the best intentions of planners, designers, and builders, there are always a few parts of a starship that end up being modified for some reason or other—usually to suit the specific needs or personality of that ship's complement. The *Enterprise* was no exception.

Ordinarily, a starship's historical section is a minor file in the ship's library—a reflection of the fact that starship captains tend to make history more than they study it. But James T. Kirk was an exception in this regard as well. Before taking the *Enterprise* out on her first patrol, he had ordered the ship's library upgraded to a primary storage level equal to the main banks at Starfleet command. The ship's third gymnasium had been rebuilt to house the additional memory tanks.

In explanation, Kirk had said only, "If you can learn from the mistakes of others, you don't have to make them yourself."

Thereafter, whenever the *Enterprise* made rendezvous with any other starship or starbase, or returned to Starfleet Command, the ship's librarian automatically requested updates and upgrades for all library sections, freely trading whatever unclassified information was requested in exchange. The *Enterprise* also routinely gathered libraries from other sources as well, particularly from whatever alien cultures they encountered in their patrols,

For the first year of Kirk's command as captain of the *Enterprise,* Starfleet's Admiralty had regarded this policy of his as an interesting quirk, a harmless aberration of command. Some captains painted for relaxation, others played chess; James T. Kirk collected the sum total of human knowledge in the universe.

Then, of course, had occurred the famous MacMurray Encounter.

MacMurray had been a freebooter who had discovered an inhabitable planet in a most unlikely place. He called it Noah because it had three suns. The suns themselves, he named for his three cats: Signpost, Shadow, and Fred.

Shortly thereafter, he established an empire for himself on the coast of the planet's single continent—actually a colony of several hundred misfits, malcontents, and deviants, but it was empire enough for MacMurray. He and his followers declared themselves an independent technocracy, raised a flag over the courthouse and put a brass cannon on the front lawn.

For the most part, the Federation paid little attention. In fact, when Emperor MacMurray requested a Starfleet ambassadorial vessel to transport his diplomatic envoys to the Federation the request was ignored. For whatever reason, the subspace message was not even acknowledged.

MacMurray had no other options. This snub could not be tolerated. The insult would have to be avenged. He declared war on the Federation.

The MacMurray empire then proceeded to capture the next three trading vessels to arrive at their single port.

The fourth ship to arrive was the *Enterprise.*

James T. Kirk assessed the situation quickly, and immediately surrendered.

Not just the *Enterprise,* but all of Starfleet and the entire Federation as well. He surrendered on behalf of all humanity and allied races. He signed over control of all the known universe and all those parts still to be discovered. And everything else that the aforementioned failed to include.

MacMurray saw what he had done and was pleased. He declared an immediate end to all hostilities, and beamed up to assume control of the *Enterprise* in person.

Before relinquishing final control to Emperor MacMurray, James T. Kirk felt it necessary to brief the new ruler of the galaxy on the state of its affairs.

He took seven minutes to list all the local wars and disagreements that were presently being contested with open hostilities—not explain them—just *list.* He took another seven minutes to impress upon the about-to-be-king-of-everything the need to keep every single one of the billions upon billions of individuals living on all the known planets—not just humans, but all sentient species—happy, satisfied, and fulfilled; else he would surely have a revolution on his hands; he spent an extra few moments detailing some of the specialized needs of certain cultures, particularly certain meat-eaters who preferred their prey live. Finally, he pointed out that there were several problems that would require the Emperor's immediate attention and would he please advise what should be done in regard to these? He mentioned the collapse of the Romulan Treaty negotiations, the troubling new Klingon alliances, the drug-spice trade out of Orion, and of course, the budget considerations for the upcoming fiscal year and certain inflationary policies that had been established three administrations previously that had not been reworked because they were politically very sensitive.

Emperor MacMurray listened for exactly forty-five minutes, and then abdicated.

Well, not exactly *abdicated*. Kirk refused to accept the Emperor's resignation. It would throw the galaxy into chaos to be so suddenly leaderless.

MacMurray considered his options for two minutes. Then he appointed James T. Kirk to a new duty to run concurrent with his present assignment as captain of the starship *Enterprise*. He was requested to accept the position of Royal High Minister Plenipotentiary in Total Command of the Universe. And not just the known universe either, but all those parts still to be discovered as well. He ordered a parchment to signify the appointment.

Kirk accepted the post graciously. He immediately signed a document granting to all subject races and planets the autonomy they had previously enjoyed, and directed them furthermore to continue dealing with their local problems to the best of their abilities. The Emperor had more important concerns.

He hung the parchment in the ship's recreation room, so that the entire crew of the *Enterprise* would see that this was no ordinary starship Captain they were dealing with.

And then, in celebration, a huge fiesta was held.

The entire incident had lasted less than two days. The party lasted a week.

No one was killed. No one was hurt—unless you count a few hangovers and two ensigns who had somehow disassembled a thermal converter in the confusion and reassembled it with themselves inside. (They had to be beamed out in pieces, much to their chagrin and Dr. McCoy's annoyance.)

The trading vessels and their crews were released with full cargoes of Noah's main export, Krystallin-G, an industrial wax, as reward for their courage under duress. Furthermore, they were granted charters signifying that they were now part of the Royal Merchant Marine, acting under the benign protection of the Emperor of the Galaxy (in absentia).

Upon returning to Starfleet Command, Kirk discovered that MacMurray's original message *had* been received, but was never acknowledged because it was believed to have been a prank.

Shortly thereafter, the Starfleet policy was changed to mandate an acknowledgment for *all* messages, no matter how outlandish they might seem to the receiving officers—unless *specifically* authorized to do otherwise by an officer of rank equal to or greater than that of captain.

In his report Kirk noted that he had gotten the idea from studying eighteenth century foreign relations. Various ship captains had found it convenient to pay homage to local Hawaiian and African kings on behalf of their own respective monarchs—*even though they had the weaponry to wipe them out*—because it was more convenient *and practical* to respect each other.

MacMurray hadn't wanted a war, he couldn't have fought one even if he had wanted to—he just wanted to be *noticed*. And respected. That was all.

If playing a little charade for a few days could make an old man happy (and provide an excuse for a party on a planet that was otherwise fairly grim), then who's to say that space law should not be bent in favor of compassion.

Starfleet Admiralty agreed with that view and Kirk was suitably commended. He was confirmed in his position as Royal High Minister Plenipotentiary for the Emperor MacMurray.

At regular intervals thereafter, Starfleet would send an ambassadorial delegation to Noah (officially listed as a Ward of the Federation) to report that the galaxy was being run as well as could be expected under the circumstances. Emperor MacMurray always asked after the health of one James T. Kirk, and when reassured that his Royal High Minister Plenipotentiary in Total Command of the Universe was out on patrol, actively fulfilling his responsibilities, would then declare another royal celebration and bestow gifts and proclamations on everybody within reach. The MacMurray Empire also sells enough honorary dukedoms throughout the galaxy each year to pay for the maintenance of its own ambassadorial fleet, a forty-three-year-old war-surplus shuttlecraft.

Other than a gaudy parchment on the wall of rec room six, the only other reminder that James T. Kirk possesses is a notation in his record that he is the only captain in the history of Starfleet ever to surrender in the face of the enemy.

It was shortly after the MacMurray encounter that Starfleet ordered the libraries in all starships, cruiser-class and above, to be upgraded to *Enterprise* standards. Further, the free exchange of libraries as practiced by the *Enterprise* was to become the model for the Starfleet Dissemination of Human Knowledge policy as practiced by all Federation member vessels.

James T. Kirk was never certain that there was a *direct* relationship between one incident and the other, but it was an interesting coincidence nonetheless.

16

The ship's library was directly opposite the main briefing room. Due to the designed symmetry of the disk, it was the same size and shape of room, but instead of a single large table in the center, it was divided into computer stations, each terminal a specialized access to the ship's library.

Actually any terminal on the *Enterprise* (and there was at least one terminal in every room, and quite a few in various corridors) could be used to access the library, which was stored entirely in the starship's memory tanks. The room which was called "the library" was therefore neither a storehouse nor necessary access as much as it was a primary control center for large-scale information handling: a set of terminals with specific data-processing functions. The room also doubled as a video control studio for the ship's internal channels and occasionally as a secondary mission control for specialized operations.

The "historical section," such as *it* was, was not so much a place as a state of mind. Set off from the library was a data tank, a small theater holding ten seats and a control console at the rear. A large wall screen dominated the front of the wedge-shaped chamber.

The ship's historian preferred to use this particular room as his main terminal because the large screen facilitated the easy examination of details in visual data such as photographs or paintings. Occasionally, however, he also used it to play some of the ancient games in the ship's library, such as Space War and Dungeon. He was fascinated by the past—perhaps because it seemed such a terribly romantic time, especially in contrast to the mundanity of contemporary existence.

He was a thin fellow, skinny, and with an uncontrolled shock of brown hair. He looked too young to be serving in Starfleet, but if he was here, then he was obviously capable; the competition was too fierce for the inept to last long at the Academy.

He stood up as the Captain, the First Officer, the Chief Engineer, and the navigator stepped into his tiny retreat. He brushed some crumbs off the front of his uniform and pushed a meal tray aside, then came to sloppy attention. He was mostly nonplused at the appearance of the top brass. "Sirs?" he said.

Kirk nodded an acknowledgment, then remarked

sideways to Spock, "I don't think I've been down here since I took command. No need to until now—hm, perhaps I'm overdue for a surprise inspection in a lot of parts of this ship." He looked at the young man standing by the console. "What's your name, crewman?"

"Uh—everybody calls me 'Specks,' sir."

"Specks?"

"Uh, yes, sir."

"Specks," repeated Kirk slowly, holding the unusual name up to the light to see if there was a secret message hidden in it. If there was, he didn't see it. "Well, Specks, your Captain needs you to do some research—"

"Yes, sir!" Specks resumed his seat at his console and punched the big screen up to life. His hands started flying over the controls.

"Uh—" Kirk was taken aback. He hadn't even voiced his request yet. Then, on second thought, he realized he didn't need to. It was obvious what he must want information on. It would have been obvious to anyone aboard the *Enterprise*. He half-shrugged in acceptance and looked to Spock. Spock raised one eyebrow at him.

Kirk said, "The origin of that ship may be the Earth system. At least, that's what Mr. Chekov has suggested. If that's true, then you should have some record of its construction. It would have left the Earth-system about one hundred and eighty-five years ago, plus or minus ten."

"Hm," said Specks. "I think he may be a little off there, just a minute—" He reached across the console and grabbed a wire framework holding two lenses. He adjusted the odd device on the bridge of his nose and peered through the lenses at the screens in front of him.

Kirk and Spock exchanged another glance. "Uh," said Kirk. "What are those things?"

"Badge of office," the historian said noncommittally, not looking up.

Spock put in, "Glasses, or spectacles, as they were commonly called, were a popular form of prosthesis for the correction of simple visual disabilities well into the twenty-first century when corneal reshaping finally became widespread. Now, glasses are used only for special viewing purposes, such as close or distant amplification of images, or for protection. I would suggest that the name 'Specks' is an abbreviation for 'spectacles.' At one time, it was a common nickname for those who wore such devices. They are probably bifocal to help the crewman focus on both his control board and the wall screen more easily."

"Thank you, Mr. Spock." One thing about working with a Vulcan, Kirk realized, you pick up a lot of trivia.

"Sirs? If you'll look forward?"

All four officers turned to face the big screen. It had become a window onto space. A gigantic cylinder turned majestically in the light of an unseen yellow star. Despite its lack of engines and ramscoop, the structure was immediately familiar. Behind it a blue and white planet shone like a drop of spring rain, and behind the planet a crystalline white moon, speckled with twilight craters.

Scotty stepped forward angrily. "That canna' be—I know every ship that came from my shipyard—"

"But that isn't a ship, Mr. Scott—" Specks was momentarily confused. He looked from one officer to the other. "Don't you realize what you've found? That's the Lost Cometary Colony!"

Kirk was startled; Scotty looked like he'd been kicked; Chekov spluttered unreadably. Mr. Spock nodded slowly. "Of course . . . " he said. "It's the only answer that makes any sense." He turned to Kirk. "Captain, I apologize. I should have recognized it."

"That's all right, Spock. We all make mistakes. It must have been your human half."

"Undoubtedly."

Specks was still babbling—"It's like finding the ten lost tribes of Israel—or the lost colony of Roanoke, Virginia. I thought you'd realized it right away, sirs. I couldn't understand why you hadn't buzzed me for the rest of the story—"

"All right, hold it—," interrupted Kirk. "Let's take this from the beginning—" He interrupted himself to note for Spock's benefit only, "I'm going to have to brush up on recent history myself. Now then . . . ?"

"Sirs?" The historian pointed to the seats. "If you'll make yourselves comfortable, I took the ah, liberty of preparing a brief presentation of this material ahead of time for just this, ah, eventuality."

Kirk looked to his officers. "Gentlemen? Be seated."

Specks began with a series of blueprints. "The early design concepts for the structure," he explained. "It was built to be the first L5 structure. Here, you can see the plan for the farms, this huge open area in the center. The structure is a giant hollow cylinder with a landscape established on the inside wall of the hull. In addition, there are anywhere from five to twenty-five levels of offices, theaters, plumbing, air shafts, industrial plants, life-support machinery, recycling stations, and the like, built in shells around that inner section. The number of levels is varied depending on the sculpting of the interior landscape. They wanted mountains, hills, lakes, and so on. A real wilderness. So they put their city and industry 'underground,' sort of.

"With appropriate construction—" Here, Specks switched to another series of photographs, these showing the framework of an unfinished "mountain range" within the inner shell. "—they could simulate a wide range of gravities, pressures and temperature conditions across that wilderness. Just by controlling air circulation, lighting, moisture patterns, isolation by natural features—rivers, mountains—they could put a rain forest, a desert, a mountain meadow, and a temperate zone all within a few kilometers of each other. Pocket environments. Very clever. They could also control the seasons for their farms, having as many as three summers a year to increase crop production. They pioneered low-gravity farming. Giant vegetables."

Now, Specks punched up images of the colony vessel as it neared the completion of its primary construction phase. It looked strangely naked without its huge fusion engines at each end and the giant hoop around its waist. Nor were there many of the additional devices studding the hull that would be added later. Instead, there were two huge solar panels, extending from the ends of the cylinder; as it rotated, they maintained a constant orientation to the sun.

"You really have to admire the ingenuity of those people," Specks said. "Here it is, near completion. Look at the size of those solar collectors. So primitive, and yet they still accomplished so much."

Kirk whispered to Spock, "I wonder if that's what some future historian is going to be saying about *us* in two hundred years?"

Spock said dryly, "More than likely."

If Specks heard, he gave no sign. He continued his lecture happily. "The original intention, of course, was that this structure was to occupy the L5 Trojan position—forming a triangle with the Earth and the moon. It was to be the first large-scale industrial base in space. Ore would be catapulted from the moon—because there's less of an energy penalty to pay for climbing out of the lunar gravity well—to the L5 position where it would be used as the raw material for the construction of the station, solar power satellites, and associated technology. You see, to put this in the proper context, this project was viewed as the last best hope to break the energy deadlock of the twenty-first century. Energy resources were particularly scarce at the time and the construction of orbiting solar power stations was recognized as the best way to meet humanity's growing appetite for electricity on a *permanent* basis—"

"Is all this background necessary, lad?" interrupted Scotty.

"Well, it's a pretty interesting story, Mr. Scott, sir—and it does have some bearing on *why* that ship is way out here on the edge of nowhere, and—"

"Scotty . . ." Kirk put a hand on the Chief Engineer's arm. "Let him tell his story," he whispered. "It's his one chance to be a part of this operation." A little louder, he said, "Go ahead, uh, Specks."

"Yes, sir. Well, what happened—wait a minute, let me call up the appropriate—ah, there—you can see in this picture that there's another structure, a larger one, under construction here. I'm jumping ahead just a bit to show you this. I know this is going to get confusing, but let me try to explain something of what happened here—you see, there were these three nations, the United States, Japan, and the Soviet Union—they built the L5 as a joint effort, with some help from their allies. At one time they had been political opponents, but their mutual energy needs led them into this cooperative venture. It was either that or continue to let their respective economies be held hostage by the energy-exporting nations—at that time, they used mostly fossil fuels. It was fairly primitive and dirty stuff—oil, coal, some natural gas. It played hell with the atmosphere and the weather. Anyway, even before the L5 station was fully operational as a self-contained environment, the industrial sections were operating; they built and installed four solar-energy satellites in the first eighteen months. Total energy imports to the member nations of this alliance were reduced more than three percent. The governments involved were so pleased with this early success that they increased their satellite construction appropriations, hoping to speed the progress of the project."

Specks switched to a series of world maps now. "Of course, all this had quite an effect on the energy-exporting nations who now saw their own economies threatened by the loss of revenues. Solar energy is clean and cheap; the sunlight is free, and in space it's a constant uninterrupted source; all you have to do is collect it. On the other hand, fossil fuels are expensive, inefficient and dirty; the pollution problem alone is reason enough to avoid them. Every solar-power satellite increased the energy independence of the member nations and decreased the total amount of fossil fuel pollution. Three percent this year, five percent next year, eight percent the year after—it's the closest thing to a free lunch in this universe."

Specks cleared the screen again. "Now—," he said, "—here is where a very bad decision was made. I think that it is this decision that made subsequent events almost inevitable. The developing nations of the Earth tried to contract with the new 'solar powers' for satellites of their own—but the solar powers, after considerable political debate, refused to sell satellites, only electricity. They would beam it to any spot on the Earth the purchaser wanted, all he had to do was build a receiving station and the power would be cheap and plentiful—but the collecting satellite itself would belong to the solar powers.

"To the developing nations, this looked like they were trading one bad deal for another. They were still buying their electricity from someone else. Either way, their economies would be at the mercy of whoever sold them their power. And after as many decades of international blackmail as they had already experienced at the hands of the various world powers, the Third World nations had become fairly suspicious of *everyone's* motives.

"The Third World nations had no alternative but to form an international cartel of their own to build their own industrial station in space to build their own solar power satellites; otherwise the growing space industry would forever be controlled by the solar powers. Of course, the solar powers said they welcomed the effort, but they really didn't—there were those (on both sides) who saw space as just one more political weapon by which to gain power over others—and many of those individuals had quite a bit of influence at that time. So the Third World project was offered everything but help. It was a very shortsighted decision on the part of some politicians, and I suspect that this is where the colloquialism, 'Earthbound mentality' comes from.

"Anyway, despite their own lack of resources, the Third World nations persevered. They formed an alliance with the oil-rich nations who then joined the venture as financial partners. It was a mutually beneficial arrangement, and the fact that it was also a way whereby they could pay back their respective grudges was just icing on the cake. There was quite a bit of resentment there."

Specks switched back to photos of the L5 station, now in a more advanced stage of development. Ships could be seen docking with it, but there were still no fusion engines or ramscoop collar. "Now, it's important to realize that all this took place over a period of two decades. By the end of that time, the L5 station had established itself as a city in space, almost a nation unto itself. It had its own government, courts, taxes, customs, and a large and very *intelligent* voting population. If nothing else, you had to be either very smart or very rich to get aboard the L5. If you were smart, you could work. If you were rich, you could be a tourist.

"Despite the station's legal status as a 'cooperative protectorate,' it functioned much more like a pocket democracy and the solar powers really had very little control over the L5 station—after all, how could they enforce it? But the legal fiction existed for twenty years because it worked and there was no pressing reason to change it. At this point, nearly thirty percent of the member nations' electricity was coming from space—of course, they owned their own satellites—and they were all in much stronger economic positions. Fusion power was finally off the drawing board; as a practical reality it was a viable alternative to both oil and solar energy—and there was some concern that large-scale microwave beaming of power back to Earth might also create subtle, but adverse ecological effects. Also, the oil-exporting nations had begun to reduce their prices to stay competitive with solar energy, and the new fusion power. Perhaps they even did that deliberately to hold back further development. It was for all these reasons that the solar powers began to cut back on their satellite appropriations. The pressure to build was no longer as severe.

"You see how complex this is getting? The cutback hurt the economy of the L5 station. More than a thousand workers were scheduled to be sent back to Earth—and they didn't want to go. By then, the L5 was a fairly nice place to live. Clean, uncrowded, and with a variety of recreational environments unmatched anywhere else. They had even simulated a section of Martian terrain as a training area for colonists heading out to the new Martian settlements. They didn't want to lose such a large part of their own community, so they made a bid to the Third World Alliance—which had been having a lot of organizational troubles—that they would contract to build their projected L5 structure for them. A project of that size would enable them to maintain their present economy, and actually expand it and grow. Again, it would be a mutually beneficial arrangement, were it not for the political realities—the solar powers didn't exactly veto the bid, they just became very obstructionist, finding all sorts of reasons, financial, legal, political, why the L5 should *not* commit its energies toward the construction of a station for the Third World Alliance.

"The wrangling went on for seven months, with tempers rising on both sides. Finally, the L5 station declared its independence as a nation unto itself. In the space of twenty-four hours, thirty-three of the Third World Alliance nations had formally recognized their existence as a nation and the contract for the construction of a second L5 had been signed.

"By the time the solar powers had finished being outraged, it was too late. They had no choice but to accept the situation. The alternative would have been war—and in that case, the L5 government had the strategic advantage. After all, they were on top of the gravity well. They didn't need bombs, they could have dropped rocks. And they could destroy all of the solar satellites if necessary—that act alone would cut off thirty percent of the electricity available to the solar powers. Or, they could have used the microwave beams of those satellites to selectively and precisely destroy whatever military targets they chose.

"So," said Specks, finally returning to the photo of the two stations in space, one finished, the other still under construction, "the outcome of that particular crisis forced *all* the nations of Earth to realize that they were at a disadvantage against political blackmail from space—but from a historical point of view, they had brought it on themselves through their own use of political blackmail. They gave their opponents no other option. It was a very touchy period of international relations. Within two years, for example, there were no less than five military space stations under construction—all of them well away from the L5 station's easy surveillance. Some of these military stations were as grandiose in concept as the original L5.

"Now we jump a few more years ahead. I won't trace all of the individual events that led up to it—it was just one more political crisis in a long string of crises—but the Third World Alliance began to fall apart. Part of it was that several years of drought and famine had exhausted the resources of the developing nations, and part of it was that with the widespread growth of fusion power, hydrogen-, methane-, and alcohol-fuels, plus assorted other sources like biomass, geothermal, wind-power, ocean current-turbines, and so on—all in addition to solar energy—the world's appetite for oil had dropped dramatically. The oil-rich nations no longer had the resources available to them to continue financing the L5 construction. The cartel collapsed. Some said it was the victim of its own bad planning—others said that the collapse was given a good push by agents of the solar powers who had worked to undermine the economies of the cartel's member nations. None of the allegations were ever proved—if they had been true, the evidence would have had to be destroyed because of the extreme potential for war such allegations carried.

"All right, so now we have one functioning L5 station and one nearly completed structure. The solar powers offered to purchase and complete the second unit, but the L5 nation turned down this offer; instead, they mortgaged themselves heavily and completed the construction on their own. Now, as you can see, just about every decision that has been made here, has been made for political reasons: the search for power in one form or another. And now there were some thirty years of long-standing grudges waiting to be paid off. Several of the military stations were operational now, a lot of bills were coming due for the L5 nation and they were not in the best position to pay these debts off. Earth's economy had taken a real beating—the collapse of the cartel had triggered a worldwide recession—and there just wasn't the financing available for the construction projects needed to keep the L5's economy on sound footing.

"They couldn't look for aid anywhere else in the solar system either. These were a proud and independent group of people and they had run out of friends.

"Now, I have to interrupt my story here to give a little more background information—I'm sorry for going on so long, sir—"

"No, no—" said Kirk. "Please go on, uh, Specks.

To borrow a phrase from Mr. Spock, I find this piece of history . . . fascinating."

"Yes, sir. Thank you, sir. Well, what I was going to say was that going on all this time there were quite a few psychological studies of the inhabitants of the L5 nation, because no one knew what would happen to a population as isolated as they were and living in such a totally artificial and structured environment. What would be the effect of being separated from the—the *karmic* link with *home?* So, throughout that entire first generation, the entire population was being psychologically monitored, every one of them to one degree or another. And now that they were on the threshold of the second generation in space, certain long-range and recurrent patterns were beginning to become . . . ah, recognizable.

"Ship-dwellers, for instance, seemed to have different perceptual 'spaces' than land-dwellers, especially as regards the sense of territory. The theory was that the mutability of gravity in the ship environment—that is, the fact that you can structure your interior ecology for whatever gravity you want or even no gravity at all—makes for a more three-dimensional perception of relationships. A holistic view. It's almost impossible to 'defend' a personal territory in a volume as opposed to being on a plane. That's why three-dimensional chess never caught on as big as everyone thought it would.

"Anyway, the lack of territoriality in a ship-dweller tends to produce the ah, 'starside syndrome'—which is sometimes called the 'million-light-year-stare.' Starsiders seem to be able to see forever. And somehow, they always seem at peace with themselves, their bodies, and the spaces they move in.

"Today, this is normal for most of the human race, we take it for granted that we have been 'expanded' by our exposure to the wonders of the universe. In fact, we call it the 'sense of wonder'—but at that time, you must remember, it was something *new* to most of humanity. The land-dwellers, the ah, 'dirtsiders'—"

Kirk studiously ignored the colloquialism. Starfleet discouraged the suffix "-siders," because used in the wrong context it might seem elitist or derogatory.

"—were beginning to become aware of this *differ-*

ence between themselves and the space-dwellers. It wasn't even a conscious realization, just a vague resentment. I like to imagine it as something like the situation between the last Neanderthals and the first Cro-magnons—"

"Ahh—Specks," Kirk interrupted, "—you can get on with your story. We pretty much know about the starside syndrome."

"Yes, sir. The point I wanted to make was that there was a very real fear on the Earth that the starsiders might begin to feel so *detached* from the rest of humanity, somehow lose their sense of responsibility to the species, that they would begin to regard themselves as . . . uh, gods. It was thought that the long-term isolation in an environment that they could totally control might produce that kind of perceptual difference. Uh, the question was never fully answered, as I will get to in a moment.

"This, combined with the various jealousies, grudges, and resentments—particularly the awareness of the 'favored'-status of just living in the sky—worked against the L5 dwellers. A lot of people felt that they had been somehow subsidizing the L5 nation for a good many years—or at least subsidizing their economy—and they felt that perhaps it was about time that the L5 nation began repaying some of its debts to the Earth. And so on and so on.

"It was a bad time for those first colonists.

"It was the biggest crisis they had ever faced, and they were no longer in the same position of strength they had been in ten years earlier when they had declared their independence.

"What they did was unorthodox—but it was their only out. They 'colonized' the second L5 unit. Then they granted the colony independence, allowing them to become their own nation, just as the first L5 unit had done a decade earlier. So now there were two nations in the sky, one debt-ridden, one free and clear. Most of the Earth nations were reluctant, but they went along with it and recognized the new nation because they didn't realize what the L5 colonists were planning to do.

"What they did caught everybody on Earth by surprise. First, they closed down their port facilities and redirected all traffic to the second structure; shortly thereafter, they summarily evicted all nonresidents and nonresident businesses to the second facility. They were selectively removing everyone from their world who did not have the million-year vision. Some very strange stories of the last days there began to come out with the refugees and there was a great deal of mystery about what was going on.

"For one thing, there was quite a bit of importing going on—all kinds of strange things. Seeds, libraries, blueprints, rare metals, industrial supplies, various animals—agricultural mostly, but enough for a small *zoo* —enough supplies, equipment, and information as if they were hoarding up for a very long siege. Nobody quite knew what the L5 nation was preparing to do.

"Intelligence agents on the second facility were able to see quite a bit of industrial activity on the hull of the ship, but no clear hypothesis had yet suggested itself. Most of the industrial activity was centered around six fusion units they had contracted to build for the Third World Alliance. The units were originally planned for a fleet of long-range spacecraft which would travel to the outer planets, and if possible, establish bases on suitable moons. That deal, of course, had collapsed with the alliance and the units had been waiting unfinished ever since.

"Now, however, the units were obviously being finished—even though there was no fleet of spacecraft for them to be installed in—umm, there was a legal problem here. The ownership of those six units was tied up in litigation with a number of parties bidding for the right to foreclose—so when the word got out that the L5 station was *finishing* the drive units, all sorts of howls of outrage were raised by all sorts of corporations, alliances, governments, lawyers, and politicians.

"The L5 station refused to respond for five days, then issued a terse statement that they would have a statement to make in five more days, and then five days later announced that they had nationalized the drive units and would be testing the first two of them in three days.

"Of course, this created a whole new uproar, and

three warships of the Solar Alliance even broke out of their lunar orbits to rendezvous with the station. But they were too late. Instead of testing the engines, the colony fired them up at full power and began to accelerate out of the L5 position.

"Within a few days, it began to be obvious what their intention was. They were injecting themselves into a long cometary orbit. The three warships chasing them couldn't follow; they had neither the fuel nor supplies—although they did make a valiant try. One of the warships took all of the extra fuel and supplies of the other two ships, but even so, it could not catch up. The L5 station had, in effect, an *unlimited* range because it was completely self-contained and self-supporting.

"Well, if there had been an uproar before, what followed now was a political riot. Outrage from those who had felt wronged—and applause from those who liked to see someone get away with something against the major powers. But all the words tossed around were just words. The L5 nation was effectively beyond the reach of every known human agency.

"Their cometary orbit would take them out almost as far as the orbit of Uranus, then eventually bring them back in as near to the sun as the orbit of Venus. It was quite a loop.

"And they wouldn't be back in the neighborhood for slightly more than ten years, more than enough time for the rest of humanity to cool down in their feelings. And humanity needed a lot of cooling down.

"But the L5 planners had been very canny in their choice of orbits. They passed close enough to Mars for a number of ships to make rendezvous, and they exchanged quite a bit of cargo and even a few passengers came aboard while several others off-loaded. A year later, as they passed over the asteroid belt (they were slightly above the plane of the ecliptic here; on the way back, they would be slightly under it) they made rendezvous with various mining craft and again traded supplies for ore, industrial goods especially.

"A year after that, they were nearly close enough to Jupiter for the Jovian colonies to attempt a rendezvous. This was a particularly crucial operation for them too. The collapse of the Third World Alliance had interrupted the supply pipeline to several of the colonies on the Jovian moons.

"So you see, the colony had created a new situation for itself. They were a traveling world—the interplanetary equivalent of a nomad caravan, bringing rare goods from faraway places. They were able to take on passengers and provide gravitational and climatic conditions identical to those of each individual world they visited. And this was especially important because the passengers could now acclimatize themselves one step at a time to the higher or lower gravities to which they were traveling. The medical facilities on the L5 were unmatched.

"A round trip on the cometary shuttle might take as long as ten years, but for some kinds of travelers—especially colonists—the slow trip was preferable. The shuttle was a clean, healthy environment. More pleasant than most places on Earth at the time, and more pleasant than most of the colonies. It was a world safely out of reach of war, weather, and politicians. Consequently, many of those who traveled on the shuttle were hesitant to leave, but the only ones granted permanent resident status were those who could prove that they could enrich the quality of life aboard ship.

"In the ensuing thirty years, the cometary colony made three complete laps from the inner to the outer planets and were individually responsible for increasing the volume of interplanetary trade by some 5000%.

"And that, of course, brings me to the final political decision in the story.

"Nobody argues with success. And the financial success of the L5 nation in this new role was undeniable. Halfway through the second lap, there were four new L5 structures under construction—three being financed by Earth-based corporations, and one Lunar-sponsored one. The economics were obvious. There were markets that could only be effectively serviced by this type of slow travel. A city in space may be slower, but if you have the extra time—and if you're in constant communication with the rest of the solar system anyway—then it's far more comfortable than either a torchship or a catapulter.

"But, of course, with this heavy investment in interplanetary travel, the *interstellar* development program was temporarily shelved.

"The *Wanderer*—as the ship was now called—had developed into a fairly closed, but visionary society. The wanderers insisted that humanity needed to expand into the universe. Even though the answers would not be known in their own lifetimes, they felt that there were mysteries that humanity absolutely *had* to investigate. The cancellation of the starship effort for more shortsighted goals was a refusal to accept the challenge.

"On the last half of the third lap, the Wanderers unaccountably stopped taking on passengers and made a point of evicting as many tourists and other nonresident inhabitants as they could. The story was that they needed the room to transport colonists and equipment to a new base on Titan. They certainly took on enough equipment and supplies for a colony. It wasn't until afterward that the Tri-Planetary Titan Development Corporation was exposed as a dummy operation—to hide the real purpose of all those supplies they had purchased.

"The Wanderers looped around the sun and disappeared.

"They weren't where they were supposed to be after transit. At first there was some speculation that they had somehow miscalculated their orbit and fallen into the sun—but that was dismissed as unlikely. It was a hobbyist on Luna who spotted them with a homemade four-meter scope. They were nowhere near where they were supposed to be.

"Instead, they were much farther out—and accelerating. They had spread a twenty-kilometer solar sail, and when they passed the orbit of Earth, they switched on their fusion engines full power.

"They didn't add the ramscoop until much later. Probably they dismantled their drydock strurture. If you'll compare that section there, with this one here on this other photo, you'll see that the sections are remarkably similar.

"For the next three months, they accelerated continuously. They bade their farewells to our solar system, and dedicated themselves to the stars. A brave and bold adventure. Their final message included the words, 'Our grandchildren will wait for yours among the stars.'

"Laser contact was maintained for quite some time —in fact, even until after their loop around Sirius-B. Then it stopped. And it was never resumed. It was assumed that some kind of major misfortune had happened to them."

Kirk leaned forward and tapped his navigator's shoulder, "Good job of tracking, Chekov." He swung around in his seat to face Specks, "A very nice presentation—uh, Specks. It answers a lot of questions. In fact, it tells me *more* about the *Wanderer* than I wanted to know. My compliments. If you would put that presentation on the library channel, I'm sure the rest of the crew would be interested as well."

"Uh—sir? It's been on the library channel since yesterday." Specks looked embarrassed.

"Mr. Spock? Did you know about this?"

Spock's gaze slid sideways. "Events have been moving rather quickly, Captain."

Kirk nodded. "Right. Even Vulcans make mistakes." To Spock's insulted stare, he added, "But only very rarely, right?" And he grinned.

Spock turned to Specks. "Is there more, Ensign?"

"Not really, sir. There was never any attempt to search for the lost colony; it was always considered impractical. Either they were alive, but out of contact —or gone. Either way, there was nothing anyone could do for them. There was quite a bit of speculation though. A few novels and films were even produced which purported to tell the story—but of course, that was impossible. No one knew for sure. Aside from the political intrigues of its construction, and the fact that they pioneered slowship travel, the colony's chief claim to fame has been its mystery. I can tell you quite a bit about that, if you wish."

Standing, stretching a bit after the prolonged briefing, Kirk shook his head. "I think we've pretty well reached our saturation point for today, Specks. You did a good job. I think we have quite a bit to consider now." To his officers, he said, "Gentlemen? Shall we adjourn?"

17

Outside the library, Kirk turned to Spock. "What do you think, Spock?"

"I think the Ensign could have shortened his presentation considerably."

Kirk glanced over. "Why? Did you have something better to do?"

Spock shrugged.

Kirk opened his mouth to say something else, then thought better of it. One of the things they teach you at the Academy is that the large part of leadership is waiting for the situation to mature before acting. Knowing you have to wait, you might as well make good use of the time. Instead, he said, "No, I meant about the *Wanderer*—is that the official name?"

Spock nodded. "I believe so. I hadn't yet begun formulating options for your consideration, Captain."

"It seems to me that at the very least we're going to have to install a cultural reorientation team, then take a delegation back to the nearest starbase to pick up a warp-tug to bring that ship into port. Let's have Chekov find the closest appropriate base. Have Uhura code the log entries and squirt them ahead. And have a new contact team briefed. We're going to have to go back in and find the Captain of that ship—" They began heading toward the elevator. "And we'd better talk to that young woman and find out what kind of people we're going to be dealing with."

McCoy looked dour as they entered the sick bay, but then, McCoy usually looked dour.

"Well, Bones? Is she awake yet?"

McCoy said, "She's on hold. She started to show signs of coming around a little while ago, but I put her on the buzz box until you could be here."

Kirk nodded knowingly. "Why don't you keep her mildly sedated when you bring her up?"

"If you want—but she's liable to be more confused."

"I was just thinking of you, Bones. She does seem to be quite the warrior. I don't like having my Chief Surgeon thrown around the sick bay like that."

McCoy rubbed his cheek. "Yeah, I can still feel the pain."

Kirk peered. "In another couple hours, you'll be wearing it too. Should be a beautiful shiner, Bones."

They stepped into the other room, and McCoy touched a control on the side of the med-bed. The young woman moaned and twisted under the blanket. Then she yawned, and was still again. Her breathing was shallow.

Kirk looked to McCoy. "Is that it?"

"The buzz-box is off. She can wake up anytime she wants to."

"Obviously, she doesn't want to."

Kirk touched her shoulder and shook gently. "Uh—miss? Hello?"

"Uh—" She yawned, then rubbed at her eyes, then rolled over. "Just few more minutes—"

Kirk, Spock, and McCoy exchanged glances.

Kirk tried again, "It's time to wake up."

She slapped clumsily at his hand. "Leave alone—" And then stopped.

And came instantly awake. Sitting up suddenly. And staring. She looked from one to the other—doing a sudden take at the *alienness* of Spock. "Who you?" she demanded. "And where in hull this?"

Kirk said, under his breath, "Here we go again." To the young woman, he said, "I know this is going to be difficult for you to understand—"

She peered suspiciously. "You demons? Savages?!! Kill me? Eat me? Make me slave?"

"It would be difficult to do all three," said McCoy. "Especially in that order."

She frowned at him. "Is joke? You mock?"

"We're *friends,*" Kirk interrupted. "We mean you no harm. You have us confused with—someone else. We're not demons or savages. And we're not going to hurt you. My name is Kirk. And this is Spock. And that's Dr. McCoy." He deliberately avoided identifying the *Enterprise*. "Do you have a name?"

"But—" She was confused and anxious. She pulled herself backward on the bed, and pulled the blanket up in front of her. "Is must be—savages. This lower levels, yes?"

"No. Is not. I mean, this is not the lower levels of your ship."

"I know Ship! I am warrior. I am guard. I know Ship. This not place I know—therefore, is lower level!"

Kirk looked at Spock for assistance, but Spock remained impassive. "Miss? Do you have a name?"

She only glared at him.

"We're not really communicating here, are we?" He spread his hands wide in a gesture of peace and friendship, and took a gentle half-step toward her. She flinched and shrank back. "I am not a savage. I know I've been accused of acting savagely once in a while, and I know that our appearance is unusual to you—especially Mr. Spock—but I assure you that we are neither savages nor demons. My name is James T. Kirk, and I am the Captain of a starship—but not the same ship that you are from. This is a different ship. Your ship is the *Wanderer* and my ship is the *Enterprise*. The *Enterprise* is a starship capable of traveling faster than the speed of light—and we're from Earth."

"You make nonsense," she said, but her resistance was lessening. "How—how can we be anywhere if not in Ship?"

And then his words hit her. "Earth? You say Earth?"

"A planet. Our planet. Your planet. Once. Your ancestors' home world." And suddenly he thought of something. "Do you remember a—a message that the first wanderers sent back to Earth? 'Our grandchildren will wait for yours among the stars'? Well, we're the grandchildren—we've come to meet you."

She considered that thought. A long moment passed while she turned it over in her mind. Kirk, Spock, and McCoy looked at each other.

At last, she looked up. "Where we?"

"We in—excuse me. We are aboard the United Starship *Enterprise.* It's a starship, and it's capable of traveling from one star to another."

"Is mad story," she said. "Is madder still. *Three* madmen. Old fables. Worlds. Skies. Other ships—"

"There *are* other ships—" Kirk was beginning to look frustrated. "Bones? Spock?"

"Don't ask me. I'm a doctor, not a theologian."

"Bones!"

"Sorry—"

"Child-talk," said the girl. "I hear these stories before, long time back. Is legend, yes? But you believe, no? Is confuse. Is truth or lie? If story is true, then I am mad. But I am not mad, so you must. Is madmen or demons."

Kirk was beginning to show some anxiety himself. "Look, uh—Miss—what can I do to prove to you that we're not demons?"

"Is nothing. Is told that madmen, savages, and demons will tell half-truths more convincing than whole-truth. Is demon tricks to make me think I mad yes?"

"Bones? Spock?" Kirk gestured the others over to him. He lowered his voice, "What would you—ah, think if we took her up on the bridge and showed her the outside of her own world?"

Spock looked thoughtful. "It seems the only logical course, Captain. This way has produced little or no useful result."

"On the other hand, Jim," McCoy put in. "You're asking a lot from this girl. You're asking her to just set aside in a few moments everything she's known all of her life. She can't do that any more easily than you or I could. Maybe Spock could do it—in the face of superior logic—but human beings aren't so calculating, and you have to be gentle with her."

Kirk considered both points of view. He turned back to the girl. "Listen, you—ah, know what savages look like. Do we look like savages to you?"

She looked at each of them carefully. Then shook her head.

"Do we look like demons? Or madmen?"

She looked at each of them again, then pointed at

Spock. "He is demon-look." Then another look. "But only little. Is kind face."

Both McCoy and Kirk turned to look at Spock's face. *Kind?* Spock looked impassively back without comment.

Kirk turned to the girl again. "You seem to think that savages always hurt people—have we hurt you yet?"

She thought about it. "Is trick?"

"Is no trick."

"Is not hurt."

"Then—why don't you trust us—for just this little bit. You have nothing to lose."

Kirk stopped himself. Realizing something inside. Nothing to lose? She didn't know that.

"Um—listen, I'll promise you something. I promise you that you *will* return to your own ship—to your home. And nothing bad will happen to you. We just want to show you some things first. We'll answer every question you want to ask. All we ask in return is that you do look at what we want to show you, and look very carefully. Do you understand that?"

She looked insulted. "Is understand! You think I child?"

"Well—I, uh—it's just that—" Kirk looked flustered, looked to Spock and McCoy, then back to the girl again, "—it's just that you haven't exactly been what we would call cooperative—ah, until now."

She looked thoughtful. "Is how long here?"

"For a few more hours. Whenever you're ready."

"Is ready now. Is warrior. Always ready."

A thought occurred to Kirk then as she slid off the med-bed. "Let me ask you something. We understand your talk only with some difficulty. Can you understand us?"

"Is easy. Is talk like old tapes. Nobody talk like that. Except in game. Or church."

Kirk looked at her. "Can *you* do it? I mean, can you talk to us like we talk?"

She met his eyes with a curious stare. And said, "Sure. If I want to. But it seems very wasteful of energy to use so many extra words in a sentence to say the same thing."

18

The elevator door whooshed open. The girl stepped onto the bridge with wide eyes. She was flanked by Kirk and McCoy. Spock followed discreetly. "This," said Captain Kirk, "is the nerve center of my ship."

"Is taught—excuse me. We're taught that there is only one ship. The *Ship.* There are . . . legends, stories of the old days—and pictures—" She lapsed into silence, brooding over something, then abruptly said, "—but nobody ever really *believed* those stories. They were—fantasy. They didn't have anything to do with *real life.* And—even if they did—none of us are going to live long enough to see Journey's End. So, the whole question of—planets and stars—is, oh, I don't know word. Is sorry. Is difficult. I not actor. Not able do—to do this."

"It's alright. I think we get the idea. You're more—that is, you communicate more than you think you do." Kirk took her by the hand and led her to the Captain's chair. "Now, you stand here and look forward at that big screen. Mr. Sulu?"

The helmsman touched a control on his panel and the forward viewscreen lit up.

"Is stars?"

"Yes," nodded Kirk. "Those are stars."

"Is pictures. I see pictures of stars at home. We have stars too. One year, I serve on crew to replace burned-out stars in ceilings. Is important job."

"Uh, I can believe it—but these are different. These are *real* stars. Your lights are only imi—um, your lights are simulation stars, meant to look like the real things."

She weighed the statement. "But—stories all say that *real* stars are big—"

"Yes, they are—"

"But these stars are small—"

"—but that's because they're so far away that they look small."

She turned to stare at him incredulously. This is logic?

"Captain?" said Spock. "This girl has lived all of her life in an environment where the farthest object that she has ever seen has been only fifty meters away. If that."

Kirk understood. He turned to Sulu again. "Helmsman, do you have something appropriate from the library?"

"Coming right up, Captain." He touched the keyboard in front of him, looked at the screen, then touched again. The image on the forward screen scrambled, then cleared to show the surface of Capella, the red giant, as seen from a close-approach satellite. A seething, churning inferno. A vast boiling surface of tortured light.

The girl shrank back in fear from the screen—then realizing it was only an image, and nobody else was demonstrating anxiety, she stiffened her resolve and stared at the screen again, her nervousness diminished. After a moment, the image shrank to a pinpoint.

"And that's what a star looks like from far away," said Kirk.

"But there are so *many* of them—," she said. "How is that possible?"

"There are more stars than you can imagine," Kirk said to her. "I can't begin to show you how full of light the sky is—but I'd like to try."

She looked at him oddly. "Is what?"

Kirk said, "I would like to show you the stars."

"Is showing now—" Her face was perplexed. "Is showing, yes?"

"I meant—I would like to show you from the surface of a planet, someday."

"Planet?"

"A world. Not like a spaceship. A ship is like a—a container. It holds in the good things and keeps them safe from the bad things."

"Like upper levels keep out demons of lower levels."

"Ah, something like that—but a world, a planet—"

He stopped himself, searching for the right words. "A planet doesn't have walls."

"Is no protection then. Very bad. I don't think I like planet."

"Yes. Well—I guess after all, a planet is very much a matter of individual taste, isn't it? Mr. Sulu, do you have some pictures of planets?"

"Aye, aye, Captain." He punched up a new series of images. A whirling, dazzling kaleidoscope of light—a pastoral wonderland of landscapes—a lighthouse on a stormy seacoast lashed by crimson breakers—blue and purple clouds streaking across a yellow sky—rays of light piercing the gloom of a forest of giant yarrows, all green and dusky—a ten-meter stingfish leaping high out of the ocean of Satlin—a sterile desert under a blue-white pinpoint of brilliance—a rolling field of red-orange blossoms stretching toward a distant city of emerald spires—a soaring glider making lazy turns against a carpet of yellow cirro-cumulus clouds—a tarantula scuttling from its shelter beneath a jagged outcrop of shiny black crystal.

The girl stared, amazed. Entranced.

"Is trick. Is must be—but—" She fell into silence, biting her lower lip. And stared a while longer—

—a silver moon above a magic sea—a slope of sparkling aspen, a glittering golden harvest underneath a towering range of awesome and forbidding mountains—a canyon layered in shades of brown and red, ochre, black and amber; at the bottom, barely visible, a tiny aircraft hovered above the silver ribbon of the river that had carved it—

"No—is not—is not possible—is simulated image, right? Is model—is all must be demon trick! They warned that demons would do trickery. I did not know it would be so—so—" She whirled to Kirk. "Why you do this to me?"

Kirk made a mistake. He took a step forward to reassure her. He reached for her hands—

She leaped back, crouching into an action stance. The crewman at the engineering station came over the railing at her, but she rolled him over her shoulder like so much falling meat—a sidewise leap and she was at the elevator door—which opened with a whoosh behind her. She slid sideways into it—and the door slid shut behind her.

Kirk and Spock exchanged a knowledgeable glance.

"She can't escape."

Kirk nodded, annoyed with himself anyway. He stepped to his control chair.

McCoy shook his head. "I warned you that the possibility for cultural shock was severe—"

"We didn't have any choice, Bones." Kirk switched on the ship's communication channel. "Security alert. All decks. A girl from the *Wanderer* is loose aboard the *Enterprise*. Do not hurt her. I repeat, do not hurt her. Bring her to the bridge."

Abruptly, behind him, the elevator door opened again. A badly frightened and flustered young girl stood there, almost in tears. "It won't go up—it won't go up—" And then the door whooshed shut again.

Kirk and Spock exchanged another glance. Kirk moved toward the door. But it did not open a third time.

"Obviously, Captain, she believes she is still somewhere aboard the *Wanderer*. The idea that she might be on another ship is as difficult for her to accept as it might be for a medieval monk to comprehend the idea of being on another world. In other words, very nearly impossible."

"This is going to be a harder job than I thought." An old memory bubbled up to the surface of his mind—the night a dragonbird escaped from its temporary pen at Spiderport. They had tracked it by its trail of mangled dogs and monkeys. Why did this situation remind him of that—? Probably because the girl was a warrior in her own world—and a good one. They had already seen proof of that in the sick bay.

Spock was saying something. "—How would you feel, Captain, if you were to come face to face with the historical truth that formed the basis for the common human conception of God? It would be difficult for you to accept that what was previously a specialized kind of belief—one that does not seem to have *direct* influence over day-to-day events—does in actuality have a very real and tangible existence that *must* be accepted and dealt with. And in so doing, your conception of the way the universe works would have to be totally restructured. And if you couldn't handle that—you would probably go quite mad."

McCoy turned to look at him angrily. Then to Kirk. But he didn't speak. There was nothing that needed to be said. The look on Kirk's face said it all.

19

She was lost and she was running. The world was suddenly—ripped apart. It was filled with faces she had never seen before! And it smelled different! Not bad—but *different*.

And when she tried to make the elevator go up—there was no *up*. How could she get back to the upper levels if there was no *up?*

She was sobbing. "I want to go home—Please! Take me home!"

And a soft voice, almost a pleasant one, answered, "Where do you wish to go, please? You'll have to be more specific."

"Anywhere—away! Safety!" *Who was that?*

The voice said, "I detect anxiety and stress. Sick bay is on residential deck 6."

And then the elevator did move. First downward—and then *sideways!* She grabbed the handle on the wall in terror and screamed and screamed and screamed—

When the door finally opened, she fled without looking, past startled white faces, turning suddenly, past open hallways and doors—*but the curve of the floor was all wrong*—it didn't curve at all! She made a ninety-degree turn down the first corridor on her right and continued running—but still the floor didn't curve upward under her feet! Instead, the corridor curved *sideways,* taking her around and around and back to the place she began.

There were men there, in red shirts, and holding those strange-looking weapons—she skidded past them in fright.

They saw her—"Hey!"—and came running after.

She barreled through a knot of men and women, sending them sprawling, and then down another corridor—and another, a safe-looking darkness—she charged into it and—it was a dead end!

She turned around to face her pursurers—she would die fighting—

—but behind her, there was only the bright square light of the end of the tunnel. The hallway was empty —and then, a single figure stepped into the light—thin and holding his hands high.

"Hello, there—," he called. "Remember me? I'm Kevin Riley, the fellow who—no, I guess you wouldn't remember. Um, look—I'm sorry you're so scared."

"Don't come any closer."

He spread his hands wide in a gesture of acceptance. "No problem. I won't hurt you. Honest. Neither will anyone else here. Captain Kirk is on his way down."

"Is no Captain Kirk. Is only one Captain."

"Look—Miss, uh—you're going to have to trust us a little bit—"

"Cannot trust demons!"

"We want to take you back to your own world. We want you to help us talk to your people."

"Prophet—? You want me to be prophet?"

"Eh?"

"In legend. End of journey. The wanderers will be met by the visitors. The visitors will pick one to be prophet."

"And who will these visitors be—?"

"They will be the—the children of those who were left behind."

"Oh, I see. Well, that description sort of fits us, I guess—uh, look, I don't like shouting down this corridor. Can I come a little closer?" He didn't wait for her reply, he just took a few steps forward. "Is this all right?"

She didn't answer.

"We're the descendants of the people of Earth."

"But, story is not true. Is fable. Is for studying for meaning, not for—for actual event. Is impossible. How can we be met by those we left behind? Unless we travel in circle? And we not do that. So you must be savage demon."

"Uh, not exactly, although I am something of a terror when I get a little drunk—but you can call me Kevin, honest. We've traveled very, very fast to catch up to you. Faster-than-light."

She snorted.

At the end of the corridor, three more figures appeared; silhouettes—but she could tell by the way they stood who they were: the one who called himself Captain, the tall one with the strange ears, and the one called "Bones." She shrank back. "Keep them away from me. They tell lies."

Riley turned around, faced the others. "Sir? Could you just keep back a minute? Please?"

Kirk and Spock exchanged a glance. Then, shrugging, backed up.

"You see?" said Riley. "We *can* be trusted. Now, if you want, you can stay here in this corner for as long as you feel you need to—and nobody will bother you—but, ah, sooner or later you're going to get hungry or want to—clean up a little or—what I mean is, I'll stay by you and make sure that nobody hurts you, if that would make you feel better."

"Who are you?!!" she demanded.

"I told you. I'm Kevin Riley."

She shook her head. "Not that. I know all that. I want to know *who are you.*"

"We're human beings, like yourself. Like your people. And we're the crew of a starship. Another ship. And you're on that ship now."

"How can I get back?"

"We'll take you back. There are two ways. We can beam you back or we can—" He stopped and thought. "Yes, perhaps—we should show you—" He looked back down the corridor to Kirk and Spock, then to the girl again. "Wait there, please—don't go away." And he moved back down to the end of the corridor to whisper with the others.

She eyed them suspiciously, but she waited. She could not get past them—and even if she could, where could she go?

And then—Kevin Riley was coming back. "It's all

right. I've talked to them. If you're ready, we'll take you back to your own world now."

"Is truth?"

"Is truth. Scout's honor." He held up his right hand.

She stared. *Scout's* honor? "You—are scout?"

He nodded solemnly. "Wolf Pack number 11340, Van Nuys, California."

She took a half-step forward, then caught herself and pulled back. She asked, "What is motto?"

"Be prepared."

Her eyes went wide—this could *not* be a trick. Savages couldn't possibly know—

—And then she broke down and cried. She couldn't contain it anymore. So much had happened to her, strange and terrifying, and all so confusing—she buried her face in her hands and began to sob in great heaving, racking gasps of air.

Riley looked at her and saw—not a frightened woman—but a frightened little girl whose world had just collapsed. He couldn't help himself. He moved forward and gathered her into his arms. "It'll be all right," he whispered. "It'll be all right—what's your name?"

She didn't answer at first, just kept crying—although she did turn and cry into his chest, holding onto him as if she needed to reassure herself of his solidity—then, after a while, she managed to say, "My name—is Katholin."

"Katholin—that's very pretty—" He stroked her hair as he held her.

She sniffled. "My friends call me—Katwen."

"Katwen?"

"Katholin Arwen."

"I'll take you home again, Katholin."

"Not yet—just a minute." She held him tightly for a while longer. Riley managed to steal a glance toward the open end of the corridor to see Spock, Kirk, and McCoy nonchalantly studying the craftsmanship of the ceiling, the walls, the floors—their gaze was anywhere but here.

"I—I'm ready now."

He looked down into her face. There were tear-streaks down her cheeks. He brushed them away with his fingertips. "I won't let anyone hurt you, Katholin Arwen—Katwen." And taking her by the hand, he turned her toward the dead end of the corridor. He hit a security hand-panel on the wall, and the end of the tunnel split and slid apart to reveal—

Shuttlecraft bay 3. A wide open space. Blazing and brilliant. And flat—absolutely, geometrically, distantly, and terrifyingly *flat*. It was a room like none she had ever seen before in her life.

A single tiny craft waited before her.

She stood and stared, unable to move. Riley had to physically guide her forward into the light.

Behind them, Kirk, Spock, and McCoy followed bemused.

20

There were actually three shuttlecraft bays on the *Enterprise*.

The main bay was at the tail of the ship's engineering module, but the two smaller auxiliary bays were located in the bottom section of the main disk, toward the edges. Taxis didn't launch from these bays so much as they "fell" out.

The auxiliary bays were rarely used except by maintenance crews, and the craft they held were of extremely limited range. They could be used for traveling from one ship to another, or for transporting passengers or cargo to a nearby space station, but journeys beyond 1250 kilometers or lasting more than six hours would exhaust a taxi's fuel and life-support systems.

A taxi could hold six passengers comfortably, more if they were friendly.

As they dropped out of the bay into darkness, Katwen's hands tightened on the arms of her seat. But she held herself steady. She was a warrior and would not betray fear.

"It's all right," whispered Riley. "Captain Kirk is one of the best drop-jockeys in the fleet. When he was in the Academy, he won the gold crown two years in a row." Riley was genuinely enthusiastic. "He invented the Tiberian reverse—and who do you think the Kirk evasion is named after? That's the one with the mandatory double victory roll at the end—because if you survive it, you've won."

She just looked at him blankly.

"Never mind."

She turned back to the forward ports. The single lighted frame of the shuttlecraft bay was receding rapidly. Kirk spoke into his microphone—"Now, Sulu"—and suddenly, the exterior lights of the *Enterprise* came on revealing the great ship in all its proudest glory.

Katwen gasped at the size of it.

Kirk turned around and grinned. "It always touches me that way too." Then he turned back to his controls. The gentle sidewise nudge of acceleration was the only clue that he was bringing the taxi into a new heading. Now they were rising in relation to the giant starfleet vessel, moving up beyond the main disk section. As they did so, the *Wanderer* became visible beyond it.

The great cylinder turned slowly in the void, the shadows of its superstructures moving lazily across its hull. The lights of the probes lit the vessel with a silvery glow.

Katwen gasped, crying out suddenly—"That's it! That's the world—" And then she stopped herself and stared at the *Enterprise* again.

She looked to Kirk amazed. And then to Riley. And even to Spock and McCoy. And finally back to Kirk. "You spoke the truth, didn't you?"

He looked at her, and his eyes were compassionate. "The hardest part was that we knew how difficult it would be for you to comprehend."

But she was looking out the port again. "The world—it's so tiny."

"No, that's only an illusion. It's really very big."

Kirk touched his controls again and the taxi began to move forward. The distant vessel began to swell in the port as the *Enterprise* dropped past them.

Katwen's eyes widened with wonder as they approached. She never took her eyes from the port.

"Those are the aft fusion units—they've been inactive for generations. Oh, and that must be the ramscoop—and there are the deep-distance radar antennae and—"

Kirk stared at her. "You know what all of that equipment is?"

"Of course. Everybody does. I studied my geography. Don't you study your own world?"

"Worlds. Plural. We study all of our worlds. But do you understand what all of those things are supposed to do?"

"Of course."

"Um—let me ask you this. Who do you think built those devices?"

"Human beings did, of course. Men and women like ourselves."

"And the hull of the ship as well?"

"Of course."

"And where were all of these people before the world was built—?"

She stopped and looked at him. "In the other ship. There was another L5 structure, you know."

"But where did that other ship come from? Who built that?"

"Human beings, of course. I thought you knew your history." She was honestly puzzled. "There were little ships before there were big ones."

"But—where did the *first* ships come from?"

She shrugged. "I'm not a theologian. I don't think about things like that. Questions about the origin of the world are best left to those who—who—" She stopped. "What are you trying to tell me?"

Kirk turned back to the controls and studied them again. Riley touched Katwen's shoulder. "I think he wants you to understand that the ships—*all* of them—are artificial environments. They had to be built. And that means that there was a time before they were built. And the people lived on planets. On one planet. Called Earth. You'd like it. It's the best world for human beings in the whole universe."

"But it's generations away—"

"Not anymore. We were on Earth less than seven months ago."

She looked into his eyes as if somehow the truth of his words could be determined there. "Really? Earth? The legendary home world really exists?"

Riley nodded. "I was born there."

She started trembling. "You—you're—gods—if you're not demons, then you must be gods!" She fell to her knees and grasped at Riley's hands, burying her face in his lap. "Forgive me, my lords. Forgive me—"

Behind them, McCoy put one hand over his eyes and made a sound in his throat. Kirk, at the controls, coughed gently to cover his embarrassment for her. Spock remained impassive.

"Uh—" said Riley, pulling her up to her chair again. "No, we're not gods—"

"The legends speak of the end of the journey. The most fanciful story is that someday we will be met by those we left behind—the visitors—and they will be as gods to us."

Riley held her hands. "Then you are a god too—because your ancestors are from Earth too." He began to speak to her of the journey, the vast distances between the stars, and the dream—the singular vision that propelled the human species outward. He spoke of the hope of discovery, and the joyous wonders of the sky. He told her of the million-light-year vision, and how there were those who wanted the stars so badly that they would die in space so that their distant children might know them.

"And there were questions to be answered, *hard* questions—is it morally right to condemn several generations of your descendants to a hard life alone in the void between the stars? Because without faster-than-light travel, it will take at least three generations to reach another sun."

But then he spoke again of courage and daring and dreams, and how the story of her world—the *Wanderer*—was a legend throughout the worlds of humanity. The lost colony. The first brave men and women to dare the stars. The ones who sailed the sea of night. "If we are gods to you, Katwen—then you and your people—you are gods to us, because you are the first star-travelers in all of human history. If it weren't for the unanswered question that your world represented, no other human beings might have dared to follow for centuries more."

Riley was fibbing a bit on that last point. The preliminary work on faster-than-light travel had already been well under way the day the *Wanderer* had crossed the orbit of Neptune (at that time, the outermost planet because Pluto was on the inner lap of its orbit), and left the solar system forever.

But those aboard the *Wanderer* had never heard about the secret warp-drive development projects then in progress. Even the impulse engine was only in the first testing stages at that time. The technology that would make the *Wanderer's* journey unnecessary had already been moving off the drawing boards. But for political reasons, nobody told the men and women of the colony.

And when Starfleet vessels finally were able to begin looking for the lost colony, so many years had passed that there was no way to know where it might have disappeared to.

Until now.

Katwen listened in silence, only occasionally asking for clarification of some minor point. There was so much that she did not understand. "I—I am discovering that I have lived in a single corridor of the universe —and the universe is more than corridors." There were tears running down her cheeks again. "I am joyous, Kevin Riley, at being given the gift of so much knowledge—but I am sad too—because I begin to see a little better now—" She pointed at the *Wanderer* still swelling in the forward port. It filled their view and still was many kilometers distant. "My world—we're at war. We have been at war for so long that no one now alive remembers a time when there was not a battle. There was mutiny many generations ago. A terrible battle."

Kirk and Spock exchanged a meaningful glance. Spock's extrapolation had been correct.

Katwen continued, "The rebellion was crushed—but not without great damage to the world. And strict controls established. The rebels who survived fled to the lower levels, where they have lived ever since. Sometimes they raid the civilized part of the world. But the frontier is well guarded. As you have seen."

Riley nodded. "We saw. I—I was the one who... captured you, Katwen."

"You?"

He nodded. "I'm sorry if I hurt you—but I can't say I'm sorry to have brought you aboard the *Enterprise*. Else we would not be talking now."

She accepted the information without judgment. She turned back to the port and stared again. "My world—I thought it was a good world, a proud place. And I believed in it and I believed in my life as a warrior. Now—I—I'm not so sure anymore. It's such a tiny little thing, isn't it? So fragile . . . "

"All worlds are fragile," said McCoy. "Even Earth. That's why we must cherish them. And live in them wisely."

"My people—perhaps we are not so wise any more—" she added. "In the schools, we are taught our history, the dream of stars, the journey, the mutiny, and the new order of life. Our—our national purpose now is no longer so noble. No one talks of stars. When someone speaks of the original dream, there is always someone to answer him that we cannot look for stars until the last shred of the rebellion is crushed. The journey is canceled until the mutiny is suppressed. But nobody really tries to conquer the savages. There are too many of them, and the world is too large, and they have too many places to hide. So the war continues forever. And no one dreams of stars anymore."

Kirk had been strangely silent all this time, concentrating on his piloting it seemed. Now, with the tiny craft moving along the great hull of the *Wanderer*—a giant wall of metal in the port—he turned around and looked at Katwen. "How many people are alive aboard your world, Katwen?"

"I don't really know—"

"Take a guess."

She thought a moment. "Not counting the savages—and nobody knows how many of them there really are—although I would think there aren't as many as there used to be—not since the auxiliary fusion units were shut down, plunging that part of the world into darkness—I would guess that there are perhaps three thousand people in the world."

Kirk looked to Spock, alarmed. McCoy's face too showed concern.

It was on all three of their minds, but it was Spock who said the words aloud. "When the *Wanderer* left Earth's system, there were thirty thousand people alive on it. And it had the facilities to support three times that many."

Katwen looked at him. "What are you saying—?"

"The implication is obvious—your world may be dying."

She didn't answer. She turned and looked at the vast metallic landscape beyond the window. Her expression was unreadable. After a moment, she said, "I don't think I'm ready to go back to my people yet. I—I wouldn't know what to tell them." She looked at Kirk, at Riley, at Spock, and McCoy. "Can we go back to the *Enterprise?* I have questions I need to ask you."

Kirk swiveled to face her, smiling gently. "That was all we ever wanted from you in the first place. I guess we had to wait until you wanted it yourself."

She looked at him curiously. "I have a right to change my mind."

"Isn't that just like a woman—," McCoy started to say, but Spock cut him off. "Under the circumstances," the Science Officer said, "it's a perfectly logical decision."

21

The briefing room again: Kirk, Spock, McCoy, Scotty, Uhura, and various other section chiefs.

"Where's Chekov?"

"He'll be late, Captain," said Uhura. "He's waiting for the computer to confirm some calculations."

"All right," said Kirk. "We'll start without him. Let's go over our options—"

"Ahh, I think—," interrupted a youngish female

Lieutenant. "I think—we ah, have to ah—remember the ah, prime directive here—and it ah, seems to me that ah—ah, after everything else is considered—ah, ah, a strong legal case could be made for ah, the fact that ah—these people consider themselves an autonomous world—and ah, ah—in such a case, the prime directive would ah, certainly be—ah, applicable."

Kirk nodded thoughtfully. Munker was the *Enterprise's* legal advisor, and despite her tendency to dither, she was considered to be one of the sharpest lawyers in Starfleet. He said, "I don't think the prime directive is particularly applicable here, though. What we have is a clear case of an inhabited derelict. And in such a case, we *must* make ourselves known to the inhabitants and offer immediate assistance."

"But ah—ah, considering that these people do not easily accept the existence of other ships, the mere act of making ourselves known to them is—ah, in effect, a clear and present case of interfering with ah, the stability of their culture, and that ah—would be ah—ah, a violation of the prime directive."

Kirk leaned back in his chair and looked at her. She was not bad looking; she had dark curly hair and perky features—but she wore a perpetually confused expression. He exhaled loudly, the closest thing to a sign of annoyance he would make in front of an underling. "How come—," he addressed the group at large, "—how come every time we discuss the applicability of the prime directive to a situation, we end up having to break it?" He made a wave-away gesture. "Never mind. It's only a rhetorical question. Perhaps that's the reason for the prime directive, to make us think twice before we do meddle. In any case, we've already invoked the local autonomy section, and in my opinion, there is sufficient reason to warrant the attempt at contact so that we may offer technical aid. Of course, it will mean that the inhabitants will have to give up their war—" He smiled. "—but under the circumstances, that will probably be a step in the right direction. Now, aside from the legal question—," he nodded to Munker, "—are there any other reasons why we should not try to contact the Captain of the *Wanderer?*" He looked around the table. "None? Good. All right, then, let's proceed to the next consideration, the mechanics of the operation."

Spock noted thoughtfully, "Captain, we've already seen the extreme reaction of the young woman from the *Wanderer,* Katholin Arwen, when confronted with the fact of the existence of the *Enterprise*—and it took drastic steps to convince her of the truth of the situaion. I suggest that we stop for a moment and consider what effect that kind of cultural shock will produce when multiplied by three thousand individuals."

"That may be a risk we have to take—"

"Jim—," interrupted McCoy. "It's not a risk that *we* have to take. It's a risk that the people aboard the *Wanderer* have to take. And they don't have any choice in the matter."

"Bones, I'm well aware of the problem. By the mere act of going in to contact them, we will inevitably produce a cultural shock. But we *have* to contact them to offer assistance. There isn't any other way—if you know a way to ask them if they need help without actually letting them know we exist, I'd like to hear it."

"Jim, there's got to be a better way. The girl, perhaps—?"

"But would they listen to her? Consider the dynamics of the situation. She's going to have to have some very convincing proof or they'll think she's been brainwashed by the demons."

"Ah, I think, ah—perhaps we should—ah, consider another ah, possibility—"

Kirk looked to Munker. "Yes, Ensign?"

"Ah, due to the ah—extreme uncertainty—ah, of this situation—and ah, the unusualness of it—ah, perhaps it would be best to—ah, hold off on a decision until we—ah, can secure—um, Starfleet authorization."

A visible flicker of annoyance crossed Kirk's face, but he erased it quickly. "That's not the way we do things on the *Enterprise,* Munker," he said coldly. "We have been granted the authority to make decisions on behalf of Starfleet because it is expected that we will apply our intelligence to make the right decisions without having to check back with base. There are situations where the time-lag—even with subspace radio—

would be prohibitive. If we cannot make these difficult decisions ourselves, then we should not be commanding the power of this Starfleet vessel—and that philosophy applies to everyone aboard this ship from the Captain on down."

"I—ah, understand that, Captain, but ah—ah, perhaps this is a situation that is ah, beyond our ah, capabilities. And ah, I think we have to ah—ah, consider that possibility."

Kirk closed his eyes and thought for a moment. First, he had to force himself to get past the dithering of his legal aide. "Look—" he turned to her. "Starfleet insists that we have a space lawyer aboard to advise us on our legal position. And that's as it should be. But let me make one thing very, very clear right now, Lieutenant—failure to make a decision is a decision in itself. And it is almost always the *wrong* one. We are here to *make* a decision, not postpone it."

"Ah—I understand that, sir. But—ah, ah, this is not a situation where ah, there is extreme urgency—and ah, that does affect our legal position. And there is a precedent in the case of—"

The briefing-room door whooshed open then, and a disheveled Chekov came bursting in. Kirk was grateful for the well-timed interruption. "I'm sorry I'm late, *Keptin,* but I had some calculations that had to be completed and I wanted to be sure, so I ran them a second time and—"

Kirk lifted a hand in cheerful benevolence. "It's all right, Mr. Chekov. You didn't miss anything."

"Thank you." Chekov moved quickly to his seat.

Munker was already continuing, "Ah, there is a precedent for ah—referring back to starbase—"

Kirk was about to stop her when Chekov interrupted—he hadn't even finished sitting down. *"There isn't time,"* he said flatly. And the expression on his face was one of near terror. As heads swiveled in his direction, he said, "That ship—the *Wanderer*—in thirteen months, it will be beyond all help."

"Eh?"

"They're headed for Ellison's star—a catastrophic variable—in fact, it's the largest catastrophic variable in this spiral arm of the galaxy."

"But—ah, ah—that's almost two light-years away—ah, certainly there's time."

"—and it will take thirteen months of full power from that ship's fusion engines to make enough of a course correction to save it—" Chekov continued right over Munker's objections as if she hadn't spoken at all. "—and if they're going to achieve any kind of workable trajectory, they have to begin accelerating within fifteen days. And that means they're going to have to start powering up their fusion engines *immediately*. This is not a question of law, *Keptin*—unless, of course, you count Newton's three laws of motion. And all the rest of modern physics."

"But ah, ah—surely we can do something to keep them from hitting the star—"

Chekov shook his head. "It's not quite that simple. If it were only a question of them being on a course where they might hit the star, then we would have as long as a year—but they're not even going to pass close enough to the star to be endangered—at least not by Ellison's star. What is going to happen is that the star will exert just enough pull on them to make an alteration in their course—a *significant* alteration. They're going to be pulled into a new course a hundred and eleven degrees off their previous heading. And that new course will put them headed straight toward—," Chekov paused, and Kirk could see the beads of sweat on his forehead, "—straight for . . . the *galactic maelstrom.*"

There was a stunned silence in the briefing room. Captain Kirk half rose to his feet and stared down the full length of the table at Chekov. "What—?"

"I'm sorry, *Keptin*—that's why I was so late. I had to double-check my figures. There's no doubt about it."

Kirk sank back into his seat, stunned.

He had known they were close—but *this* close?

Imagine a black hole.

If you can.

A place where the bottom drops out of the universe; where gravity is so intense not even light can escape. A place where time and space are sucked into a vortex of impossibility and even the laws of physics are twisted beyond recognition.

Now, imagine a second one.

Imagine the two of them tumbling about each other in the classic two-body problem of astrophysics.

Only the tumbling isn't stable. The two singularities come rushing at each other wildly, loop around each other, and then go whirling back out into space. The interlocking ellipses of their orbits are like a vast propellor, three light years in diameter.

Imagine this propellor turning lazily, slicing through the nothingness of space, a giant grinding wheel of destruction.

Imagine this wheel sweeping through the galaxy for a billion years, its intense gravitational waves creating disastrous effects on everything it passes near.

Stars explode into supernovae at the merest brush of its presence, solar systems shatter into dust. Lost planets go spinning through the darkness, frozen and alone.

The churning whirlpool is a one-way funnel without a bottom. Fragments of stars can be seen caught in this maelstrom—long streamers of still-burning gas. Some of the dead bodies are glowing balls of neutronium only a few kilometers wide. Cherenkov radiation glows like a beacon around the two great holes. Matter streaks across space to disappear into nothingness. An oblate red giant flattens into a disk and then becomes a crimson ring around one of the holes. A blue-white pinpoint is ripped apart between the two opposing pulls.

A whirligig of three neutron stars goes spinning past, then pulls apart as they funnel down toward bottomless terror.

A hundred stars are caught in the gravitational whirlpool, a thousand planets follow. This is no easy death—some of these worlds have been caught for as long as time has flowed forward.

Uncountable thousands of objects whirl around this horror. Once caught inside, time slows to a crawl and they tumble forever. The light is so twisted, the radiation so fierce that not even the most sophisticated detectors known to Starfleet can determine exactly what is occurring within the vast sweep of the propellor blades described by these two orbiting black holes.

This cosmic whirlpool—the galactic maelstrom—goes on and on and on, growling down through time, eating everything in its path, cutting a swath thirty light-years wide through the galaxy.

In just a little more than three million years, it will eat the Earth.

Kirk's problem, however, was a little more immediate.

"The maelstrom," Chekov was saying, "is fifteen years beyond Ellison's star. That is, the center of it is. It's at its most extended now, with the two singularities at their widest distances apart. That puts the nearest edge of effects quite close to us. Cosmically speaking, that is."

Spock said quietly, "Even at this distance, we are still well within the E-ring of detectable events. In fact, we are most likely experiencing second degree time-dilation, and will probably have to reset our inertial clocks when we next return to base. My calculations suggest a seven microsecond discrepancy has already piled up."

"That much?" asked Kirk.

Spock nodded. "The maelstrom's primary area is just over four light-years in diameter, but the hard radiation put out by the component bodies is enough to be lethal even at a range of six light-years from the center. There are quite a few novae and supernovae in the maelstrom. Space in the immediate neighborhood is noticeably curved as far as ten light-years from the center."

Chekov nodded in enthusiastic agreement. "And the *Wanderer's* loop around Ellison's star is going to be enough to point them straight at the *center* of it. That's the problem. If they were only going to approach at an oblique angle, they'd have a fighting chance—if they could shield themselves from the radiation somehow. But the maelstrom is going to catch anything that passes within ten light-years. And at the *Wanderer's* present speed, they will be inside that range three years after they pass Ellison's variable."

"Three years—?" That was Munker. "Oh, now—I really can't assent to ah—"

Kirk ignored her. "Go on, Chekov."

"Even assuming all six of their fusion engines could be brought to full power, it would take them four years to decelerate. It's the broadside of a barn problem, *Keptin*—only in reverse. They can't miss it, no matter what they do—it's too big—unless they back up. And they're going too fast to do that. Our only hope is to keep them from looping around Ellison's variable. If we can do that, then they'll miss the maelstrom—just barely. And if they're going to change their course, they have to start powering up their engines yesterday."

Kirk put his head into his hands for half a heartbeat. Then he looked up and around the table, stopping when he reached Munker. "I don't think there's anything left to be discussed. Circumstances have forced the decision on us. We have no choice but to go in and find the Captain of that vessel. And as far as the legal objections go—" and he looked straight at Munker when he said this, "—the Starfleet code allows those considerations to be set aside in situations of the gravest importance. And this is certainly one of those cases." He paused, then added with just a hint of a twinkle, "In every respect, this is a matter of the highest gravity."

22

Katwen hesitated at the door to the room. Riley looked at her. "What's the matter?"

"Scared," she said simply.

"It's all right," Riley said. He took her by the hands and looked into her eyes. "I'm with you."

She swallowed once and nodded. Then she said, "All right," and pushed on through the door.

There were only a few people in the room. They looked up curiously, then returned to their conversation. "They don't want to be impolite," Riley whispered. "That's why they're all trying so hard to act normal."

"Oh," said Katwen, staring very hard at Lieutenants Arex and M'ress. Three arms?!! And a talking lioness?!!

Riley pulled her over to a table and sat her down. "No, they're not demons either," he said to her unspoken question. He tapped the table and said, "Menu," and the surface of it lit up with a three-dimensional display of words and pictures.

"Is food—?"

"Is pictures of food. If you see something you like, just point."

"Is all unfamiliar—"

"All of it? How about some fruit?"

"Fruit is good."

"And a salad perhaps?"

She nodded.

"And maybe something cold to drink?"

She nodded again. "You pick."

He tapped the top of the table quickly, spoke a few code phrases and the tabletop became a tabletop again.

"Where food?"

"In a minute. It takes time—"

"Oh." She sat there, staring at the table, not knowing what else to say. She looked around the room—on the wall beside Kevin there was a gaudy, badly calligraphed, over-gold-leafed proclamation sealed into a wooden plaque with veriglass. She stood up to get a better look.

"Oh, uh—" Riley stood up quickly. "It's something the Captain had presented to him—"

"May I see?" She stepped up close to it, squinting slightly as she peered, and traced the illuminated letters with one finger, speaking the words aloud as if she were having difficulty with them. When her expression turned serious, Kevin began to feel uneasy.

"—'grant this patent to'—'Ambassador Plenipotentiary to the Universe, both Known and Unknown'—that . . . that means—" She turned back to Kevin, looking upset and betrayed. "You *are* Gods! You *are!*"

"Uh—uh—"

"Is proof here! Says, 'Signed, Emperor of Universe—' Only a God can use such titles. Emperor of Universe. Ruler of Planets—"

He held out his hand to her. "Katwen—no, we are *not* gods. That is a joke."

"Is joke—?" Her expression was incredulous.

"Is joke."

"What kind of joke is blasphemy? You are testing me, perhaps?"

Riley shook his head again. "Look, Katwen, there are too many worlds—it's a big universe and—oh, hey! Food's here!" Riley was grateful for the interruption as the sparkle of the in-ship transporter began to pile up on the surface of the table. Katwen turned and stared. The sparkle cleared and there was a crisp green salad, a bowl of fruit and a tall glass of iced tea.

"You *are* Gods—"

Riley closed his eyes for a moment, said a silent prayer, then opened them up again. "Katwen, a long time ago, there was a very great man—he lived even before your world was built. He said that any sufficiently advanced technology will look like magic. Airplanes—you know what airplanes are, don't you? Television. Computers." He pointed at the table. "Transporters."

She looked suspicious, but she sat down at the table again. "I will trust you," she announced. "For now." Then she remembered the plaque. "But what about—that?" She pointed.

"Um. I was afraid you'd ask about that. There are lots and lots of planets. Thousands. No one single government can rule all that many planets. There's another old saying, 'Law stops with atmosphere—' "

"I know that one. Was first said by First Captain when he declared independence." She brightened. "I am indirect descendant of First Captain."

"By now, I would expect everybody on the *Wanderer* would be."

"Oh, yes—is so. Everybody related to everybody else. That why it so hard to keep secret."

"Now, I know *who* said that one first. Solomon Short. Only he said, every *thing* is connected to everything else."

"I have wrong?"

Riley was embarrassed. "No. Just different. Different is not always wrong. In fact, maybe different is hardly ever wrong."

She nodded, and looked at the food in front of her. Idly, she took a carrot stick from the dish and crunched into it. "Is sweet—," she said. "Is good. Not quite as good as ours, but you are not farmers, yes?"

"We are not farmers."

She put the carrot stick down and asked, "Kevin Riley, tell me—what is like to live Earth?"

"Huh?"

"What is it like—," she spoke slowly to be certain of her words, "—what is it like to live in Earth?"

"Is—," he started, then stopped himself. "Um—," he said. "On. Not *in*. On. *On* Earth."

"Oh. What is like to live *on* Earth?"

"Ahh—we live on the surface of the planet. We live in buildings. We go outdoors. We ride in vehicles. We fly in airships, we sail in boats—"

"Boats?"

"Boats. Uh—boats. A boat is—well, there's a lake in the middle of Hollywood. That's water. A lot of water. There was a big hole there. And they filled it with water, and called it Lake Marathon. And there were little wooden shells—called boats—that you could sit in, and they would float on top of the water—"

"Is silly, no? Then what?"

"Well . . . you don't do it alone. You go with somebody you like, and you sit and you talk, and after a while, you lean over and you kiss and—"

"Hi, guys—"

Riley and Katwen looked up, startled. "Oh, uh—this is Specks. He's our historian. He probably knows more about the *Wanderer* than anybody else aboard the *Enterprise*. Hi, Specks." Riley said softly, "You don't want to join us, do you?"

"Don't mind if I do." Specks pulled up a chair and dropped easily into it.

"I was just trying to tell Katwen here about Earth. She wanted to know what it's like to live on a planet."

"You've seen pictures, haven't you?"

Katwen looked at this stranger, at the funny wire frames he wore on his face. "Yes. Kevin Riley showed pictures. But we have pictures on *Wanderer*. Is blue. And round. And streaked with white swirls."

"That's weather."

"I know. We have weather too. I served on weather crew once. Made winter last three extra weeks. Then turned up suns for short but hot summer. We make very humid weather that year."

"Uh—not quite, Katwen. We do have weather control on Earth—but even if we didn't, we would still have weather. Weather is a natural phenomenon."

"Natural?"

"Outdoors. Everywhere."

"Outdoors. Kevin Riley used same word. What means outdoors?"

Specks looked at Riley. "Outdoors?"

"Outdoors," Riley confirmed. Katwen looked to him expectantly. "Well, it's a—a—you see, we live on the surface of the planet. On the outside of it. If we go inside into a house, we're indoors. If we go outside, and there's no house around us, then we're *out*doors."

"House. Is underground?"

"No. Is structure. Like little ship, but it doesn't move." Riley stopped himself. "I'm starting to talk like you. It's like a—"

But she didn't wait for him to finish. "If is true, then where were people in pictures?"

"Huh?"

"You showed me pictures of Earth. Blue, round, streaked with white. Remember? Where were people. Inside Earth? Inside house? Where was house?"

"Yeah," said Specks to Riley, "I see your problem."

Riley picked up an orange. "Now, look—try it this way. The Earth is round like this, right?"

"If you say so," Katwen said doubtfully.

"I say so. Now, people live all over the planet, but the planet is so big and the people are so small in relation to it that if you are far enough away to see that the planet is round, you're too far away to see the people anymore. The planet is *so* big that when you're standing on the ground it looks flat. You can't tell it's curved."

Katwen took the orange from him and pondered it. "Now, you say people live on surface of this?"

"The Earth. That's right."

She knit her brow in puzzlement. "And I can stand on it here, right? With nothing between me and space—?"

"Atmosphere. There's atmosphere."

"But what holds atmosphere?"

"Gravity."

"Oh. But, if I stand somewhere else, *here*, say—" and she indicated the bottom of the orange, "—then I fall off, right? Atmosphere falls off too?"

"Huh? No. You can stand on the top or on the bottom. Whichever you like. Gravity holds you down."

Katwen raised an eyebrow at him skeptically—and suddenly Riley felt the same internal doubt as he did when Mr. Spock gave him the same expression. She said, "Your gravity work inside out?"

"Huh? What? Say again, please?"

"Gravity in *Wanderer* pushes everything on the inside toward the outside." She indicated with the orange.

"Uh huh." Riley and Specks exchanged glances. "Go on."

"Now, you tell me that gravity on Earth is backward and pulls everything on outside toward inside. Right?"

"Yes—"

"I'm confused."

"You're confused?" Riley turned to Specks. "Uh—I know there's an explanation, Specks—I really do. But how do I explain it to her?"

"Very simple, Riley. You just have to define the problem." He reached over and took the orange from Katwen. "Now, follow this very carefully. In the *Wanderer*, you get gravity because the *Wanderer* is spinning, right?"

"Right. Is called centrifugal force."

"And because it's spinning, all the gravity is going from the inside toward the outside, right? So people live on the inside." He spun the orange in his fingers. "Now, on the Earth, all the gravity is backward. It *pulls* from the inside. And this—," he said with a flourish, "—is because the Earth is spinning in the *other* direction!" He bit into the orange and grinned at Riley.

"Hey—!" said Riley, after a startled moment, but Specks was already out of his chair and walking away.

"Is smart man there," said Katwen. "Is making logic very clear."

"Uh, yeah, right." Riley decided not to reopen the question. If she was satisfied, then so was he. Somebody else could try to straighten her out. Later. *Much* later.

Idly he picked up another orange and began spinning it in his fingers. *But, wow*—Riley thought—*what a terrific explanation!*

"Lieutenant Riley?" said a soft voice in the air. It seemed to be right behind his ear.

"Who that?" Katwen looked up, startled. "Is heard voice before. In sideways elevator."

"It's the ship's computer," he explained. "Yes?"

"Captain Kirk would like to see you and Ms. Arwen in the briefing room. Immediately. Thank you."

"Thank you," said Riley. He sighed and pushed his chair back from the table. "Come on, Katwen—"

23

Kirk was waiting for them in the briefing room. He was alone, and there was a grim expression on his face.

"Katwen," he said. "I'm sorry. We're out of time. There's bad news. And there's *worse* news." He indicated a chair. "Please, sit down. You too, Riley." He sat down himself and faced them across the corner of the table. "Katwen—we've had a—a meeting here. There's a problem. Your world—the *Wanderer*—is in very great danger. You have to tell your Captain of this. You have to go back."

She met his gaze without fear. "What kind of danger?"

"There's a place—a place in the galaxy called the galactic maelstrom—or the galactic whirlpool—"

Riley nearly came out of his chair. *"Polo's Bolos?!!"* he cried.

"Sit down, Lieutenant. Yes, Polo's Bolos."

Katwen looked confused.

Kirk reached across and laid his hand on hers. "There was an exploring ship a hundred and fifty years ago. It was called the *Marco Polo.* The Captain got curious about the irregularities in a certain X-ray burster, a neutron star. So he came out this way to investigate. There was nothing unusual about the neutron star itself—insofar as *all* neutron stars are unusual—but the irregularities were coming from a point *behind* the neutron star. The neutron star was directly in line with this *thing*—whatever it was—and the Earth, pretty well blocking the view of what was on the other side." He stopped and poured himself a tumbler of water from the pitcher on the table. "What they found when they moved out far enough to see past the neutron star can only be described as literally 'a galactic horror.' I don't know how much of this you can understand, but there are two black holes in orbit about each other. Like bolos. Do you know what bolos are?"

"Yes. We use them against savages. I was on bolo team too."

"These are on a much vaster scale," Kirk said. "Any ship that approaches too close to the bolos is doomed. It isn't even a question of being sucked into this terrifying gravitational whirlpool. Long before that, everybody aboard the ship would be dead from the intense levels of hard radiation. Even the *Enterprise's* own shields wouldn't be enough. The tenth of a percent of radiation that still got through would still be a thousand lethal doses."

His voice was strained. "I'm sorry, Katwen—but unless we convince your Captain that he must immediately power up his engines and change the course of your ship, the *Wanderer* will be headed straight for the bolos in thirteen months."

"Thirteen months—?? But—"

"I know. It sounds like a long time. But the *Wanderer* has got to start changing its course now. There's a star almost directly ahead. Its gravitational pull is very intense. It's going to pull the *Wanderer* into the deadly orbit—and into the bolos a few years later. I know it doesn't sound as if the danger is immediate, but believe me, it is."

"Is demon trick?" she said softly.

"Eh?" Kirk looked confused. Was this the *old* Katwen speaking?

Katwen said, "Is what they will say. Is demon trick. Is no way I can say. How can one person prove?"

Riley reached over and took her other hand. He held it in both of his.

Kirk said, "We've thought about that. Some of the members of my crew think we should just go on in there—*break in*—take control over the *Wanderer* and do whatever is necessary to get that ship under way. But other individuals, myself among them, think that that would be a dreadful mistake. Your people have a long history of guerrilla warfare. You know your own world. You know how to make it run. You know how to shut it down. If we used force, your people—both sides in your war, your side and the savages—would fight us. That's not what we want. The alternative plan is for you—a respected citizen—to inform your Captain."

"But—but savages control the drive engines. Is reason for whole war. Was mutiny. Rebels wanted to stop at planet. Crew wanted to go on. Rebels fought. Finally shut down engines. War has continued ever since. Cannot power up engines while ship is divided. War must end before ship will move. I ask you, Captain Kirk, how I end war? I tell my people that world is doomed unless we stop war, is that what you ask? You think they believe?" She brushed a hair back from her eye unconsciously, and said, "Is story. Is man who captured by demons. Live with them for long time. Why they not kill him, he not know. But he learn that they are good, kind people who want peace—just like us. Or so he say. He come back to real world and tell people. Savages not savages. They brothers. We make peace, no? What you think happen? *We* kill him. We try him for blasphemy. He be brainwash by savages, so not real human any longer anyway. You know penalty for blasphemy? Is very old. Is called crucifixion. You know what message this man try to bring? Love one another. We tell him, you recant this belief and you not die. He say he cannot recant. Truth is truth. Recant not change truth. Someone must speak truth or no one ever know it. He die. *He willing to die for three words.* Love one another. Is crazy, yes? Maybe not—I not know anymore. Story is very old. Maybe not even true story, just fable. But I do know this. If one say war must end, one is blasphemer. And penalty for blasphemy is death. Either way, Captain, I die. If I have choice, I prefer it to be later, not sooner."

Kirk looked at her. He looked to Riley, then back to Katwen. "I understand your problem. We will give you proof. Mr. Spock is putting together a package now. A viewer, some tapes, a couple of simple devices that represent our technology—and whatever else you think might be—"

"Captain?" Riley spoke up. "I can go too. If there are three thousand people aboard the *Wanderer* then everybody will know everybody else by sight. What more convincing proof than a person they have never seen before?"

Kirk opened his mouth to say something, then closed it. "Lieutenant Riley, you're right. Only, I should go."

"Sir? With all due respect, it could be dangerous. Extremely dangerous. That's why there are contact teams. Starfleet doesn't like their captains endangering themselves. Not that they care if a captain gets himself killed—they just don't like their investment in his training and skills to be wasted. Sir."

Kirk raised an eyebrow at him. "Lieutenant Riley, I was *teaching* that course before you were in Starfleet."

"Yes, sir, I know. Then you must also remember the section about the hardest job of all for a contact team—holding back the captain and reminding him that his *first* responsibility is to his ship. That's part of the job too."

Kirk was annoyed. He drummed his fingers on the table. "Damnit, Riley. You've been trained too well."

"Yes, sir. Thank you, sir. I studied your own thesis. And also the report you wrote for the investigation into the circumstances surrounding the accident that crippled Captain Pike. In that latter document, you firmly stated your conclusion that Captain Pike's only error was in not allowing his contact team to fully bear the risks that were part of their job."

"Riley, I'll tell you something—no captain likes to risk the lives of his crew. But it's part of the job for all of us. The risks. I was wrong when I wrote that report because I had never been a captain at that time, never had the responsibility of command, and simply didn't know. It's this easy: if you can save a life by being a little more cautious on his behalf, and a little more daring on your own—then you do that, and you don't question."

Riley accepted the Captain's argument at face value. "But," he replied, "there's also the fact that the man best suited for captaincy of a Starfleet vessel is a man willing to take personal risks to reach through to the answer to a problem. And such men frequently have to be reminded to give their crews a chance to work on the situation first. That's why there are crews aboard Starfleet vessels, sir. So a captain doesn't have to do it all. His job is to know *when* to delegate authority."

Katwen was looking back and forth between the two of them. "I not understand this argument," she said. "But if my people are in danger, should we not be doing something more than arguing? If is question of who should go with—" She pointed, "I choose *him.*" And poked Kevin Riley in the chest with her forefinger. "Not insult to you, Captain Kirk. But Kevin Riley show me his world. Now I show Kevin Riley mine."

Captain James T. Kirk of the starship *Enterprise* closed his mouth. He had lost an argument. Aboard his own ship. "Tiberius!" he said under his breath.

"All right," he said, standing and pushing back his chair. "Let's go to work then."

24

To her, the *Enterprise* seemed a world of rooms, too many rooms—each one more unusual than the last.

And now, this room—empty, except for a console facing a circular alcove—it was the most disturbing of all.

She asked about a ship—like the taxi.

They told her this was a "transporter" room. And then they tried to explain the transporter to her.

She looked from one face to the other, from Spock to McCoy, to Kirk, to Riley. They all nodded. The one called McCoy twinkled a bit and admitted, "I find it hard to believe too."

She turned to Riley. "Sometimes, Kevin Riley, I think is all trick by savages. Dumb show to make me think something different from truth. We do dumb shows in my world. Is very good. I was star once. Was very good because no one recognized me until I took off make-up. Is sometime difficult to believe in *Enterprise*—I have thought sometimes that perhaps all I must do is find *right* elevator and I go home. Now, here is elevator. You call it booth. What if all this is some kind of trick? I think—do I betray my people? I worry, Kevin Riley—but then I think of you, and how well you treat Katwen. Is no savage action. I think I trust."

Riley swallowed hard. "I—I'll try not to betray your trust, Katwen Arwen."

She looked at him gravely. " 'I'll try?' In *Wanderer* we have saying. When someone says 'I'll try,' the part he doesn't speak aloud is, '—but I'll probably fail.' Will you let me down, Kevin Riley? Is that what you tell me?"

Riley shook his head. "I won't let you down, but—I do have my duty to my ship, and that must always come first."

"Is good. Is my duty to my world comes first too. Is

good we understand. Now, how does transporter work?"

Riley said, "It's just a larger version of the device that delivers the food to the table after you order it."

"Is not know how that works either."

Spock said quietly, "It is a multi-stage process. First, your body is entirely mapped—that's what produces the sparkle effect—then the component molecules are disassembled and converted into photonic waves—"

"Photonic waves?"

Spock said drily, "Photonic waves: the interference pattern in a coherent transporter beam—which is a much more precise and controlled development of the same principle that produces a phaser beam—phased light, but of a very high frequency. In fact, the frequency approaches the theoretical limits of the vibratory ability of matter in this particular configuration of space-time. The beam has the ability to penetrate some kinds of materials. If the target is well-shielded, however, or moving too rapidly, focusing becomes problematic. Anything less than 99.9999% accuracy is usually—," he hesitated for only the briefest of instants, "—less than desirable. At the point at which the interference patterns coalesce, the transported object rematerializes."

"Eh?" She blinked.

Spock explained further. "It's really quite simple. The locus of coalescence is controlled by the separate frequencies of the individual beams that make up the mega-beam of the transporter. This is usually handled entirely by the transmitting station, but in particularly difficult situations—as beaming aboard the *Wanderer* —it is handled with the aid of a coordinating module which functions as a beacon by which to target the locus. The information being sent on the beam exists not within the beam itself but in the harmonics of the various interference patterns that the separate beams produce. Although there are three-dimensional harmonics produced throughout the length of the beam, they are chaotic orders, out of tune with each other. At the point at which all the harmonics come into phase again—that is, the point of focus—all of the separate frequencies are once more tuned exactly as they were at the point of transportation, and the photonic waves collapse back into their material equivalents—forming an exact replica of the pattern that they held at the moment of disassembly. I hope that makes it all clear to you."

She turned simply to Kevin. "Can we take taxi instead?"

"It's perfectly safe," he reassured her. "Really."

"Is not sound so."

"It's safer than the taxi. If for any reason there's a problem, the polarity of the monitron beam can be reversed and instead of transporting *to* a target, the beam brings you back."

"Oh."

"So, as long as the *Enterprise* can hold a focus on a location, we can beam into or out of anyplace at all."

"Is weapon too? No? Beam explosive to enemy? Boom! Big joke on demons—everybody laugh."

"Katwen—" That was Kirk. "We are *not* a warship. Our weapons are for *defense*. Our mission is to seek peace."

She narrowed her eyes at him. "Is saying in my world, Captain—is many sayings, but this one applies here. If you carry weapon, is because you expect to use it. Whether you intend or not, you have demonstrate ability to destroy my world. I must tell my people that. Is what I meant when spoke of duty first to own world. My message—the words that I must bring to my Captain—is that our world is going to be destroyed. One way or another. If he will not listen to reason, you will use force, no?"

Kirk looked to Spock, alarmed. How had she heard of that contingency plan? It was supposed to be secret—

"No one told me, Captain. I figure out myself. Is understand this—all of you. I am not puppet. I am warrior. I follow orders. I will deliver your message because I love my world and do not want to see it destroyed. But whatever decision my Captain ultimately makes, I will follow his orders because that is my job as warrior. Next year, I may be something else. If ever I become philosopher, I will argue with Captain and not follow his orders—even at risk of expulsion from upper levels. But whatever, I follow oath of duty. Today, I think like warrior. I look. I listen. I think like one who sees man with weapon. I think *hard.* My world is end. I know that. I don't know what come next. Am not sure is my decision to make. Am certain that I not like having burden placed on me. But part of job as warrior is to accept burden. No matter how unpleasant." She looked to Riley. "You make job less unpleasant. But is still no delight." To Kirk again, she said, "Is understand?"

He nodded. "I understand."

She turned to Riley. "What we do now?"

"We stand on the stage there."

She stepped up onto the dais without fear. "Is adventure. You not harm me yet. I try."

"Stand on the focusing node—" Riley pointed.

She looked to see how he placed his feet on the plate and did likewise. She looked down at Kirk and Spock and McCoy. "Is forgot to ask one thing. Why *he* have funny ears?"

"I'll tell you later," Riley said quickly. "We have to go."

"Hokay-dokay. How?"

"He does it," Riley pointed. "That fellow behind the console. When you're ready, say 'energize.' "

"Energize—?" She started to ask—but before the word was finished, they were standing among the tanks of the *Wanderer*'s farm—the exact same place where Stokely had planted the coordinating module.

Katwen looked around herself, amazed. "Is same place—!! How he do that?"

"I thought Mr Spock made it all clear."

"Oh, yes. Like mud. Is old saying. Clear like mud. Not know what it mean, but everybody use it." She took him by the hand. "This way. I see your world. Now you see mine."

25

Once past the farms, there were long stretches of deserted, dimly lit corridors with cross-branches curving gently upward in the distance. There were distant pools of light, and sounds of activity. There was music, oddly discordant—but compelling and complex; a baroque texture of sound hovering just above the threshold of consciousness.

She caught him listening and explained, "Is season of thoughtfulness. We have seasons in *Wanderer*—marked by color of lighting, temperature, humidity, and music. In thirteen days, begins season of hope. Is fine time, preparing for season of joy."

"I hope so," said Riley. "All we have is thirteen days." He hesitated for a heartbeat, then added, "But if we do succeed, then it will be a season of hope, won't it?"

She didn't answer.

They came to an elevator shaft, a vast open space lined with tracks for eight different cars at once. The rails glowed with the bright reflections of the many lights lining the huge shaft. They stretched upward until they disappeared into a luminous blur. Downward, they disappeared into gloom.

"Is only two cars running here," Katwen explained as they boarded. The elevator was glass walled and as they rose toward the lights above, Riley was given quick tantalizing glimpses into each of the levels they passed.

"Are you getting all of this?" he asked his communicator.

"No problem," came back the reply from the *Enterprise*. "We're already into single-frame analysis on the early stuff. The whole ship is tuned in, Riley."

(That's all I needed to hear,) he thought. (Lord, don't let me do anything stupid now—)

The elevator stopped.

They stepped out onto a busy concourse. The people stood tall and they moved with grace. They wore bright-colored, lightweight clothing; mostly shorts, singlets, tunics, kilts, and simple robe-like wraparounds. Footgear was mostly sandals and slippers. There did not seem to be a specific style for either sex. Rather each person seemed to wear what he or she felt most comfortable in. Or if there were a pattern, Riley couldn't detect it. Hair styles were mostly long and flowing.

And then, the "wanderers" began to notice him.

At first, there were quick, curious glances. Then a child pointed and asked a little too loudly, "Mommy—*who* that?"

Other people turned then, startled by the very question.

Someone called, "Katwen!" More in shock than recognition.

And someone else wondered aloud, "Is that a savage?"

"Maybe is captured one—"

"—Katwen is must escaped—"

"—does not look harmed—"

"—is probably damaged now—is well-known what vileness practiced in lower levels—"

"Is must be hell—"

"Is handsome—even for demon—"

"Hush! Is want to be turned in?"

Katwen ignored the murmurings. She took Riley by the arm and moved purposely through the concourse. The crowd parted before them like a sea. A few people stared after them, but no one moved to follow.

Once past the worst of the crowd, Riley stopped Katwen and looked at her. "Are you all right?"

Her lower lip was quivering ever so slightly. But she said, "Is functioning. We must go. Captain will know we are here. No time to waste—but we must see Dr. Hobie first. Head of Science Council. Is must explain to him." She drew him aside into a narrow deserted hallway. She pointed at his communicator, then placed a finger to her lips.

"Huh—? Oh!" Riley realized and switched off his monitor. "What is it?"

"Listen to me, Kevin Riley. Is very dangerous. Is not even tell your Captain this. Not want to give him reason to not take this chance. But Captain Frost is dogmatic man. Old-fashioned. Very religious. One-world doctrine. Not believe in old stories. Calls them divisive fantasies. Old ways much suppressed. Old beliefs illegal. Old tapes destroyed. Is dangerous to speak of other worlds except with contempt. We risk our lives to speak this heresy. Is must convince Science Council, our only hope. Else Captain Frost simply refuse to listen." She looked at him intensely. "Is much scared. Is much to be scared for."

He took her hand. "I'm with you. Whatever happens, I promise, you'll be all right—believe me?"

"Is want to believe."

"Is good enough," Riley said. He switched his monitor back on. "Sorry about that," he said to the *Enterprise* autolog operator. "Private business."

"Yeah, Riley," came back the laconic reply. "You want to run your love life on your own time in the future? We've got a job to do."

Riley didn't answer. "Let's go," he said to Katwen.

26

Dr. Hobie was a genial-looking man, heavy-set and graying at the temples. He looked from Katwen to Riley and back to Katwen again. "Katwen—is thought you had been—taken by savages."

"Is more frightening than that. Is perhaps end of journey."

"Eh?" Hobie looked startled.

She told him what had happened to her, where she had been for the past thirty-six hours. Hobie listened quietly, only occasionally asking for clarification of a detail. He looked at Riley with curiosity at several points in the narrative, and studied the tapes with eagerness, but also a great deal of anxiety. "Is possibly demon trick?" he said, then looked to Riley again.

"No, is not possible. Is too convincing. Savages would not have resources for such a ruse. But—if story is truth, Katwen, is most disturbing truth since mutiny—no, since world began. This—this confirms heresies and destroys Captain's doctrine. Would also destroy Captain's power. He would not allow. And even if Captain could be convinced—which is doubtful—cultural shock would destroy us. World would not accept such inside-out perception."

"You don't have any choice," said Riley. "If you don't, then your world will die. It's that simple."

"Is no proof of that," Hobie said, "except what you provide. If we not accept your story as true, then we not accept your proof of danger to world."

"But you have living proof—!" Katwen pointed at Riley. "This is no demon!"

Hobie shook his head. "He is outsider. By definition, all outsiders are demons. And not to be trusted."

"Wait a minute," said Riley. "You're supposed to be a scientist, aren't you? That means you follow the scientific method, right? You tell me what proof you need—whatever you want—and I'll supply it. I have the resources of the *Enterprise* at my disposal. You tell me, Dr. Hobie."

The man's eyes were troubled. "Is want to believe—because it would answer many questions. Much knowledge has been lost. The book purges . . . the new doctrines—we are an impoverished people in the midst of wealth. Is heresy even to suggest such, but a rational man cannot help but wonder. We have gone many generations trying to convince selves that this is best of all possible worlds, but is it? What was world like *before* mutiny? Is dangerous to suggest that it was better place. Is better to believe that we are stronger for having cast out unbelievers and heretics—but are we really?"

He ran one hand through his hair. When he lowered it again, it was shaking. "Is too much, Katwen. Is too much to ask. Throw away all beliefs because world will end if we don't. Is too convenient a package. Is feel like trap. Captain Frost wants to dissolve Science Council. This could be excuse he need. Is must think. Is must think."

"Is no time!"

"Is must have time!"

Riley asked again, "What proof can I give you?"

"Is already given more proof than I need." Hobie turned to Riley. "You think I not already wonder about these very questions? Is long, troubled hours of private torment. Science Council free to hypothesize on origin of universe, on evolution of stars, on mechanics of body—but not allowed to consider *real* questions—like where we came from? What is soul? Where we headed? How we get to where we are today? Those are dangerous questions—and now you drop them in our lap and demand that we decide immediately. Is just too much. We spend lifetime learning how to avoid these questions so we can survive. Now you say we no survive anyway—unless we do confront. Is dilemma, Kevin Riley. Is no easy answer. You must understand."

Riley opened his mouth to speak, then closed it suddenly. No, the harsh answer was not the right one. He thought of Katwen scared and huddling in a darkened *Enterprise* corridor. He said quietly, "Yes, I understand. Is wish I knew way to make it easier. But the truth is, Dr. Hobie, there just isn't any time to do it the easy way. It has to be done immediately."

Hobie thought for a moment. He turned away from them and toyed with a block of lucite on his desk. There was a spiral of glitter imbedded in it. Pinpoints of light sparkled and glowed within the spiral. "Is supposed to be honor," he said. "But honor is worthless unless one is willing to be worthy of it. Is always wondered why truth is so dangerous. You know that proverb, Kevin Riley? 'Truth *always* dangerous.' Is because truth always threatens someone's cherished falsehood. Always knew this day would come. Hoped it would not come in my lifetime. The day that truth must be spoken." His eyes were moist. "I never once thought that courage would feel so frightening. I guess that's why it needs be courage—to overcome fear." He put the block of lucite down. "I will come with you to see Captain. I will try to protect you from his wrath."

Riley and Katwen looked at each other and exchanged hopeful smiles. Riley reached out and took her hand in his. Maybe, just maybe, there was a chance—

And then all hell broke loose.

The door exploded inward in a shower of sparks. Smoke was everywhere—things were flying in the air amid flashes of light and roaring blasts of sound—and then what seemed like a thousand black-clad stormtroopers poured into the room like a legion of agitated army ants.

One of them caught sight of Riley and raised his weapon—and then the lights went out completely.

27

Watching the replay for the fifth time on the big screen, Kirk's lips tightened into near-invisibility, his only sign of emotion.

Just behind him, McCoy wore his usual dour expression. Spock was quietly impassive.

The replay wound toward its end; the sudden whirling of the image, the bulky warriors, the flash of muzzle fire—then nothing.

Kirk turned to Spock. "Analysis?"

"Primitive stun weapons. Obviously, low-level electron interrupters. Not particularly dangerous to life, but they can inflict significant damage to microelectronic devices. Such as the interface between the power supply and the light-guide processing chips in Riley's tricorder. Fortunately, it is a simple matter to recalibrate to the standby interface."

"Right," said Kirk. "How do we tell him?"

"Assuming he is still alive—" Spock ignored the sudden startled looks of Scotty, Uhura, and Chekov. McCoy looked irked; but Kirk was too familiar with his First Officer's dispassionate manner to react. "—He may be able to figure it out for himself. Otherwise, the best we can accomplish is a remote-triggered activation. We could reach through with a tight-focused transporter beam—"

"Aye," interrupted Scotty. "But that presupposes that we can locate him. And we can't locate him without the signal from his tricorder or communicator."

Spock acknowledged it with a nod. He continued, "Because Mr. Scott is so quick to point out his own inabilities, I might suggest that we try to trigger the unit back to operation with a direct signal. The tricorder unit that Riley was carrying had a short-range subspace capability. If the light-guide circuits are not completely inoperative, we could bypass the electronics of the device and communicate directly with the main processing elements and reprogram them directly."

Kirk nodded. He said almost abstractedly, "Go ahead, Spock. Do it." But his eyes remained narrowed on the forward screen. "But I think," Kirk added quietly, "that we may have a more immediate problem than reestablishing contact with Lieutenant Riley. That ship. Her fusion reactors have to be brought back on line. And it doesn't appear as if we're dealing with a rational command."

"Obviously," said Spock.

Kirk turned to Scotty. "We have no choice. Start beaming your boarding crews over to the shuttlecraft link. Have them wait for my command. And I want a security squad standing by in the main transporter room. Lieutenant Uhura, I want you to brief them. Show them Riley's tape. And have Specks give them maps of the *Wanderer*. I'll want them to go straight in and immobilize the ship and seize the control room. Arm all crews with sleep-bombs. And phasers set for stun. The same for your reactor teams, Scotty. All teams are to stand by for my signal. Chekov, if that Klingon ship shows up again, we'll go to immediate red alert—and in that case, Sulu, I'll want the shield parameters extended to include the *Wanderer*."

Sulu turned to look at his captain. "That's dangerously over-extended, sir—"

"We don't have any choice," said Kirk. He glanced quickly around the bridge. "Any questions? Good. Let's go."

He turned back to the viewscreen and studied the

Wanderer again. "Mr. Spock, did you ever hear of Robert the Wise?"

Spock shook his head. "I can't be expected to be familiar with all of Earth's culture, Captain."

"He lived a long time ago, but he said something very appropriate for this occasion. 'There is no problem that can't be made more complicated with just a little effort.' "

Spock nodded. "A very intelligent observation."

"Very," Kirk agreed.

28

Riley came to in a dark unfamiliar room. He was lying on his back. He tried to move and found that he couldn't lift himself. His arms were bound. The effort made his head buzz uncomfortably and he felt distinctly nauseous. There was a bright light shining down on him from just above his feet. Behind it, he could just make out three silhouetted figures.

"Is not as ugly as most," a soft male voice said. "Perhaps should display it in zoo."

"Is not good idea. Someone might feel sorry for him."

"Is awake now," noted the third. "Wait. Is lift."

Riley felt the table move beneath him, swiveling to bring him upright to face his questioners. The light was directly in his eyes now. He squinted at the intensity of the glare. "Would you turn that down please?"

"It speaks?" asked one of the silhouettes.

"Is probable mimickry. Pay no mind."

"Damnit!" said Riley, then stopped himself and lowered his tone. "I am not a savage," he said as mildly as he could manage. "I am Lieutenant Kevin Riley and I want to talk to Captain Frost. And where is Katwen? And Dr. Hobie?"

The silhouettes ignored him.

Riley pressed on. "Listen to me. Your world is in

danger. You could all of you be dead in just a few years—I have proof. You've got to listen."

The silhouettes were discussing something quietly among themselves; they refused even to look at Riley.

"Look at me!" Riley screamed. "Listen to what I'm saying! This is important! Your world has been lost—separated from the rest of humanity for hundreds of years—we've finally found you! But if you don't listen to us, it could be the end of the journey!"

One of the silhouettes looked up at that. It—no, *he*—stepped into the light and looked straight into Riley's eyes. "Listen to me, savage. Do you understand what I'm saying?"

"Yes, yes, I do—please—"

The man—he was wearing a green lab smock—put one hand over Riley's mouth. "Shut up. Stop talking. Preach us none of your foul blasphemies. Or we shall be forced to put you back to sleep. Don't speak. Not at all. If you understand, nod your head."

Riley bit his lip—and nodded slowly.

"Good," said the man and stepped back out of the light to the console where his two colleagues still worked.

Abruptly there was a sound in the darkness, the sound of a door whooshing open. Three figures stepped into the room. Riley wasn't sure, but he thought that one of them might be—

The newcomer in the lead said something to the three figures at the console; they nodded and exited quietly. One of the others stepped to the console and did something there. The light in Riley's eyes faded and the rest of the room lights came up. Riley blinked in confusion. He had been right; one of the newcomers *was* Dr. Hobie. He looked uncomfortable. The figure at the console was a black-suited technician. It was the third person who drew Riley's attention. He was—almost—pleasant-looking. He was pear-shaped, paunchy, balding, with a frizz of bright red hair around his temples. He was apple-cheeked and smiling. "How do you feel?" he asked. "It's all right. You may talk now."

Riley hesitated, choosing his first words carefully. "Will you unbind me?"

Frost smiled, "I'm sorry, that isn't possible. I'm sure you can understand why. Security."

"You haven't bound Dr. Hobie."

"Dr. Hobie is my Science Officer. It isn't good practice to bind one's crew. You, on the other hand, are an alien."

"Did Dr. Hobie tell you why I'm here?"

"Yes, he did. And he showed me your pictures too. I must say, it's a very convincing presentation. Not that I'm convinced, of course, but I can understand how you were able to trick Katwen. She is only a child, and not really sophisticated or mature enough to understand the complexities of the savage mind. She is gullible—but now you are dealing with your superiors, savage, and we can see how foolish your story truly is. This nonsense of faster-than-light travel, for instance. Do you think the builders would have embarked on the journey if it were not necessary."

"But—but—," spluttered Riley. "The warp drive *is* possible! How do you think I got here?"

Frost sighed regretfully. "How you got here is obvious. Where your delusions come from is something else. Hobie, tell this poor devil about faster-than-light drives."

Hobie looked troubled, but he stepped forward and said, "It is possible to prove that faster-than-light travel is impossible with an Einsteinian 'thought-experiment.' Do you understand what an Einsteinian 'thought-experiment' is? I will explain. A philosopher named Einstein postulated that some experiments can be performed entirely in the head. These are thought-experiments. Now then, one of the classic experiments is to prove that faster-than-light travel violates the law of conservation of energy—"

If Riley could have moved, he would have leaped from the table. "No!" he shouted. "That's wrong! That's not the scientific method! You don't set up an experiment to prove or disprove a fact, but to test a hypothesis!"

"Hush now," said Frost. "Let him explain." Frost

nodded to the technician at the console and suddenly Riley found himself paralyzed, unable to move or speak, and barely able to breathe. Every gasp was an effort.

Hobie continued. "Postulate an observer who receives all of his information about the universe around him via the light that reaches his scanners—just as you and I perceive our environment with our eyes. Now then, one light-year away from this observer there is a spaceship. He can see it through a very powerful radio-telescope—we assume it is emitting a signal for the purposes of this thought-experiment."

Riley wanted to scream, but the air was constricted in his throat. He was terrified that he would choke, but Hobie droned on, unaware of his discomfort.

Hobie said, "Now, postulate that this observer moves toward our observer at a speed that is faster than light. Obviously it will arrive in the vicinity of our observer long before the light waves that originated at its departure. So our observer now sees not only the light waves of the ship at its original position—that is, the light still enroute—but also the light generated by the ship at its new position. To him, a second ship has appeared out of nowhere. To our observer, it will seem as if the first ship has duplicated itself. Out of nothing at all! And of course, that violates the law of conservation of energy. This is a classic example, and one cannot argue with the law of conservation of energy." Hobie finished his recitation glumly. He looked unhappy.

Frost nodded to the technician again, and the pressure on Riley's chest eased somewhat. "Now then, savage, what do you say to that?"

Riley took a moment to catch his breath. He wanted to phrase his next words carefully. He said slowly, "But the fact remains that I am here. How do you account for that?"

Frost folded his arms. He said calmly, "A demon will tell any lie."

Riley felt his anger rising like a storm. Oh, for just one moment of freedom—just one chance to punch this self-satisfied oaf—but no, he had to remain rational, whatever effort it took. "Just *what* do you think I am here for?"

Frost's eyes were deceptively gentle. "Let me ask *you,* savage," he said, perching himself on a stool, "what *is* the purpose of this charade? What do you think you are trying to accomplish? You couldn't possibly have expected such an outrageous story to be believed, could you?"

Riley answered in a deliberately conversational tone. "As a matter of fact, Sir, it is that very outrageousness that proves the story. Can you imagine someone *making* all that up?"

"Clever," commented Captain Frost. He looked to Hobie. "You see, Hobie—it is dangerous to argue with a demon. They have an answer for everything."

Hobie looked embarrassed. "Is true—yes, but even half-baked idea deserves fair hearing. Perhaps we can learn something."

"From a savage? Don't be ridiculous."

Riley's mind was racing. What would Captain Kirk say if he were here? How would Spock handle this situation? He said quickly, "Listen to me, for just one moment, that's all I ask, Captain Frost. You've heard my story from Katwen and Dr. Hobie, haven't you? Now, you tell me—what do you think the purpose of my mission really is?"

"To undermine the authority of the Captain, of course. The rebellion continues. You should know that —it is your credo, is it not?"

"If I truly were a rebel, it would be—but consider this: isn't it possible, just barely possible, that there could be some menace, some threat to this vessel so vast that it could require both you and the savages to cooperate in order to survive it?"

"Is barely possible," Frost admitted. "But not very likely."

"What would I have to do or say to convince you that such a thing is actually happening?"

Frost thought about it. "But *I'm* the Captain. If there *were* a danger to this vessel, *I* would be the first to know about it—not some illiterate savage."

Riley repeated, "What can I *do* to convince you?"

Frost smiled genially, "Why nothing at all, dear boy. When the day comes that the Captain of this ship starts listening seriously to savages, it'll be time for a new captain. I have only come down here to *observe* you. You are a curiosity, you know—a savage who can mimic the functions of a human being with remarkable accuracy. If you are representative of some odd new mutation, we shall have to become ever more mindful of our defenses. We dare not risk additional contamination of our population. Poor Katwen. She was such a dear child."

"Was?"

Frost ignored Riley's question. He turned to Hobie. "All right, Hobie. I have come. I have listened. I have given this tale as much credence as it deserves. It is an amusing novelty. But I have seen nothing here that would suggest that any further consideration of this nonsense is necessary. The most remarkable thing I have seen today is that this savage has been bathed recently. While this is unusual, it is hardly . . . world-shaking. Have him disposed the usual way."

They started for the door—

"No—wait!!" Riley screamed.

They stopped, looking back with curiosity. "Is something else?"

"It's the end of the journey. You've got to take a chance, Captain Frost. *Please!* Your people trust you—you control their lives. You can save them!"

Frost shrugged and turned away. "Is ranting. Is more of same."

"Dr. Hobie—" Riley cried. "We thought you believed us!"

"Was only willing to listen," Hobie mumbled. "Is part of job as scientist, but—" He looked troubled. His eyes flicked to Frost, then back to Riley. "—but reason always prevails. Is sorry. Is actually *liked* you, Kevin Riley. Is nicest savage ever met." He shrugged apologetically and followed Frost to the door.

"I'm not a savage!" Riley bellowed. "You fungus-brained baboon!"

Frost touched Hobie's shoulder. "You see? The savage always reveals his true nature sooner or later." He looked back to Riley. "I am the Captain of this vessel. When the savage tribes are willing to accept my authority, then we shall have reunification. You can begin by restoring control of my reactors. Then we can talk of trust." Frost looked hard. There was bitterness in his eyes from some long ago hurt.

Riley struggled in his bonds. "We can restore power—we *can*—but there has to be trust *first* so we can start—Captain Frost, please give us a chance—"

But Riley was talking to emptiness. Frost had already turned and exited the room. Hobie gave Riley an embarrassed look, then bustled after. The technician at the console did something and Riley went out like a light.

29

They wouldn't leave him awake. He came to in another room, surrounded by more indistinct silhouettes. They asked him questions and he answered. He wanted to *tell* the truth, not *hide* it. Then they put him to sleep again. Then he was in another room and they drugged him with something and asked him more questions—or the same ones again. They wired him to somatic scanners and asked more questions. They shuttled him in and out of consciousness as casually as one would switch on a computer program. He lost all sense of time and space.

And then—after what seemed like an eternity of questions—he was brought into a large open place filled with light and strangers. They did something to him and he started to hurt. The rational part of his mind identified the sensation as one of the irritability factors. They must have given him one of the left-handed adrenaloids. The hurt became stronger and every sensation became an agony. He began to hate, he couldn't help himself. He wanted to smash these ignorant grinning apes into sensibility—but they had too strong a grip on his arms. He was being locked into some kind of binders. He began to thrash and scream—

"Save it for the show," one of them said. "It'd be a shame to waste your energies on us. We've seen savagery before."

"Eh?" Riley turned to look, but whoever had spoken to him had already turned away.

Control! Riley told himself. *Don't lose it!* He took a deep breath, then another and another. "Listen to me," he said calmly. This world is going to be destroyed. It's going to fall into a cosmic maelstrom. There's a black hole—you're not aimed for it yet, but you will be. There's a star. Its gravity is going to deflect the course of this ship toward the gravitational whirlpool. It's so big and we're already so close that there's only one chance to alter the course of this world, but it has to be done immediately. Oh, please listen to me—what can I do to get you take me seriously?"

"See?" said one of the strangers to another. "Is fascinating stories it tells. Is perhaps one more proof of linkage between storytelling and madness. Storytellers have lost grip on accuracy of perception; next step is schizophrenia and complete personality dissolution. Poor fellow. Savage environment must breed nothing but madness."

Riley couldn't help himself. He began to rage again. And scream. He started swearing. "You clot-faced chimpanzees. You're going to deserve everything that happens to you!"

They brought him into a larger place, so vast he couldn't make out the farthest walls, so bright he couldn't bear to look. He had been in darkness so long, the light was painful, and tears came streaming to his eyes. He blinked and squinted and tried to rub his eyes, but couldn't because his hands were chained in front of him. Likewise, his feet were hobbled.

There was a sea of faces around him. A roaring gabble of voices swirled around him. The level of boos and catcalls increased as he was pushed out into the center of the stage.

Stage?

He looked around.

He was on some kind of wide raised platform. And there was Katwen!! She was bound as he was. She looked haggard. She saw him at the same time and called out, "Kevin Riley! I thought you were—" And then one of the stormtroopers slapped her into silence.

Riley flinched at the violence of it. "Stand tall, Katwen," he called. And then added impulsively, "I love you!"

He hardly felt the blow when it came. When they jerked him back up to his feet, he was grinning, and Katwen was smiling back at him. A smile in the midst of terror.

Abruptly, Captain Frost was there. He was draped in a glittering robe and crowned by a sunburst of light.

He raised one hand, and the crowd fell immediately silent.

He looked at Katwen. He looked at Riley. He spoke and his voice was like dust and velvet, but his words were carved in ice. "You have sinned against the Ship. And you have been brought before this, the highest of high tribunals, to answer for your crimes. You have both been determined to be enemies of the Ship. You have committed the blackest of blasphemies. Your heresies are the most sinful of all heresies, beyond even the redemptive cleansing of recanting. For what you have attempted, there can be no forgiveness."

He looked to Riley, "As a rebel from the lower levels, you are guilty of sinning against the Ship because you have failed to work *for* the Ship. You have lived off the energy of the Ship without ever once working to repay that debt. You do not help maintain, hence you are a parasite. You and your kind are guilty of stealing the fruits of our labors."

He looked to Katwen. "And you, Katwen, were entrusted the duty of guarding those who do work for the ship against those who would destroy us and steal the fruits of our labors. We the people trusted you. Yet, you betrayed that trust and formed an unholy alliance with our enemies."

He paused, he clasped his hands, and looked sorrowfully downward. "It is a grievous occasion. We do what we must, not in anger, but in sorrow. But we *must* do this because the survival of the ship is the singular goal that must take precedence over all other concerns."

"You pious oaf!" Riley screamed. "If you really believed that, then you would listen to what I'm trying to tell you. Your whole world is going to die! Everybody—even the savages. Upper levels, lower levels, everything is going to—"

The blows were blinding.

"You will not speak," said Frost. "We have tolerated your blasphemies long enough."

"And I have tolerated your stupidity long enough!" Riley shouted back. "Your people are going to die! Why don't you ask them how they feel about it? Why don't you give them a chance to decide for themselves?"

They struck him down again, but he still refused to be quiet. "You hypocritical, self-serving, gold-plated phony—"

The crowd was roaring. The world was raining hysteria. The room was spinning. Riley felt dizzy and collapsed to his feet. But he kept his head and came up still shouting. Still trying to make himself heard against the wall of sound washing over him from a thousand separate throats.

"Gag him," said Frost. "No more this nonsense."

Riley struggled and bit and fought, but there were six of them, and they held him in a grip of iron. And still he screamed behind his gag.

Frost ignored him. "If you will not serve Ship in life," he said, "then you will serve in death. Is the will of this authority that two of you shall be cast out with rest of the refuse of world. Your bodies will be broken down into their component substances for use by the Ship as needed. In that way, you repay your energy debt to society!"

He looked at each of them in turn. Riley felt himself being jerked sideways onto a red-painted circle. He looked and saw a guard shoving Katwen into position too. Her eyes were wide with fear.

"You belong to the molecular converter now," said Frost, and this time when he looked, there was the slightest hint of a smile on his face. He turned forward to the still-hushed crowd and said, "Let it be done."

Riley looked across to Katwen, and then—

The floor jerked out from under him and he was in free fall. He heard Katwen screaming somewhere near him—and then the darkness swallowed them both—

30

There was a tumble of sensations—

—*it's only free fall!* Riley's mind was shouting—

—but even before his reflexes could seize that information and respond to it, something caught him—yanking him out of the air. Somehow, he could sense that the same thing was happening to Katwen too—her scream was cut off by a *yowp* of surprise and there was a tangled sense in the net that held them. And somewhere an alarm bell was ringing.

They hung there in the blackness, the net still throbbing with the impact of their fall. "We're still alive," Riley managed to gasp. "Don't move, Katwen. Stay still until we figure out where we are—"

"Is net!" Katwen screamed back. "Is lower levels! Savages! Your kind of people! Is must get free before they catch us—" Already she was trying to fling herself sideways toward the wall of the shaft.

Riley's eyes were becoming used to the darkness. Far above there was the faint luminescence of the shaft opening. It seemed more like a distant moon than the top of a well.

"If savages catch us, will kill us and eat us—"

Abruptly there was light, flickering and orange. There were torches and grinning faces peering at them out of the darkness.

Katwen gasped, then stifled her scream of terror. Riley held his bound hands aloft and said, "Is friend! No kill! No kill! Is must speak with leader! Is understand?"

"Is no friends on upper levels!" one of the faces snarled back. "Keep silence!"

Another one hissed something else and jabbed him with his weapon.

Riley shut up and waited to see what would happen.

For a moment there was confusion as the savages—there were at least six of them—began to pull in the net. As they worked, they talked among themselves. Riley couldn't understand all of what they said, but the general tone of their voices was less hostile than he would have otherwise expected.

The savages tumbled them out onto the floor of a dusty corridor, then examined their bindings carefully, nodding with satisfaction. "Is still holding. Is good job does Captain, no?" And then they all laughed. They were dressed in shapeless black jackets and shorts. All were armed with knives and crossbows. All of them were short and stocky.

"Wh—what you do to us?" asked Katwen.

"Is simple choice," grinned one of the younger savages, he couldn't have been more than sixteen. "Is join rebellion or die. Eh?"

Katwen bit her lip and turned away. Riley said, "Look, fellas, don't get me wrong—I don't like the Captain any more than you do—but—"

"Silence!" snapped the group leader, a slightly taller man, fortyish. "Is no talk!" He prodded Riley in the back with the crossbow he carried.

"Ow! Hey! Watch that pigsticker, will you! I'm friendly!"

The officer—for that's how Riley was beginning to think of him—stuck his face close to Riley's and said, "Is one of invaders, no? We see your ship. We see where you break in. You try to reach upper levels, yes? From alliance with Captain and hunt down rebels, yes? Is not succeed, right? Captain throw you out with garbage. Captain famous for throwing out. Is joke—Captain is our best recruiter. Now, you in *our* hands; you call self friend? Is already kill three men. Is hypocrisy, no? Do not think us also stupid! You come with us, we listen to your story. Is better be good, alien! Is better be good." He prodded Riley again, pushing him forward.

"Ow! Hey! Watch the kidneys!—"

The officer pointed at two of the men, including the sixteen-year-old who had spoken earlier. "Is escorts. Come with me. The rest of you, continue patrols of disposal shafts. Is must meet higher quotas now."

Then, grabbing one of the torches from its improvised wall socket, he started down the corridor. Riley and Katwen exchanged a quick uncertain look and followed after. The two men detailed as escorts fell in behind them.

They marched silently through empty corridors. Some of them were blackened by signs of battle. Others were stripped of paneling down to the bare support structure. All were dark and dirty.

They moved through corridors that were puddled with water, they jumped across a stream that trickled out of the darkness toward an open shaft where it poured out as a steady fall of water. There were dank areas of decomposing matter. There were places where fungi streaked the walls. Mushrooms were growing in the corners.

They came to a wide, down-sloping ramp. There were four sets of rails set into its floor. An ancient looking cart was anchored to a wall. The officer brushed a tired-looking drifter off the seat and looked to Riley and Katwen. "Get on," he said.

As they did, Riley looked for a motor in the cart, but there wasn't one. It was just a simple platform on wheels, a box with four benches for passengers and a space for cargo.

Once they were seated, the officer released the cart's locking brake. It began to roll forward down the slope, picking up speed slowly. "Of course," Riley said. "The track spirals out from the central axis of the ship. It doesn't need a motor—it's all downhill. At the bottom, there's probably an elevator to lift the carts back to the top. Right?"

The officer turned around to look at him. "Is very perceptive for an alien. Is must be careful, eh?"

Katwen was studying Riley perplexedly. "Kevin Riley, you really are alien, aren't you? These people not know you. You not know the lower levels. You speak truth."

"That's what I've been trying to tell you!" Riley said to her. "Don't tell me you've been doubting again."

"Is sorry, Kevin Riley, but is been told so many different things by so many different people. Is wanted to believe you, then is not wanted to believe you, then is wanting to believe my own people—they took me away, Kevin Riley; is asked me questions, is told me you lied. Is told me that there was no place as *Enterprise*—I was victim of lower-level plot. Is not wanted to believe. Is not know who to believe. Is begun to doubt everyone. But is—I am beginning to understand better now. In upper levels, is not want to understand, not know how—they fight the truth as determinedly as I did—they will not listen, even when *I* tell them. Tell me, Kevin Riley, is world doomed now?"

"I hope not, Katwen." He tried to reach over for her hand, but the cuffs on his wrists made it difficult. "Captain Kirk doesn't give up easily."

The cart was moving faster now. Periodically, the officer would apply the brake to hold their speed down. The wheels squeaked unmercifully. The man had a thoughtful expression on his face; probably he was considering the meaning of Katwen and Riley's conversation.

Even though they were rolling *downward,* the corridor ahead of them had a gentle upward curve. Now, as they peered forward, a faint glow of light began to be visible. The reflection of some distant source as it bounced its way up the shaft. The officer frowned and picked up his crossbow as the glow of light ahead became stronger. "Everybody get down," he said. He armed the bow and released the brake, letting the cart build up speed alarmingly.

Then, abruptly, there was blinding light ahead of them. "Your people!" he snarled at Katwen. "Another raiding party from the upper levels!" He fired off a bolt toward one of the blinding lights, shattering it in a shower of sparks.

Something whooped and flashed over their heads—a

phaser beam?!! The cart squealed as it rocketed downward.

Riley stuck his head up long enough to see a party of men scattering sideways, trying to aim their weapons—and a barrier hastily thrown across the tracks and—

—was thrown violently against the bench in front when the cart crashed suddenly into the obstruction—no, *through* it—they were still rolling, but slower now—

Riley looked backward—there were stormtroopers running after the cart—

—one of them pitched suddenly forward, an arrow through his chest—

Another one of the stormtroopers raised a familiar-looking weapon, a stun-rifle—and as Riley recognized it, one part of his mind was already screaming, "Oh, no—not again!"

And then everything went out. Again.

31

Something was rumbling. And squeaking. And vibrating.

He was moving.

He rubbed at his forehead—it buzzed like a photonic crystal in an oscillating matrix. Where was he?!!

And then he came alert instantly—they were still on the cart and it was rocketing wildly downward! And still accelerating!

The darkness blurred past them—occasional patches of light flashed past, and once Riley thought he saw startled faces looking their way—but the gloom ahead was unbroken. They could be heading straight into anything! A brick wall—another empty shaft—whatever they hit, at this speed it would not be pleasant. How fast were they going anyway? Perhaps as fast as a hundred kilometers per hour? Riley couldn't tell.

They hit a bump then and for a brief terrifying

second, Riley thought they had come off the tracks and even now were hurtling into death—but, no—the car was still screeching downward through darkness.

Riley turned around on the bench. "Katwen!"

"Unh—" There was a muffled sound on the floor of the cart. He reached for her and pulled her up into his arms. She was still unconscious from the stun-rifle's blast. Probably their two escorts were still unconscious too; they had taken the full force of the beam.

Still cradling Katwen, Riley peered forward, looking for the officer who had been piloting the cart. He too was sprawled on the floor. Riley stretched and grabbed for the brake lever, but he couldn't reach it. He lowered Katwen back to the floor and scrambled over the bench ahead. He grabbed the braking lever and pulled it upward, hard. But nothing happened. It felt . . . useless. Perhaps at this speed, the brakes didn't work. Riley wasn't too certain about some kinds of mechanical devices. Things with moving parts always seemed so *complex*. He pulled at the lever again. It made a ratcheting sound, but still the brakes did not take hold. "I must be doing something wrong."

Riley grabbed at the officer on the floor and pulled him upright. He slapped at the man's face. "Come on, guy! Wake up! Wake up!" The man's head lolled loosely.

And then there was light ahead of them, dim, and orange-looking. It circled down into view and became —a station of some kind! There were three lower-level women crouching there, crossbows held at the ready— they stared in confusion when they saw Riley holding one of their own warriors—

And then they were past them and just ahead Riley could see some kind of a framework—*a net!*

They hit it at full tilt and for a moment they were pitched ahead and Riley thought the cart was about to flip over forward—and then there was a terrifying ripping sound and they were through the net and still rocketing madly down an endless roller coaster ride.

Riley jerked at the brake again—and the handle came off in his hand. He said a word and dropped it back on the floor. He pulled the officer over the bench with him, and began working his way toward the back of the cart. Perhaps if he moved all of them backward they would have a better chance of surviving when the cart smashed into its final destination.

He glanced forward just in time to see—

—a place where the track pitched suddenly upward. And before the fact could even register on his brain, they were already onto that slope and climbing it. The cart was already slowing as their momentum disappeared against the simulated gravity of the *Wanderer*.

Riley was only slightly relieved. Of course there would have to be some kind of safety backup in case a cart went out of control—the cart was slowing now—but what about the downslope? In a moment, the cart would be rolling back down from here.

Riley turned and looked at the steepness of the slope behind them—and immediately wished he hadn't.

Something occurred to him then and he scrambled around on the bench to scoop up Katwen again. She was just stirring—

The cart came to a momentary hesitation, and then—

Riley shoved Katwen out onto the floor and tumbled out after her.

The cart began to slide backward.

And something clicked.

And clicked.

And clicked.

And clicked.

And continued to click as the cart lowered itself gently backward one click at a time.

Another braking system. Some kind of ratcheting device set into the floor designed to catch a runaway cart and keep it from rolling back down into the main tunnel.

Riley lay there on the steep slanted floor, gasping for breath, and watching as the cart clicked steadily down and away from them.

He tried to roll over and see where Katwen was, but it was difficult to move. And then he realized something—he was still wearing the binders on his wrists and ankles. Everything he had just done, he had done while bound!

He couldn't help himself, he began to laugh. He had

just demonstrated the ingenuity and heroism of the human animal in extreme crisis—*and there were no witnesses!*

And of course, nobody would ever believe him when he told them the truth.

He sighed ruefully.

A sound behind him caught his attention.

He rolled over and saw Katwen struggling to pull herself into a sitting position. "What is happened?" She asked.

"Is explain later." Riley replied. He pointed, "They're all still on the cart. Unconscious."

"Is chance to escape!" Katwen said.

Escape? Riley hadn't really thought about escape. He had only wanted to get off that cart before it smashed into a wall. He considered it. "To where?" he asked. "Back to the upper levels? Not likely. Do you know your way around this part of the ship? I doubt it. And even if we did find our way to a ladder or an elevator or a staircase, it probably wouldn't be safe. Troops from one side or the other are bound to be watching it."

"Is not necessary to find ladder. We just walk spinward. Levels not concentric, but spiraled. Is makes for greater sense of space. Is learned that in geography. Is probably take much longer, but we still arrive at top."

Riley stared at her. He couldn't help but marvel aloud. "Katwen, your knowledge is the most amazing patchwork of ignorance and gold," he told her. "Sometimes it's hard to believe."

"Is some information privy only to Captain," she shrugged.

"Huh?"

"Is some things for commonfolk not to know. Is perhaps too dangerous. To commonfolk. And to ship. Rebellion proves that dangerous knowledge must be controlled."

Riley held himself back. He thought very hard and very carefully about what he should say to that.

Perhaps he thought too hard, for Katwen said, "Is frowning, Kevin Riley. Why?"

He said, "I'm sorry, Katwen. Sorry that you have

been deprived—of the right to know even unpleasant truths."

"Huh?" She looked confused. "But that's why there is Captain, Kevin Riley—to bear responsibility."

"And what if the Captain makes a mistake? What if the Captain is wrong?"

"Captain is never wrong. Is law. Captain is always Captain, and Captain is always right."

He looked at her sharply. "Isn't that what started the rebellion?"

"Is not know, Kevin Riley. Rebellion is one of those things not discussed. Is dangerous."

"Um. And who decides that something is too dangerous for people to know?"

"Before rebellion was job of Captain and Council—but Council started rebellion, so now is Captain sole authority. No more Council—except Captain's Science Council."

Riley thought about that. He knew what he wanted to say, but this wasn't the right time or place. He levered himself to his feet—and not without difficulty. The binders made it hard to maneuver. "Come on," he said.

"We escape?"

"No," he sighed. "We turn ourselves in. We go after that cart." Far below them on the slope, it was still clicking steadily downward. "We can't go back to the Captain. There's only one chance left. Down there. The people of the lower level may be the last hope of this world, Katwen."

"Is savages—" she protested, but not too convincingly. Reluctantly, she followed after him.

There were stairs at one side of the shaft. Holding onto the railing with both bound hands and hop-jumping downward one step at a time, they began their slow descent after the cart.

32

At the bottom of the shaft a crowd had gathered around the now-motionless cart. The men were scruffy and unshaven. The women were gaunt. The children were sullen and sickly. They turned as one person as Riley and Katwen came hobbling toward them.

In the center of the crowd were the three guards who had been in the cart with them. They looked shaken and confused. The officer was just taking a drink from a jug. He lowered it to look at them. "Is not try to escape?" he asked.

Riley shook his head. "We have a message for your people. Is not our purpose to escape. Is purpose to deliver message."

The officer nodded and said, "Come with me."

Riley held out his hands so the man could see the plastic binders. "Is possible to remove these first?"

The man said, "Is not procedure to release prisoners without authority, but—" He grinned. "—is obvious you not planning escape." He spoke to someone in the crowd and almost immediately a box of tools was brought forward. In moments, Riley and Katwen were free of their hobbles and binders.

Riley saluted then, "Lieutenant Kevin Riley of the United Starship *Enterprise,* Captain James T. Kirk commanding."

The man nodded in acknowledgment. "I have seen your ship, Lieutenant Kevin Riley. It is . . . impressive. Is true that your people travel faster than light?"

"Is true . . ."

"Is almost makes me cry. Our journey has been for—what?"

Katwen stepped forward then. "I am Katholin Arwen, known as Katwen, oath of Warrior, protector of the Captain's Republic of the *Wanderer*. Upper Levels. And then she added, "But excommunicated . . ."

"Is lucky for you," the man said grimly, but without

explanation. "I am Squadrant Commander Lasker, at your service." He returned Riley's salute. "Come with me. You must meet *real* Captain."

The crowd parted for them, people staring curiously, and they entered one of the side tunnels off the transport shaft. Riley couldn't help but notice that the lower-level people were all dressed in similar drab clothing; tattered shirts and shorts, sandals, and ponchos. Most of the people were short and stooped—and thickly muscled too. They were a hard-looking population and Riley puzzled over the physical characteristics he saw. The people of the upper levels were all tall and graceful and—

Of course! The upper level people lived in a simulated gravity of anywhere from .3 to .9 Earth normal. These people spent all of their lives in gravities that ranged from 1.1 to 1.75 Earth normal. What he was noticing was the difference between a population that was shackled by gravity and one that was nearly free of its effects.

These people probably paid a severe penalty for trying to survive in such an extreme environment. Arteriosclerosis, high blood pressure, and assorted other diseases of the heart and kidneys. Hyperdevelopment of the musculature as compensation for the energy expenditures that just simple day-to-day activities would require. Bow legs, fallen arches, sinus trouble, and bursitis. Not to mention hypercalcification of the bones leading to problems of ossification and deformity. Emphysema was probably prevalent here too. And high pressure disease. There weren't many old people in that crowd, nor in these passages. Death probably came quickly on the lower levels. Riley thought about the sanctuary just a few levels above and felt resentful. How did such a division come to happen in the first place?

And just how did these people live anyway? What did they do for food? Riley thought about the dim orange lighting of the corridors—it looked like some kind of emergency lighting system; he wasn't certain, but the plates looked like the old-fashioned glowplates that turned ambient thermal energy into low-level lighting in the absence of any other power source. He shivered in reflex. Perhaps that was why these corridors were so cold. The glowplates were eating the body heat of the population. But they didn't dare disconnect them or they would have no light at all.

Abruptly Lasker turned and led them into what had once been a storage room, but was now something of an office and something of a guerrilla headquarters. Riley thought about that—yes, probably these people had to be continually on the move. They were too vulnerable to set up a permanent base in any one part of the lower levels. Their best defense would be to keep moving from place to place. In fact, it looked like they were already preparing to move.

A short dark man was peering at them. He had thick bristling eyebrows and a scowl like the inside of a furnace. Katwen shrank back in fear, clutching at Riley's arm. "Is Satan himself!!"

The man smiled guilelessly. "It's been long time since I've been called that. But then, it's been long time since the last execution." He helped himself to a shapeless biscuit from a plate on the table, then shoved it toward them. "Are you hungry? Help yourself. It's not very fancy, but it's the best we have to offer." He glanced from Riley to Katwen and back to Riley. "What was your crime?"

"Is done nothing wrong," said Katwen.

The man shrugged. "Of course not. Nobody ever does. What were you accused of?"

"Heresy."

"Oh ho! Heresy! Heretics are more fun!"

"What are you going to do with us?"

"Nothing. If you wish to make your life with us here in the lower levels, you are free to do so. Obviously, you cannot go back to the upper levels. If you truly *are* an enemy of the upper levels, then of course you are our ally. But if you choose to make your way elsewhere in the lower levels, you may do that also. There are a few minor settlements, but they are not very successful. Or hospitable, I might add."

"Aren't you afraid I will go back and tell Captain where to find you?" Katwen asked. "Captain has sworn the death of you, Satan."

"Please," The man held up a hand. "I am Gomez. I

am the Captain of my people, but I do not like to be called Captain. That man—upstairs—," and he rolled his eyes at the ceiling, "—has made the word distasteful to us. And no, I am not afraid of what you will tell your Captain. He has already sentenced you to death. What do you think will happen if you go back—if you could get back through your people's defenses? No, I am not worried. Besides, as you may have noticed, we're nomads. We move every three days."

Riley stepped forward then. "Sir, I am Lieutenant Kevin Riley of the United Starship *Enterprise*."

"I thought so. You don't look like the average heretic. And I am Satan, the demon of the lower levels, also known as Lucifer, Baal, Beelzebub, and I forget what else they call me. Captain Frost—is he still alive? Pity—is religiously dogmatic. Tell me, Lieutenant Kevin Riley, does your Captain understand the situation here?"

"I believe so, yes."

"More than a hundred years ago, this ship found a planet where human beings could survive. Every twenty-three years, however, its primary gave off a burst of hard radiation. The Captain at that time—Captain Shiras—felt we had no choice but to move on toward our next target. The colonists didn't want to. It was a choice between settling a real world or being one more generation who would live and die within these metal walls. And our ancestors wanted to be the first generation to live on a new world, they would not accept the Captain's assessment that the world was uninhabitable, and so was born the rebellion.

"The colonists believed the Captain did not want to relinquish his power over the world. The Captain claimed that the colonists were foolhardy and misguided. The colonists demanded that at least the world be put into orbit around the planet so that it could be observed at close range and we could determine if it was truly inhabitable or not. Captain Shiras refused and ordered continued acceleration toward the next star on our course. Our ancestors shut down four of the ship's fusion plants. This world's engines were now without power. In the fighting that followed, many persons on both sides were killed—including those men and women who knew how to restore the ship's engines to full operating status. Shiras and his followers managed to channel some of the power from the two remaining plants into the aft engines and altered the ship's course as scheduled. When the mutineers discovered this, the ship was already well under way; they retaliated by counterattacking and shutting down all power to the control room, navigation, and computer sections. They said that they would restore the power when Shiras agreed to turn back. They said that it could be accomplished in less than five years, decelerating and reversing direction. That stalemate lasted for three months and then Captain Shiras died under very mysterious circumstances. With his death, our ancestors thought that perhaps they had a chance to make peace with the upper levels—but no, the Captain who followed him, cursed to be his name, was even more hard-nosed— if such a thing is possible—than his predecessor. He claimed that the mutineers had assassinated the Captain—which was not true—and declared war on us. We have been at war ever since."

Riley said, "Captain Gomez—it is *imperative* that power be restored to this ship's engines. The *Wanderer* is headed for certain disaster. This ship is going to fall into the galactic whirlpool!"

"Eh?"

"Two black holes, rotating around each other in the most eccentric possible orbits, with a collection of cosmic debris in their wake that would give an astrophysicist nightmares. The course corrections have to be made *yesterday!*"

Gomez sank down into his chair with a sigh. "So this is the way the world ends. Listen to me, Kevin Riley. Even if we could start up the fusion engines, it would not do any good. Captain Frost controls the command sections of this ship. The orders have to be given there. And you already know what Frost thinks of your story."

"What do you mean, 'Even if we could'?"

"Just what I said. Look around. Do you see any books? No. Not even electric lights. Captain Frost controls the electricity of this ship. We have to use wallplates that glow at room temperature—our body heat powers them. And when one of our own dies, we melt down the animal fat in his body to make candles. Sometimes we raid the upper levels and try to tap into a power cable so we can recharge what power cells we have. But mostly, we have to line the walls with blankets and foam to keep our heat from bleeding off into the deserted parts of the ship.

"We have no light, no heat, and what food we have comes from the garbage of the upper levels. Yes, we have farms. But they are small and pitiful, and the light for them comes from a team of men riding pedal-operated generators. We have no manufacturing. Our clothes are cut from industrial canvas that we salvage when we can find it. Our lives are a continual struggle for survival. We do not have the time to teach our children even the simplest things—not even how to read! Can you read?!!" He looked at Katwen and Riley. "Of course you can. You don't think twice about it!" Gomez went to a filing cabinet and pulled out an old book. "Do you see this? Do you know what this is? This is the logbook of the first Captain. It dates from the day this ship first broke free of the L5 position and went into cometary orbit. It's the legal token of my office as true Captain of this ship. As elected by the people. And do you know something? I can't read it! I don't know how to read! We haven't had a captain here who knows how to read for sixty-three years!

"All the books, all the knowledge how to restore this ship to full operation, is upstairs! In the hands of those who are too blind to use it, and too selfish to let others have access to it! Yes, if we could start up the fusion plants again, we would! But we can't because we don't know how!"

"But—"

"Oh, we do know something about the plants! We've been maintaining them for generations. But what we do know has been handed down by word of mouth from generation to generation—would you trust your life to that kind of knowledge? I wouldn't."

"Have you offered to negotiate with Captain Frost?"

"We have not offered to negotiate with any captain for sixty-three years. The last time we tried to make peace with a captain of the upper levels, it was a trick. An ambush. He wiped out four of our leaders. We dare not trust a captain again. Besides, we have nothing left to bargain with. We give him control of the fusion plants in return for what? We restore power and we're giving him full control of the ship—the power to hunt us down and finally destroy us. No, Kevin Riley—is better this way. This way, at least, we survive a while longer. As long as I am responsible for my people, my loyalty is to their survival *first* above all. If we cannot survive, then it does not matter if the ship survives us."

He stopped and stared at the two of them, and Riley studied Gomez's eyes with fascination. There was the same look of hardness and bitterness he had seen in the eyes of Captain Frost, some long-ago hurt that had never quite healed.

Katwen broke the silence first. She said, "I—I did not know. May I—offer you my help? I can read. I can teach reading. Is worked as teacher once—"

Gomez blinked. "Eh? Why, yes—thank you."

Riley stepped forward then. "Sir? I think we can help each other, you and I—if you're willing to take a chance. If you can trust us—"

Gomez said, "Trust is the only thing we *do* have down here. We have it in abundance, Kevin Riley. We survive because we depend on each other. It is impossible to survive alone. So, we trust. We have to."

"Thank you," said Riley. "Perhaps I can offer you something to go with that trust—the word is *hope.*"

"Hope," said Gomez. "We have not heard that word in a long time." He sighed. "Down here, hope has been a hollow word. And yet—I admit—it is a word we want to believe in. I go to the window, Kevin Riley. I look, I see your ship. I cannot help myself. I hope. Maybe you bring change. But will it be change for better or worse? If there is something I can do that will help my people, then I will dare to hope again. Let us talk. Let us begin." He held out his hand.

33

The darkness of the corridors was unnerving. Stokely and Omara stood silent guard at the receiving bay where the shuttlecraft umbilical connected. The boarding party of twenty armed security guards stood silently clustered around the only exit. They were dressed in battle-suits and flash helmets, protection against the crossbows of the savages and the stun rifles of the upper-level dwellers.

A light had been mounted in the main corridor outside the two rooms the boarding party had gathered in. They held back the gloom of the corridors, creating a no-man's-land of brightness. Occasionally, in the deepness beyond, something could be heard moving, and tricorder scans indicated human forms—but when a spotlight was aimed up the shaft there was nothing there. It made for a spooky feeling, and the tension was almost palpable.

Stokely looked to Omara. "They're watching us, I know it. I feel like a sitting duck in all this light. It's like being surrounded by the shadow-wraiths of Malavar. You reach out for one and there's nothing there. I don't think we're going to stand much chance of surprising them."

Omara grimaced. "This is a rotten job, you know? Why should we have to invade a world to save it?"

Stokely shrugged. "It's not our job to make the decisions."

"If it were, you think we'd be here?"

"I know where I'd like to be. There's a *zaftig* little number I left on Wrigley's—"

"Please—," Omara groaned. "If I have to hear about green-Linda one more time—"

"Hey!" interrupted Stokely. "What was that?"

"Huh?"

Stokely held his tricorder out in front of him, scanning the darkness. "Something out there. No, two—three somethings."

Omara brought his rifle up sharply, crouching low against the darkness. Stokely called into the door behind them, "Security! Red alert!"

"Don't shoot!" came the cry. "Don't shoot! We're friends! It's me, Riley!"

"Huh?" Stokely punched a sequence on his tricorder and the spotlight behind him swiveled to point into the darkness— centering Riley, Katwen, and somebody they didn't recognize in a pool of brightness. All three of them were shielding their eyes from the intense battery of light, squinting against the glare.

Omara started to lower his rifle, but Stokely hissed, "Stay alert! It could be a trick." He called, "Approach slowly—and with your hands high." He studied his tricorder as they came down the corridor. There were no other human forms within its limited range. "All right," he said. "Come on in."

"Is suspicious people," said the unidentified stocky man. "You learn fast, no?"

"Put down your rifle, Omara—or I'll tell Scotty who built the still in the synthesis section."

"That was a legal still," protested Omara, but he lowered his rifle.

"Yes, but it was clumsy. Very inefficient. Scotty made us rebuild it right."

Omara grinned. "It's Riley," he said. "Hey! What happened to you? Are you all right?"

"Yes, we're fine—and this is Squadrant Commander Lasker, acting representative of Captain Jesus Garcia Gomez, the *real* Captain of the *Wanderer*—at least, by Starfleet rules, he's legal." He turned to Stokely. "Let me have your communicator. They took mine when they arrested us—on the upper levels. And you can relax your guard. The lower-level tribes are not going to attack you. At least not until after Commander Lasker here has had a chance to parlay with Captain Kirk." Riley flipped open the communicator. "Transporter room. Riley here. Three to beam over."

"Riley—?!!" came the incredulous reply, and then a crisp, "Yes, sir!"

Riley stepped away from Stokely and Omara, indicated to Lasker and Katwen where they should stand, and said, "Energize."

The air piled up in sparkles and they were gone.

Omara looked at Stokely. "People come and go in the *strangest* ways around here."

34

A com-link and two technicians were beamed immediately onto the *Wanderer*. As soon as the link was brought on-line, Kirk called an executive session in the main briefing room. The forward wall of the chamber shimmered once, then "disappeared" and became the interior of Gomez's office in the lower levels. Gomez was there with two of his advisors.

"Captain Gomez," Kirk acknowledged his presence. "James T. Kirk of the *Enterprise,* at your service."

Gomez looked a little bit overwhelmed. "Who are all those other people?"

Kirk looked behind him. "These are executive officers of my crew. Science Officer Spock, Chief Engineer Scott, Communications Officer Uhura, Medical Officer McCoy—"

"A doctor?!"

Kirk nodded.

"Captain Kirk, forgive me if I am presumptuous, but my people need help. Our children are dying. Your Lieutenant Kevin Riley told me of your Starfleet's high ideals. He used the word 'hope.' My people do not believe in hope anymore. But we would like to—can you send us your doctor? Can you send us food?"

Kirk looked to McCoy.

Bones was already rising from his chair. "I'm on my way." To Scotty, he said, "I'll need a number three med-unit, and backup. Let's go with the standard disaster-relief support modules and I'll supplement those as soon as I know the details. I'll need Chapel and a paramed squad—main transporter room." And he was out the door.

Kirk turned back to the screen. "Captain Gomez, is there anything else you need?"

"Thank you, Captain Kirk—we will need defenses against the warriors of the upper levels, but—"

Kirk held up a hand. "Let that wait. First, we must save the *Wanderer.*"

"Your priorities are not my own, Captain Kirk, but I will listen."

Kirk took his place at the briefing-room table. "Mr. Spock, your analysis of the situation?"

Spock acknowledged with a nod. "The upper-level people hold the control room of the *Wanderer.* The lower-level people have the fusion plants, but not the controls. Four of the fusion plants are inoperative. The other two are operable, but only one is currently on-line. The power output is minimal. Not enough to provide full life support for the vessel, let alone power to the mass-drivers of the ramscoop. The upper-level people have control of the library—which undoubtedly contains full technical details of the ship's construction and operation, but they seem to have made themselves *deliberately* unaware of their situation. The people of the lower levels are aware that they live aboard a ship, but they exist at such a poverty level that there is no chance of their applying that knowledge.

"The limited ecology of the *Wanderer* will remain locked into this pattern as long as the upper-level civilization controls both the resources and the knowledge of the *Wanderer.*"

Spock looked around the table. "Two goals must be achieved if we are to save the *Wanderer.* First, we must bring all six of the fusion plants back to full operation. Second, we must gain access to the *Wanderer's* control room. Captain Gomez will undoubtedly provide us with the necessary access to the plants, leaving only the problem of the control room."

Gomez interrupted Spock then. "Access to the fusion plants will *also* be a problem."

They turned to look at him, puzzled.

Gomez explained. "Have any of you stopped to think about what happens after you save the *Wanderer?* Where do we go then? You will have turned this world outside-in."

He stood up and came around his desk, revealing just how short he really was. "My people, we live in darkness. The darkness is our ally. When the first rebels fled to the lower levels, they turned off the lights to protect themselves. That's how we have been able to survive against the attacks of the upper levels. In the darkness we can hide. We can ambush them. We can hit and run and then disappear like ghosts. We are guerrillas because we have to be.

"If you bring the plants back on-line then there will be power for the lower-level life-support systems. There will be light. How will we hide then? Captain Frost will not waste a second mounting an attack on us when he learns that there is light."

"The alternative—," said Kirk. "The alternative is the destruction of the *Wanderer* and everyone aboard."

Gomez shrugged. "If my people have been destroyed and if I am dead, then I will be in no position to worry about it, will I?"

A flicker of annoyance crossed Kirk's face. He covered by turning away. "Tiberius," he muttered. He turned back. "What are you asking for, Captain?"

Gomez said slowly, "I want you to guarantee that my people will not be left vulnerable to those of the upper levels. We want the weaponry with which to defend ourselves against them."

"For what—to continue the madness of your war?!!" Kirk was genuinely angry. "Don't you realize? Either way, this is the end of your journey! If we save the *Wanderer* there will be no need for your people to continue on like this. Starfleet can find you a planet—if that's what you want. Or we can direct you to a permanent orbit in a suitable system. But no matter what the ultimate decision, your isolation is ended. The reasons for the war are going to be irrelevant. Captain Gomez, I want to give you the best guarantee of all—I want to give you peace."

"We have no experience with peace, Captain Kirk. We only know suspicion."

"But you *do* have experience with peace," Kirk countered. "I gave you a demonstration of the kind of trust that can exist between peoples when I sent you my doctor. I sent him to you without question. You needed him. The mission of Starfleet is not only to seek out new life—but to cherish *all* life wherever we find it. It's in the preamble to our charter. Every life is unique. Therefore every life is sacred. It does us no good to save the *Wanderer* if the people aboard her are determined to continue killing each other off. Our goal is to save the *life* aboard the ship, not just the ship herself." He stopped and glared across the intervening space at the impassive image of Gomez.

Gomez was glowering behind a dark brow. He said, "Captain Kirk—your words are pretty enough. But it has been my experience that nobody gives anything without expecting something in return. There is a price for everything. What is the price that you and your Federation will eventually demand from us?"

Kirk spread his hands wide. "What can you offer the Federation? The question is asked every time a ship contacts a new civilization. Sometimes, the answer is that the new civilization can offer very little in the way of knowledge or goods. Sometimes the question must be turned around. What can the Federation offer you?" Kirk turned around suddenly. "Mr. Spock."

Spock cocked an eyebrow at Kirk.

"There is a Vulcan story, the Elder and the Child—tell it please."

Spock looked momentarily puzzled, then began quietly, "There was a Vulcan Elder, many centuries old—she had reached the end of her years and made the decision to die. On the day before her death, she went out to her fields and began to prepare a patch of ground for planting. A child came by, riding on his *sehlat,* a child who had not yet learned that it is bad manners to laugh aloud. The child saw the old woman working and stopped. He asked, 'What are you doing?'

"The Vulcan Elder said, 'I am going to plant a family of *dalm* trees.'

"The child laughed out loud at the incongruity of a woman of her age planting a family of *dalm* trees. Had this been any other Vulcan, the child would have been quietly rebuked for such a show of bad manners—but this was a Vulcan Elder, and she was wise enough to know that children do not always know that their manners are bad, so she merely asked quietly, 'Why do you laugh, little person?'

"And the child answered, 'How long will it take before your *dalm* trees bear fruit?'

"And the old woman answered, 'These trees will not bear fruit for more than a hundred and fifty years.'

"The child said, 'But tomorrow you plan to die. You will not be here to enjoy the fruit. Therefore it is illogical to plant. I laugh at your silliness. Perhaps you have been spending too much time with Earthmen.' "

Kirk rolled his eyes toward the ceiling and decided to ignore the remark.

Spock continued, "The old woman continued working. She continued to dig the hard-baked Earth, loosening the soil with a three-fingered tool. After a moment, she spoke, 'When I was a small child, no bigger than yourself, little person, there were *dalm*-figs to enjoy. One day, I asked my father where these *dalm*-figs had come from. He told me that two hundred years before, one of my ancestors had been thoughtful enough to plant a family of *dalm* trees on the day before she died so that I would have them to enjoy. He told me that it was her gift to me, even though she would never know me and I would know her only as a story. Each generation provides for the next one, little person. I can never repay the gift that my great-ancestor gave to me—whether it be something as simple as a bowl of *dalm*-figs or as elegant as the whole of Vulcan learning—except to pass it on to those who will follow after me. It will be my gift to them. Someday, you will pass by here again and you will taste of these *dalm*-figs, and you will remember the old woman who planted them—and you will be grateful for my foresight. Someday, you will plant *dalm* trees of your own, even though you will never live to taste of their fruit. Illogical? No, my great-great-grandchild, I am not illogical. It is the ones who do *not* plant who are illogical because they are not repaying the debt. If you eat of the *dalm*-figs, then you must also plant.'

"The child thought about the old woman's remarks for a moment or two. Then he climbed down from the back of his *sehlat* and began to help the old woman with her planting." Spock finished and looked to Kirk.

Kirk smiled. "Thank you, Spock. Your great-great-grandmother was a very smart woman."

"Thank you, Captain," Spock acknowledged.

Kirk turned back to the image of Gomez. "Do you begin to understand now, Captain Gomez, something of the mission of Starfleet? When Vulcan joined the Federation, the Starfleet charter was redrafted—the woman in the story was one of the ones who helped in the drafting. It was she who pointed us toward the future. And that is what Vulcan did for Starfleet and the Federation. More than any other contribution, that was the valuable one. I don't know what your people can offer to the Federation—but neither did we know what Vulcan could offer the Federation until after they had joined."

Gomez's features had softened. "Captain Kirk," he said. "If I trust you, and I am wrong, my people will curse my name for generations to come—," and here he smiled. "Except, you tell me that if I *don't* trust you, there won't be any generations to come. If I believe you, I *have* to trust you. I tell you this; I believe you—but I have not had much experience in trusting. It is not easy, is it?" He looked across the gulf of understanding at the starship Captain.

James T. Kirk smiled gently, and said, "No, it isn't."

Gomez nodded. "But we must begin. Let it be done." He stepped forward, then appeared flustered. "Is confusing. I come to shake your hand, and you are not here. How we seal deal?"

"Your word will be good enough."

"And yours—but just same, I shake my hand for you." Gomez grinned and clasped his hands in front of himself, shaking them briskly.

Kirk grinned back and echoed the gesture. "All right, let's go to work—I want Specks up here, and I want the *Wanderer*'s designs accessed to this screen. Let's find that control room."

35

Scotty brought in his senior engineering staff and a set of auxiliary consoles. As Specks began accessing the *Wanderer*'s designs from the library to the screens of the different consoles, he noticed Kirk's surprise. Hardly glancing up, he said, "You always said that you wanted this ship's library to be complete, sir."

"I know . . ." replied Kirk. "But—" And then dropped the end of the sentence with a shrug. He turned to Mr. Spock. "I wonder what else we've got in that library that we don't know about?"

Spock was impassive. "Captain, the sum total of knowledge in this ship's memory tanks is so vast that even the index to the index to the index is beyond the capacity of the human brain."

"Oh," said Kirk.

"That is why I am aboard this ship."

"Oh," said Kirk again. "Thank you, Mr. Spock."

"You're welcome."

Kirk turned to his Chief Engineer. "Have you got anything yet, Scotty?"

"Aye, and it's not good. We can't just go barging in, Captain. We'd have to fight for every centimeter and they have the high ground. We could do it, of course, but it might take weeks."

"We haven't got weeks."

"Aye, I know that. I've been looking for an alternate route. I think we can send a party of men up these air ducts here and here. That doubles our chances of a group getting through."

"It looks good, but I want you to go over your plan with Captain Gomez. He knows the territory better than we do. Put the boarding teams on condition green, but tell them to keep alert just in case."

"Aye, sir."

Kirk turned back to Spock. "We're about to administer a massive cultural shock to two separate cultures.

I'd like to have our operation secured and our controls locked in quickly, before they have a chance to develop a first-level reaction. I hate to say it this way because it sounds so damned callous—but if we're going to get through to those people on the upper levels, we're going to have to totally demoralize them first. There's the possibility for mass hysteria, no matter what we do. That ship is a very fragile ecology—and if they panic, they might activate their own equivalent of a 'doomsday weapon,' destroying themselves and taking everyone else with them."

Spock nodded. "You're beginning to think like a Vulcan, Captain. My compliments."

Kirk flicked a sidewise glance at him. "Thank you, Mr. Spock. Do you have any suggestions you'd like to make?"

Spock looked thoughtful. "We should consider the introduction of some sort of phenomenon so unfamiliar to the inhabitants of the *Wanderer* that they will be paralyzed by its presence. Warriors cannot fight what they cannot understand."

"Hm," said Kirk. He thought about that for a half a moment, then turned to Uhura. "Get Kevin Riley and Katwen up here."

As soon as they arrived, Kirk took them to one side of the room. "Katwen, look—this has become an operations room. We're planning an invasion of the upper levels. We must seize the control room of the *Wanderer* if we're to save the ship. We don't have the time anymore to try to establish contact with Captain Frost. But we don't want to bring any undue harm or shock to the inhabitants of the upper levels. So what we want to do is startle your people into immobility, so that there will be no fighting. Do you understand?"

Katwen looked troubled and upset, but she nodded. "I understand."

"We have some . . . ah, devices. They float through the air and they generate large three-dimensional images around themselves. We can make elephants or dragons or any kind of other creature appear to be real. We use these devices for parades—"

"Parades?"

"Carnivals. Celebrations."

"Oh."

"—and it seems to me that perhaps you and Riley here could program these devices for us. You describe the kinds of creatures that your people put into stories—especially the stories you tell children—"

"Oh, you mean like prowlers and growlers and bears?"

"Prowlers and growlers and bears? Yes, exactly. Riley will bring these animals to life. They don't have to be scary—in fact, it's probably better if they're not. Just very big and very silly-looking. And as clumsy as a basket of puppies. Make them so the people who see them will laugh out loud."

"Captain Kirk, this will help save lives?"

"I hope so, Katwen, very much."

"Then I will do it. I will give you *lots* of prowlers and growlers and bears."

"Good. Call we when you have the first few up and running. I'd like to see exactly what these prowlers and growlers look like."

"And bears!"

"Yes, and the bears."

They exited and Kirk turned to see Spock looking at him with an odd expression.

"Prowlers and growlers and bears?" Spock asked.

"Something wrong, Mr. Spock."

"Not at all. It's just unusual to see a starship captain applying prowlers and growlers and bears to the solution of a problem."

"Especially the bears, Mr. Spock. Especially the bears."

Spock raised an eyebrow. "Captain, you may have just discovered the first logical application of illogic."

Kirk looked to his First Officer speculatively. "Makes your head hurt, doesn't it?"

"Only my brain."

36

Every second moved the two ships closer to a catastrophic rendezvous at a place where the laws of physics were tortured into incomprehensibility.

The big ship was dark. The giant cylinder turned majestically in the night. The *Enterprise* was dwarfed by this city in the sky, but it was ablaze with lights. Periodically a new point of light would appear on her hull and another pool of illumination would glow on the side of the *Wanderer*.

On the bridge of the *Enterprise*, Captain James Tiberius Kirk satisfied himself once more that the plan was workable.

This happened every time he had to order members of his crew into a situation where their lives might be endangered. He hesitated each time—just long enough to ask himself again if the risk was absolutely necessary.

This was the most important part of his job as captain of a Starfleet vessel—making the *right* decision where human lives were concerned.

"Tiberius," he said to himself, so softly that his lips didn't even move. His *deliberate* compassion spoke up inside his head then. Yes, the risk *was* necessary. It always was, or he wouldn't be stopping and asking himself if it really was.

He touched the button on the arm of his chair. "Scotty, are you ready?"

"Aye, Captain. All units are in place and standing by. And we've got two dozen of Riley's gremlins ready to go."

"Good." Kirk touched another button. "All units, go to Condition Yellow. Stand by for Condition Red. We'll move on my signal." He stood up. "Mr. Spock?"

His First Officer stood up beside him.

"We'll go up with boarding team two. If your timetable is correct, we should be entering the control room just about the same time Scotty is bringing the first of those fusion plants back on line."

"If the plan works, the timetable will be correct."

"Right." Kirk turned to Uhura. "Any traces of that Klingon?"

"No, sir. All sensors have been silent for the past thirty-one hours. We do have a blind spot dead ahead—the influence of Polo's Bolos—but any ship trying to hide in that is going to have more to worry about than playing tag with us."

Kirk grinned. "Good." He nodded to her professionally. "Fourth in command, you're in charge. Take care of my ship, Uhura."

"Aye aye, sir." She sat down in the command and control seat, already unplugging the Feinberger monitor from her ear.

Kirk and Spock stepped into the turbo-elevator. "Main transporter room," said Kirk, grasping the wall handle. "The elevator dropped in the shaft. Kirk glanced to Spock. "This time, I may finally get aboard the *Wanderer*. Think of it, Spock—a piece of living history. One of the first space-built cities. From even before the time of interstellar travel." He was going to add, "Doesn't it give you an extraordinary feeling?" But then he remembered who he was talking to. He said nothing.

Spock chose to comment however. He said, "I believe you were going to make some sort of emotional statement, Captain. Were you not? I often wonder why during moments of significance, humans feel the need to translate the experience into *emotional* terms."

"Ah, but that's just it, Spock. We *feel* the need. Perhaps because it helps us better assimilate and *understand* the experience. Did you ever stop to consider, Spock, that there might be a very *logical* reason for human beings to have emotions?"

"No," said Spock. "I never have." His expression was his usual impassive gaze.

"Perhaps you should. Ah, here we are." The elevator slid to a stop and Kirk stepped out, leaving Spock blinking in momentary puzzlement.

"An interesting question," Spock said to his back. "And quite remarkable, considering the source." He followed thoughtfully.

They stepped into the transporter room in time to see the last party of six just fading out on the transporter platform.

A number of transporter coordinating modules had been beamed over to the *Wanderer* and Gomez's men had delivered them to the locations Scotty had picked out on a master map of the vessel—because of the spiraled nature of the ship's decks, it was possible to map the entire world as either a set of cross sections or a single long strip. Once the coordinating modules were in place, it was possible to beam teams over to key points within the *Wanderer*'s hull.

Kirk and Spock stepped up onto the transporter platform. They nodded to the transporter chief. "Mr. Kyle, energize."

And then the world flickered around them and they were aboard the *Wanderer.*

37

Riley, Stokely, and Omara were waiting for them with three other security men. Kirk acknowledged them with a nod and pulled out his communicator and flipped it open. "Scotty, we're aboard the *Wanderer.* What's your status?"

"We've got the first two fusion plants opened up—aye, and these are beautiful pieces of machinery, Captain—but the ignition lasers have long since been destroyed. And we're not equipped for this kind of reconstruction."

"Scotty—there's got to be something you can do!"

"Aye, I hope so. I've got one idea working in the computer now. If we can recalibrate a medium powered phaser-cannon—and if we can get it into these mountings—we might be able to trigger ignition with it. We're going to have a bottling problem though. I'll know if it's possible when the design study is through cooking."

"How long do you think it will take?"

"There's no telling, Captain. But I've got the lads tooling up in the shop so they'll be ready to go as soon as we get the word."

"Right. Keep on it. Kirk out." Kirk switched to a new channel. "All units, Kirk here. Go to Condition Red. Repeat, go to Condition Red. Alert status. Stand by."

He turned to Riley, "Are you ready?"

"Yes, sir."

"All right, let's see what you've got."

Riley grinned. "Yes, sir!" He removed a small shining sphere from a case of them on the floor and activated it. It floated out of his hands, an aura of light forming around it. The aura swelled and grew brighter. A high-pitched humming sound began, the tone dropping as the field of light expanded, taking on hue and shape. A six-legged something was inflating like a balloon. It was colored pink and purple—no, yellow and orange—no, blue and green—

Kirk shuddered and looked away. "That's not too silly, is it Spock?"

"Too silly? How should *I* know?"

The humming had lowered in pitch to become an almost uncomfortable rumble. The big balloon-creature's head *galoomphed* around to look at Kirk; its long salami-tail swinging around the other way, bumping noisily into the wall. The prowler blinked its big moist eyes and said, "Coeurl?" in a voice surprisingly liquid and almost effeminate. "Coeurl? Coeurl?"

"That's a prowler?"

"That's a prowler." Riley stepped up to the illusion and said, "Command: *Prowl!*. Activate."

"Coeurl," said the prowler, nodding to nuzzle Riley wetly, then it turned and lumbered down the corridor. "Coeurl? Coeurl?" it called as it flubbered into the gloom.

On and on the prowler coeurled, until finally it disappeared into the murk of distance.

Kirk looked at Riley. "Good job, Lieutenant. Uh—where is it going now?"

"Oh, it'll find its own way up to the upper levels. All of the toys have been programmed with a map of the *Wanderer*. They'll go straight up the drop-chutes, that being the quickest way—some of them will be coming up through the same hole Captain Frost dropped Katwen and I. If we release now, the first ones will be there in ten minutes."

"Right. Do it."

"Yes, sir!" Riley grinned. "It'll be a pleasure." He motioned to the others; they began taking the rest of the shining spheres out of the box and activating them. The corridor began to fill with prowlers. And growlers. And bears.

"Chartreuse bears?" asked Kirk.

"And lavender too. We have all different colors. Whoops! Watch out for that one—"

That one was a looping purple python, spiral-striped with blue fringe.

"You don't think you might have gone a little overboard, do you, Riley?"

"Oh no, sir. Not at all."

"Oh. Good."

Riley looked momentarily startled. "You don't think it's too much, do you, sir?"

"Ahem," Kirk said into his fist. He kept his face straight. "No, no. Of course not. The whole idea is to—ah—disconcert the people of the upper levels. This should certainly do that. Don't you agree, Spock?"

"Indubitably."

A few moments more and the last of the prowlers, growlers, bears, boas, and bandersnatchi had galumphed and galoshed, babbled, clucked, clawed, and slithered their way down the corridors or up the shafts, and the lower levels were silent again.

"Is that it?" Kirk took a breath.

"Yes, sir."

"Good. Let's go!"

They rode upward through an access-tube. A vertical conveyor-belt ran the length of the tube, studded with hand-and-footholds. The boarding team had attached their own power-packs to the ancient linear-induction motors. The machinery squealed and whined and occasionally sparked, but the belt ran upward.

The top of the shaft was sealed.

"Can we cut through it?"

Spock scanned the dull gray surface with his tricorder. "We *can* cut through it," he said. "But it'll take several weeks to accomplish. The shaft has been completely plugged by several hundred feet of foamed concrete."

"Terrific," said Kirk. "Spock? You have the map. Is there another shaft?"

Spock shook his head. "I suggest we go around, Captain. If we take this tunnel aft, there's an access chute that should take us all the way up to the core. Captain Gomez confirms it's clear. We can follow the core space forward and come *down* on the upper levels from the central axis space."

Kirk frowned unhappily. He flipped open his communicator. "Scotty, status report."

"Aye, Captain—it's a mess all right. We can do it, but it's going to take hours. Perhaps days."

"All right, keep on it." He switched channels and contacted the other two boarding teams trying to reach the upper levels. They were experiencing the same problem. Their access chutes had also been plugged.

Abruptly, he thought of something else. "Riley—your toys! You'd better put them on hold. We're not going to want them working until just before we break through."

"Yes, sir." Riley flipped open his own communicator and punched through a code signal.

"This isn't working out as I expected," Kirk said. "Spock, you and I are going to beam back. We'll keep the teams moving inward. As long as the transporter can focus on any given communicator, we can join whichever team has the best chance of getting through. Riley, you take your men aft and try the access chute there. Contact me when you get to the top." He flipped open his communicator. "*Enterprise*. Two to beam over."

38

Back on the bridge, Kirk requested status reports from all his section chiefs. The situation was unchanged—stalled in all departments.

Kirk punched up McCoy. "Bones, what's the medical situation?"

The doctor's face peered sourly from the big screen. "It's terrible over here, Jim. We've got a whole population suffering from the long-term effects of specific malnutrition. But its roughest on the children, Jim. This isn't something that a little chicken soup is going to straighten out. We're going to need a vigorous program of long-range rehabilitation. That girl, Katwen, is a real godsend with the little ones."

"Is there anything you need?"

McCoy shook his head. "We're all right on supplies. And there are more than enough willing hands. This isn't a rabble. These people know how to work. But it's the cultural shock I'm most concerned about. To them, we're—like magicians."

"Aliens from another world?" Kirk suggested.

McCoy nodded at the *apt*ness of the comparison. "They're a little bit overawed by us. That's stage one. At stage three, they'll start resenting our technology and the superior abilities it gives us. At stage five, they'll go to impatience, backlash, and possible violence."

"I think we have a little time before that happens, Bones."

"I agree, Jim. But you'd better understand that it makes them uncomfortable to have to relinquish any kind of control to another party—even when it's demonstrably to their own ultimate advantage."

"I understand the situation."

"You're going to have to show some progress, Jim. You've made promises and they're expecting results. I can't demonstrate immediate results. It takes as long to cure low-level starvation as it did to get there in the first place. So it's up to you."

"It usually is," Kirk agreed grimly. He touched the arm of the chair. "Kirk out."

He swiveled to face his Communications Officer. "Uhura—did you ever send that subspace signal to Riley's tricorder?"

"Yes, sir—but the responses were incoherent—and then Riley came back, so it wasn't necessary to continue."

"I have an idea, Uhura—if we could get either that tricorder or that communicator operative, we could beam a crew directly through. Can you work on it?"

"It may take a while—it's not just a problem of coding and recalibration; there's the signal phase, the axis of transmission, and the fact that the focus is moving also complicates the process."

"Then you'd better get started right away," said Kirk. "Hadn't you?"

"Yes, Captain." She swiveled back to her console, already calling up the problem on her board.

Kirk sat silently for a moment. Absent-mindedly, he bit at the knuckle of his right hand. Abruptly, he hit the communicator button on the chair arm. "Scotty? I have a question for you."

"Aye, Captain?"

"We still have a transporter module in that upper-level farm, don't we? The one where Riley first met the girl?"

"Aye, we do—oh, I see. Can we beam our boarding parties through there?"

"Yes, why not? We seem to be stalled every other way."

There was silence from the communicator while Scotty considered the question. "It's the distance that bothers me, Captain," he said finally. "With the access tubes, we would have come out right by the control room. There wouldna been time for resistance. If we go in through the farms, we'll have to pay for every meter gained. And it's their territory, and they'll have the high ground."

"Um," said Kirk. "I knew there was a good reason."

"Still," added Scotty. "If we have to, it's not impossible."

Kirk grunted an acknowledgment. He asked, "What's the status of your situation there?"

"We're making some progress, Captain. But we're still a long way away from bringin' even the first of these beauties on line. Despite the best intentions of Gomez's men, they're in a terrible state. It's a sin, Captain, to let such fine machinery fall into such condition."

"I know, Mr. Scott—but these people have had other things on their mind. Kirk out." He allowed himself a gentle smile of empathy. Scotty's perspectives were occasionally . . . narrowed by his own specific concerns.

Kirk pondered his problem one more time. He stabbed another button. "Mr. Kyle, how many transporter coordinating modules have you got on the *Wanderer?*"

"We've got seventeen modules in place. We also have forty-three communicators and tricorders aboard the vessel in the hands of various *Enterprise* personnel."

"Is it possible," Kirk asked, "to coordinate all those separate point-sources as a network? Knowing the design of the *Wanderer,* can we then extrapolate a position within that network and beam through a probe which, if the landing site is viable, can then function as a coordinator?"

"It sounds good, Captain, and we've been tinkering with just that problem for some time. Mr. Spock suggested it last night, but—" Kirk looked at Spock, mildly surprised; Spock looked impassively back. "—the problem is that the vessel is spinning, and she's got too much heavy metal in her hull. That tends to scramble certain phase relationships within the beam. Even if we do have a precise fix, the lack of a coordinator makes it next to impossible to reintegrate the delta relationships, and those are the primary controllers."

"I understand." Kirk signed out. He drummed his fingers on the chair arm thoughtfully. When the communicator bleeped, he answered it almost automatically. "Kirk here."

"Riley, sir. We're at the top—and you'll never believe what we've discovered!"

"We're on our way—" He was already out of his chair. "Spock, let's go."

39

By the time Kirk and Spock beamed over, Riley and his team had already cut through. The Captain and his First Officer materialized in a small room in front of a very wide open door. Bouncing lightly on his feet, Kirk noted how light the simulated gravity was this close to the axis of the vessel.

On the other side of the door, there was twilight. A cold brisk wind whistled softly in the gloom.

"Here," said Riley, handing Kirk a pair of goggles. "You'll need these."

Kirk frowned and took the instruments without putting them on. He stepped through the open door.

For a moment, he was disoriented.

He was standing on a hillside, underneath a starlit sky. The wind plucked at his shirt. Spock stepped up quietly beside him.

They listened to the darkness. Kirk glanced around slowly. Behind them was a silhouette of light, the door in the hillside that they had stepped out of. Before them, in the distance, was a feeble glow—it was hidden by an intervening range of hills.

Kirk took a deep breath, then another. "Smell that, Spock? Earth. Soil. Water. Rain. And listen—is that a stream?"

"It sounds like it."

Something hooted softly in the distance.

Kirk remembered he was holding a pair of nightviewers. He lifted the goggles to his eyes.

And looked.

It took a moment for his eyes to focus.

And even when they did, he had trouble resolving the image. The lines of perspective were all wrong—

no, different than he was used to. Instead of stretching evenly toward the distance, they curved up overhead.

They were in a gigantic cave—

—a twilight world—

The landscape was circular. Hills, mountains, streams, trees—

Intellectually, Kirk knew he was on the inside of a massive cylinder, but emotionally he hadn't grasped the reality of it—until now.

"This is their wilderness," he whispered. He offered the viewers to Spock.

Spock shook his head. "I don't need them. Not just a wilderness, Captain—a preserve, a farm, a reminder of home, a test lab for new environments, a recreation area, a park—perhaps even, an escape."

Kirk put the viewers back up to his eyes. "Look—over there—mountains. And across the river, a desert."

"Fascinating," remarked Spock. "They have simulated a wide variety of landscapes and ecologies. The rivers are natural barriers." He pointed. "See, you can follow that one tributary for quite some distance. From here, it seems to go through three separate areas. Probably, there are more areas on the other side of the mountains. I'm sure that they would have used part of this core space to simulate the environment of any world they planned to colonize, although its primary purpose must have been as a functioning memory bank of genetic material."

They were silent a moment, then Spock asked thoughtfully, "Captain, do you smell anything?"

Kirk sniffed. "No, why? Do you?"

"No," said Spock. "And that's unusual. We should be smelling plants here. Of all kinds." He bent to examine the tufted growth on the ground beneath their feet. "It's a fungus." He unstrapped his tricorder and studied its screen. "A twilight growth, it takes most of its nourishment from the moisture in the air. Stronger light levels would probably destroy it—" He stopped, realizing.

Kirk caught it too. "This is a desert, Spock. When the lights went out, they went out all over the world. And the world died." Standing there in the darkness, Kirk could taste the bitterness of the words.

"This answers the question of what happened to their farms, Captain."

Kirk grunted. "Let's get out of here." He stepped back into the lighted room.

Spock followed.

Riley was studying a portable monitor. He looked up as Kirk entered. "Did you notice that glow, sir? We've sent some probes forward to discover the source of it." He offered Kirk the monitor. "It's a small settlement. Some farming. The lights are portable units. One of the other probes shows the glow-plates on the central axis to be almost completely inactive. Whatever lumens they're putting out just aren't strong enough to be seen."

Kirk nodded thoughtfully. "Lock down one of those probes and we can use it as a transporter focus. We'll beam our boarding team forward and enter through that settlement. They won't be expecting us to come in from above—"

40

The boarding team materialized on a shadowed hill-side overlooking a small bright valley. The slopes below were patterned into colored squares of crops, and surrounded by tall towers supporting banks of glaring lights.

"An oasis of light in a dark wilderness," Kirk mused. "It looks too vulnerable."

"It is undoubtedly well defended," agreed Spock. "We are probably not the first invaders who have tried coming in through this route."

"That's the problem. The lower-level tribes have had generations to try every available route. The upper-level people have had an equal length of time to develop every possible defense."

Stokely and Omara were already surveying the installation. The other members of the team had started spreading out into a skirmish line. Kirk tapped Riley's elbow. "Get your toys into position. As soon as we find an entrance, let them go."

"Yes, sir."

Kirk checked the positions of his team, and signaled them to begin advancing.

Kirk looked to Spock. The Vulcan Science Officer had his tricorder set for long-range scan. He looked up, "It appears to be deserted, Captain."

"Let's hope it stays that way."

They skidded down the grassy slope. This close to the single source of light in the core-space, the hills were covered with yellowish grass. The blades were wide and fragile. The footsteps of the crewmembers crushed into the growth like wounds.

At the bottom of the slope was a shallow stream. It meandered deliberately through the fields.

"Looks like we're going to have to get our feet wet," Kirk sighed. He signaled his troops to ford the brook. Fortunately, it was only a few meters wide.

Riley was the first man up the opposite side. He took three paces forward and then—

—fell flat on his face.

"What the—!?!! Something tripped me."

Kirk and Spock came up cautiously. Spock switched on his flashbeam and held it low to the ground. Very faintly, a shimmering line appeared, hanging in the air.

"Monofilament?" asked Riley, rubbing his bruised shins.

"Not likely. Else, it would have cut you off at the legs," said Spock. "However, I believe you have activated the alarm system, Lieutenant."

Riley stood up quickly, unstrapping his phaser.

"Right," said Kirk. He glanced behind, checking that the rest of the team was out of the water. Spock was still angling his beam along the wire for them. They stepped over it carefully.

"Phasers set for stun," Kirk ordered. "And watch your step."

They began moving across the field, through low ranks of yellow-leafed plants. "Tubers," noted Spock. "One of the best protein sources possible." He bent, broke a leaf off one of the plants, and sniffed it. He tasted it carefully. "The leaves are edible too. I suspected they would be. With such a limited growing space, every part of the plant must be usable." Spock dropped the rest of the leaf back to the ground.

Kirk grinned at him. "If you don't finish your salad, Mr. Spock, no dessert."

"I beg your pardon, Captain?"

"Never mind. What do you think that installation over there might be?"

Spock peered, then focused his tricorder on it. "I believe, Captain, that you have just found the entrance to the upper levels."

Spock stopped suddenly—as if he had *heard* something. He turned around slowly, cocking his head.

"Spock, what is it?"

"I don't know—"

Something was flickering above them—

They turned to look, wondering.

Fireflies?

Bright pinpoints of light were dropping toward them from the top of the mountain ahead.

Kirk held out a hand to Riley, who put the night-viewers into them almost automatically. Spock was already focusing his tricorder.

The points of light were close enough now, resolving into a flock—

"Birds?" asked Riley.

"Winged men—?" said Kirk.

"Flying machines. We should have expected it in this low gravity," answered Spock.

And even as they spoke, the first spears started falling among them, thudding into the soft earth with hard snapping sounds.

"Scatter!" shouted Kirk. He fired his phaser upward—and his target exploded in a ball of orange fire.

"What the—? Spock?"

"It's the plastic in their wings. It's unstable. Something in the beam ignites it," answered Spock.

The flaming debris was falling—slanting—toward the ground just ahead of them. The flyer's screams disappeared into the crackling of the framework collapsing around him.

Kirk held his fire uncertainly. He didn't want to kill these men—or women—he couldn't tell—he just wanted to *stop* them. The simulated-gravity here was light. A fall wouldn't kill them, though it might injure them a little, but their flying harnesses and wings would incinerate them.

But the spears were still falling. Behind him, a crewman screamed in agony as one of the missiles pierced his thigh.

"Should we fire?" cried Riley. Three flyers swooped overhead, dropping what looked like water-balloons. They smacked wetly into the ground, releasing rank clouds of evil-smelling gas.

Kirk bit his lip, made a decision, and fired off three quick shots. There were screams from the flyers as their wings ignited.

"Hold your fire!" Kirk ordered. He stood up, squinting through the smoke and gas to see if the other flyers were veering off. They weren't—

"Captain, that's *gas*—"

Kirk coughed harshly. "I can smell, Spock—" He set his phaser for scatter-focus and incinerated the nearest cloud of it, then tight-focused the beam again and phased the gas-bomb itself out of existence. The other members of the boarding team were doing the same.

"Captain—" Spock pointed with his phaser. "Look—"

Another wing of flyers was dropping toward them from the mountaintop.

Kirk said a word. Spock looked at him, surprised.

"We're going to have to withdraw. We can't get in without killing them all. And that's too high a price to pay. There's got to be a better way—"

And then suddenly, there was light.

Not just the lights from the farm towers, but dawn—a pervading glow that seemed to fill the world with mist. And it was getting brighter. It was turning into daylight, bright and glaring—

The flyers stopped their attacks, circling confusedly overhead. Two of them collided and tumbled helplessly toward the slope of the hill. Because of the rotation of the *Wanderer,* they fell sideways.

Kirk flipped open his communicator, "Scotty, what's going on?"

"We've just brought the first of the fusion plants back on line, Captain—and we've got an uncontrolled power-drain. I don't know where it's goin'—"

"I do. The lights just came on in the core-space." Kirk squinted against the glare, stunned by the enormity of the vista before him. The world curved off into the distance. The horizon was a distant circle.

"I was just goin' to call you, Captain. Whoever shut down these fusion plants also sabotaged the control networks. Aye, and that's not all—we've got lights comin' on all over the ship."

"Captain," said Spock. "The flyers are withdrawing."

"Scotty, keep those lights on. If you can."

"Aye, Captain. We have to. We're patching in a monitor now so we can install our own controls, but it's going to take a while. Heaven knows what demons we'll unleash when we bring the other plants on-line."

"Never mind that now. Just keep working." Kirk readjusted his communicator. "*Enterprise,* we've got an injured man. Prepare to pick him up. And pick up the other boarding parties and set them down with us. We're going in." Kirk snapped his communicator shut. "Riley, activate your toys. We're going to need all the confusion we can get."

41

The entrance to the upper levels was deceptively simple. A set of stairs led down into the ground to a sealed door.

The door was locked.

Of course.

Kirk nodded to Riley, who set his phaser for needle-beam and began cutting through.

After a moment, he paused and said, "It's pretty thick, Captain. This may take a while."

"I'm getting used to it, Lieutenant. Keep on." Kirk turned to Spock. "Have you noticed, every time we come to a door in this ship, not only is it locked, sealed or otherwise defended; but just about the time we do get it open, I get called away."

Spock nodded. "Coincidence often pretends to form patterns, Captain."

"It's still very frustrating." Kirk turned his attention back to Riley's progress. The Lieutenant wasn't even halfway through the job.

Kirk sighed impatiently, then turned to study the landscape around him. It was magnificent—and terrifying. Far above, he could make out the pattern of another river as it etched its way through an ochre desert. Except for the patches of green surrounding the farming area, the rest of the core-space was a disheartening vista of red and yellow earth, black hills and brown deserts. What vegetation had managed to survive was mostly lichen, fungus, and faded grass.

"This is their paradise," Kirk said sadly. "This is what they were withholding from the rebels of the lower levels."

"It became necessary to destroy the world in order to save it," noted Spock.

"I beg your pardon?"

"It's a quote from your Earth history," Spock said.

Kirk was silent a moment. Then he said, "Human beings have not had as much time as Vulcans have had to learn . . . rationality."

Spock noted thoughtfully, "Nor have you had as much *need*. Remember, Captain—the Vulcan culture is *compulsively* rational because the Vulcan race is notoriously hot-blooded. In a manner of speaking."

Kirk glanced at his First Officer. "I've often wondered, Spock, if our two races might be heading in very different directions. Vulcans tend to control—almost *suppress*—all sense of emotion. Human beings try to learn how to *use* their feelings instead. By human standards, a Vulcan is emotionally retarded."

"Quite so, Captain. And there is much to be said for both attitudes. My own—ah, feeling—," Spock chose the word deliberately, "—is that one must control one's emotions *before* one can use them."

Kirk accepted Spock's counter-argument with good grace. He didn't have an answer for it right now. He'd let it percolate for a while in the back of his mind though. He might come up with a response later on.

Riley called then, "I'm almost through, Captain."

"Good—"

Kirk's communicator bleeped.

He unstrapped it, flipped it open, and said, "Kirk here."

It was McCoy. "Jim, we've got a problem."

"What is it, Bones?"

"Light—all the lights are back on in the lower levels—and it's too intense for these people. They've lived their whole lives in darkness, and now they're as paralyzed as if they've all gone blind. Their eyes can't function in light this intense."

"Can you do something for them, Bones?"

"I don't know what there is I can do—Gomez is screaming betrayal, Jim—you'd better get down here right away."

Behind him, Kirk could hear Riley saying, "There it goes! We're through!"

Kirk exhaled softly. "I knew it." To McCoy, he said, "I'm on my way." He readjusted his communicator. *Enterprise*. Transporter room—"

42

Gomez's office had been draped with canvas. Even so, the glare from the glow-plates filled the room with a diffuse brown glow.

The short dark man had an angry expression. "I am vulnerable, Kirk! My people are unable to move because they cannot see!"

Kirk held up a hand to interrupt. He stepped over to a wall and peeled back a piece of the cloth. The glare from the glow-plate was bright even for his eyes. "I see your problem." He flipped open his communicator.

"Scotty—is there any way you can shut off the lights in the lower levels?"

Scotty's voice was frantic. "Aye, there is—but we haven't found it yet. Sorry, Captain—but whoever mangled the control network up here did a marvelous job—"

"Terrific." Kirk flipped his communicator shut.

Gomez stepped forward and peered up into Kirk's face, "What are you going to do?"

"I don't know yet. Let me finish assessing the situation—"

"There isn't time. Two of my scouts report that a raiding party from the upper levels has already discovered that the lights are on all over the *Wanderer*. It's only a matter of time."

Kirk flipped open his communicator again. "*Enterprise*. Beam over two security squads to the lower levels. Arm them with phaser rifles."

"Acknowledged," came back Uhura's response.

Kirk flipped the communicator shut and looked down at Gomez. "That should take care of your immediate problem."

"Kirk, you don't understand. The reason that we have been able to survive on the lower levels for so long is that we are divided into five separate tribes. No single tribe ever knows where more than two of the other tribes are at any one time. Each tribe shifts its position every three days. Tribes keep in touch through runners who are considered members of both tribes. You don't have enough men to protect five tribes, do you? No—I thought not—and we have no way to warn the other tribes what is happening. *All* of us are vulnerable now."

Kirk thought for a second. "But they haven't sent down any attack squads yet, have they? Can you post lookouts? Wherever they send raiding parties down, we can put men in to stop them."

"It's no good, Kirk. They can put men into the lower levels almost anywhere. They're right above us. Don't you understand—we live with them always above us wherever we are. All they have to do is open one of their hatches and come straight down!"

Kirk turned away to think. He noticed McCoy staring at him, with that wide-eyed concerned look of his. And Chapel too. And who was that—? Oh, Specks, the historian. He was polishing his glasses thoughtfully. Beside him, Katwen stood stiffly. An idea was beginning to suggest itself to Kirk—

His communicator bleeped. "Now what—?" He flipped it open. "Kirk here."

"Hello—hello—am I working this thing right?" An unfamiliar voice came out of the speaker.

"That's Dr. Hobie!" said Katwen. "He's head of Captain's Science Council! On upper levels!"

"He must have Riley's communicator," said Kirk. He opened the channel. "Hello—can you hear me? Dr. Hobie? This is Captain James T. Kirk of the starship *Enterprise*—"

"Hello—listen to me—is not much time—Captain Frost has discovered that the lights are back on in the lower levels. Is calling it a miracle. Is calling for a holy war. This is his chance to wipe out the devils of hell."

"Dr. Hobie—listen to me—can you keep that channel open?"

"Uh—I can't—they're already massing. Everybody who can carry a weapon is being armed. If they find me—"

"All right—look, there's a red button. Press it, please. That switches on the automatic transponder—do that—Dr. Hobie?"

There was no reply.

Kirk switched channels quickly. "Uhura—did you monitor that?"

"Yes, sir—and while he was on, I activated the automatic transponder from here. We've got a focus now, Captain. And it's very close to where the control room is supposed to be located."

"Uhura, I could kiss you!"

"Captain!"

"Uh—figuratively speaking, that is—of course."

"Of course," she said, but there was disappointment in her voice.

Gomez grabbed Kirk's arm then. "What are you doing? He said there's an attack massing! They could be down here in minutes!"

"Hold it for a moment, Captain—" Kirk pulled his

arm away. He switched channels again. "Scotty—you can't shut the lights down, right?"

"Aye, Cap'n. I can't shut them down."

"Can you increase their intensity?"

"Now why would you want to do that?"

"Can you do it, Scotty?"

"Aye—by increasing the output of this plant—it'll be easy enough. There's no limit to how much light those glow plates'll put out—except, of course, the melting point of the plate."

"Good. Now listen—I need some kind of goggles—filters—for our boarding teams—"

"Oh, I get it—Captain, that's a beautiful idea. I'll get right on it."

"You've got fifteen minutes."

"Won't take half that long—" And he was gone.

Kirk turned to Gomez. "Get your people all together. Get them into some room where the glow-plates are covered. Have them shield their eyes. We'll give your runners some filters to wear over their eyes. Have them warn the tribes you can reach. Can you do that?"

"What are you planning to do?"

"You've seen how your people react to too much light. We're going to push the light levels of this ship up even higher—so that even the people of the upper levels will be blinded! Now, go—get your runners!"

Kirk opened his communicator again. "*Enterprise,* prepare to recall all boarding parties and put them down again at new coordinates. Uhura has the focus. One to beam over now—energize—"

43

Finally—*at last*—the pieces were beginning to fall into place.

Kirk accepted a pair of blast-goggles from Scotty and stepped back up onto the transporter platform with Riley, Stokely, Omara, and Spock. The second and third teams were lined up in the corridor, waiting.

"Are you ready, Scotty?"

"Aye, sir. I am." Scotty was beaming proudly.

"All right, let's go."

Scotty stepped over to the transporter console and transmitted the order to his crew. He looked up. "The lights are getting brighter, sir."

Kirk looked to Spock. "Maybe this time, I'll get where I'm going." He turned forward. "Energize—"

—and they were materializing into whiteness. Hastily, Kirk slipped the goggles over his eyes.

They were in a chamber of some kind—a laboratory? Never mind, it didn't matter. Riley's communicator and tricorder were in a bell jar on a workbench. The handphaser was not with them.

They spread out in a circle with their phasers ready. Spock was scanning with his tricorder. Behind them, the second squad was already materializing. They stepped outward too.

As soon as the third team beamed in, Spock indicated a set of double doors at the end of the room. "That way, Captain."

Even through the blast-goggles, everything was white. The corridors were white. Their clothes were white. The people who stumbled past them, hands over their eyes, were so pale as to be cadaverous. The walls were warm to the touch.

And in the middle of all this whiteness, something orange and red and purple lumbered down the corridor toward them.

"Coeurl?" It asked. "Coeurl? Coeurl?" It stopped, cocked its head, blinked, coeurled again, then half-shrugged and—keeping its six legs planted where they were—it *rotated* its head and tail clockwise around its body to face in the opposite direction. And coeurled off down the hallway.

"If that didn't demoralize them, Spock, nothing will."

"It certainly disconcerts me, Captain." He pointed. "We go up here now."

They raced up a long curving ramp—skidding to a

stop, face to face with a squadron of twenty upper-level warriors. They were strung out in a line against the wall, moving slowly toward them. Each man had one hand over his eyes and one hand on the wall.

The lead man in the line saw them—somehow—and began fumbling with his rifle.

Kirk didn't wait to see what he would do—he fired his phaser. Again. Again. And again. The entire line of men collapsed, stunned into unconsciousness. "Tiberius," he said. "Come on, Spock. Which way now?"

Spock pointed and they continued on up the curving ramp, turning left at the top and rushing forward through a deserted lobby, a narrow corridor, an observation theater and—

—a dead end.

"Uh—Spock?"

"I'm sorry, Captain, but according to the design plans provided by Specks, the entrance to the control room should be right here."

Kirk sighed. "I should have expected it. One more place I can't get in. It must have been sealed off somehow."

"Or disguised," suggested Spock.

Kirk began examining the wall closely. It was patterned with a close-set series of vertical slats. If there was a seam between any of the slats, it didn't show.

Kirk stepped back, frowning. He raised his phaser as if to fire, then lowered it again. "Better not. I might damage something we may need."

"Very intelligent, Captain."

"Thank you, Spock."

Abruptly, Kirk noticed something—a solitary drifter was creeping along the base of the wall. As he watched, it leapt away sideways.

Kirk stepped over and picked up the small balloon. He replaced it against the wall. Once more, it crept along the floor, moved by the air currents of the room. Once again it reached the same vertical slat and leaped away. Kirk pressed his face close. He sniffed. "Spock? What do you think?"

Spock put his face close and sniffed also. "A draft from somewhere, perhaps?"

"Probably, the original seal was damaged when the

camouflage was added." They stepped back and Kirk refocused his phaser to a needle beam. Using both hands to steady his aim, he sketched a quick line down the seam. It smoked and melted and peeled back to reveal the outline of another door behind the false wall. Quickly, Kirk finished cutting away the rest of the camouflage.

As soon as it was clear, Spock stepped up and began punching an emergency override program into the locks.

Kirk flipped open his communicator. "Scotty, you can turn down the glow-plates now. We're at the control room. We should be secure in a few moments." He waited for confirmation, then turned to the crewmen waiting behind them. "Riley, take charge here. Split into three teams and cover all accesses to this area. Don't let anyone through except on my orders or Spock's."

"Yes, sir."

Kirk flipped open his communicator again. "*Enterprise,* prepare to beam over the auxiliary bridge crew."

Uhura's voice came back. "They're still training on the mockup, sir."

"Never mind that. In about two minutes, we're going to put them to work on the real thing."

"Aye aye, sir!"

Kirk disconnected and turned to Spock. "How're you coming?"

Spock didn't look up from what he was doing. "The control codes seem to have been changed. The override doesn't work." Spock scanned the lock-panel with his tricorder again and frowned impassively—he raised one eyebrow. "Logic demands an alternate solution." He stepped away from the door, unstrapped his phaser, adjusted the beam, and began blasting a hole into the heavy metal.

Pointedly, Kirk did not say anything.

When the door fell open, still smoking around its edges, Kirk jumped through, followed by Spock, Stokely, and Omara.

The light levels were normal here. They pulled their blast goggles off and looked around in awe. The control room was *huge.*

They were in a vast chamber with a horseshoe bank of equipment in the center. Three rows of consoles faced a diorama of screens. And in the center was a huge swivel-chair. As it spun around, they came face to face with—

"Captain Frost, I presume?"

"You are the pretender, Kirk?" Frost was holding Riley's missing hand-phaser, aimed straight at Kirk's belly.

Kirk spread his hands wide and mustered up a friendly smile. "I was when I came in. Captain James *Tiberius* Kirk of the starship *Enterprise.* At your service." He inclined his head in a polite bow.

"You will drop your weapons, please—?"

"You'd better do as he says," said a new voice. Kirk turned around to see—

"Dr. Hobie?"

"Captain Kirk— please, drop your weapon." Hobie was holding a weapon of his own, a very lethal-looking handgun, but his voice was apologetic.

Kirk shrugged and dropped his phaser to the carpeted floor. "Do as he says," he called to the men behind him. He noticed out of the corner of his eye that Spock was activating the transponder on his tricorder as he set it down. Uhura would be getting all of this on the *Enterprise* bridge.

"Captain Frost—," Kirk began; he was holding his hands not *up,* but *wide.* "This ship is in serious danger."

"*I* am the Captain here. I will decide when the ship is in danger. And it is my decision that we are in greater danger from those who presume to authority without knowledge."

"I couldn't agree more," said Spock.

"Spock, please." Kirk opened his mouth to speak again, but Frost cut him off.

"Is heard story from your Kevin Riley. Is not need to hear it again. Is come up here to look at controls. Is find some interesting things—" He pointed to one of the monitor screens. "Is that your world, Kirk?" On the screen was the *Enterprise.*

"That's my ship, yes."

"Is very small. Is silly looking. Badly designed."

Kirk exchanged a glance with Spock. Incongruously, he thought of Scotty, and was grateful that his Chief Engineer was not here to hear this.

Frost said, "My Science Officer, Dr. Hobie, has interesting theory. Ship is obviously a childish construct. Tell them, Hobie."

Hobie looked uncomfortable, but he said, "Is my opinion that a vessel that small—comparatively speaking, of course—could not possibly contain the resources to bring a human crew this far into space; at least, not without significant advances in technology. And it is impossible that an Earth vessel could catch up with us without faster-than-light capability."

"So, you see," continued Frost. "That leaves us with two possibilities. Either you have faster-than-light travel or you are aliens. But faster-than-light travel is impossible—that's why the *Wanderer* was sent on this journey—and if you were aliens, you wouldn't be so obviously *human*. We examined your Kevin Riley *very carefully*. And you speak English, of a sort. Your so-called ship is obviously just a . . . a childish construct and not a ship at all. So, the only conclusion left to us, Kirk the Pretender, is that this is some vast, impossible hoax."

Kirk opened his mouth to speak, but Frost cut him off again.

"No, I don't have to listen to you. You have to listen to me. Surely, it must gall you to see how my superior intellect can so easily dismantle your carefully worked out plan, clever as it is." Unexpectedly, Frost *smiled*. "Now, then—it is obvious to me that the savages on the lower levels could not possibly have mounted a hoax this elaborate. Therefore, this is some kind of coup—*long-planned*—being mounted by my own political enemies on the upper levels. Oh, yes, I'm aware that there is an underground movement, with hidden farms and even occasionally, an unregistered child. Have long been watching for an alliance between the underground and the lower-level tribes—"

Kirk glanced at Spock. The man's logic was *baroque*. "Do you follow this, Spock? I think he's losing me."

"I follow it, Captain. But it's rough going."

Kirk said, "Captain Frost—isn't it just barely possible that the *unlikely* explanation might have some truth to it? You have instruments here—can't you see the danger ahead?"

Frost said, "Is possible, there may be reason to change course of *Wanderer*. Is possibility only, I grant. But is more likely that changing course is only an excuse to justify your mutiny. But, even if possibility *is* true, it is decision that must be made by Captain." The hand-phaser wavered, then came back to center on Kirk's stomach again. Kirk eyed it uncomfortably, it was beginning to look bigger and bigger.

"Captain Frost, please listen to me—" Kirk kept his voice as calm as he could.

Frost shook his head. "I don't have to listen. I am Captain here. You are invader. If you truly are a captain, then you know laws and traditions of space. If you seize control from rightful captain of a ship, then you are mutineer and pirate. And I am legally justified in killing you."

"A pirate? Uh—"

"Precisely."

"Captain Frost—if we can *cooperate* with each other, it is to both our benefit. But if not—well, you may be able to kill me. But you will not be able to stop the inevitable. And the inevitable is that this ship is doomed—unless everyone aboard her cooperates for the common good."

"You speak of cooperation? You? Your men have already begun invading my vessel. You let your silly illusions growl up and down our corridors—fortunately, our disruptor pistols can easily disable your projecting devices. You pump up the light levels of our glow-plates. You fire upon my men. I have watched most of it from here. I have cameras. I have eyes. You incinerated my flyers—who were only trying to protect their fields. If you really mean cooperation, then you would not be mounting this mutiny. You and your men are zealots, terrorists, and madmen—you speak of common good and cooperation, yet your actions speak of tyranny. I have only done what I must to defend my people. That is my responsibility—and now you ask me to betray that responsibility because your self-righteous narrow-mindedness will not let you see any other solution."

Kirk nodded thoughtfully. *"I see your point.* All right, Captain Frost—you tell me. What would you have me do?"

"I would have your help in subduing the rebellious tribes who terrorize the lower levels of this ship, bring them back into the fold. Help me establish complete control over my vessel. And then we can discuss the direction of this ship as its builders intended it to be discussed."

Kirk dropped his hands to his sides and dropped into a nearby chair. "I'm sorry, Frost," he said conversationally. "That's not workable. We just don't have the time." It was a dangerous gambit, and Kirk knew it, but he had to somehow break the *adversary* relationship here. Spock and the others were watching him curiously.

Frost swiveled to face him directly. "And you dare to speak of cooperation?"

"Within reason, of course. I mean, let's face it—" Kirk kept his voice deliberately casual. "—we have to be logical about these things." Behind him, he could hear Mr. Spock's eyebrow rising straight up his forehead. He continued, *"You* have to make some compromises too. Wouldn't you agree the most important thing is to save the ship first?"

Frost looked as if he was amused by Kirk's presumptuousness. He said, "I find you charming—but there can be no compromise with treason—and your priorities are seriously disordered. First one must establish control over the ship before one can save it."

"Ah, there's the rub. I have control over the fusion engines. You have control over the bridge. You can't take my control from me. I can't take your control from you. One of us is going to have to trust the other."

"You are not as good a captain as you think, Kirk. You have never learned that you cannot trust anyone."

Kirk sighed. "You have never learned that a good captain *must* trust."

"And perhaps," said Frost, "that is the reason why we cannot cooperate. You are a fool."

"A pirate? A fool? Make up your mind." Kirk was feeling a bit impish. He swiveled to face Spock, deliberately turning his back on Frost. "I think this needs a second opinion. Spock?"

"Captain—" Spock looked about as apologetic as any Vulcan ever did—which is to say, not much. "It is really a case of six of one and half a dozen of the other—"

"Spock—?"

"Enough!" cried Frost. "All of you, up against the wall." He waved the hand-phaser meaningfully. "You too, fool!"

"Well, I guess that settles that—" Kirk rose slowly from his chair and—

—then all hell broke loose!

Suddenly, there were men in battle-jackets and helmets beaming in all over the control room! Frost stood up, whirling—*and his weapon started to sparkle with transporter effects*—

Frost panicked and fired!

The hand-phaser sparked—

—it was caught in the transporter effect!

And then it *imploded*—Frost was enveloped in flame.

The fireball whitened into brilliance—

—and collapsed with a sound like lightning. The shock knocked Kirk off his feet. The others dropped to the floor, flattening themselves against the glare. Intense heat washed over them.

And then there was silence.

Kirk was the first to look up.

Captain Frost was gone. Incinerated. There was only a light haze of ash to show where he had been—

He hadn't even had time to scream.

Hobie was screaming, "Don't anybody move!" He was pointing his pistol straight at Kirk.

Kirk stood slowly, holding his hands wide. He motioned to his security men. "Hold your fire!" He took a step forward, then another. "Dr. Hobie—you spoke to me on the communicator. You warned us about the attack that Captain Frost was going to send against the lower levels. You wanted to save lives."

"I wanted to believe in you, Kirk. I still do. But—"

The gun barrel wavered nervously. "—now I don't know if I can. All the time you were asking Frost to trust you, you were already betraying him. Perhaps, even now, you're planning to betray me."

Kirk said slowly, "Dr. Hobie, it's difficult to trust a man when he's pointing a gun at you."

Hobie looked at the weapon he was holding, then back to Kirk again. "You have a more advanced technology, Kirk, I recognize that. I believe your story. I believe your ship and your technology. The evidence is too overwhelming. But—answer me this—*what kind of a gun are you holding on me?* What are you going to do next?"

Kirk took a step sideways, slowly bent, and picked up Spock's tricorder. He held it up so Hobie could see what he was doing—and deliberately switched it off. "The *Enterprise* can't hear us or see us anymore. It's just between you and me, Hobie—you can trust me now, or you can pull the trigger."

Hobie shook his head. "That's a hollow gesture, Kirk. And we both know it."

Kirk agreed. "You're right. But I can't give you anything but gestures, right now. There are no guarantees with *trust*. You either trust or you don't. You can kill me now, Hobie—and probably one of my men here will stun you. Our weapons are all set for stun. Or, you can trust me. Either way, we're going to change the course of this vessel and try to save the lives of the people aboard her. But I'll tell you this—if we, the men and women of the *Enterprise,* have to do it by force, then it will break the spirit of your civilization. Your people will forever be ashamed of their heritage.

"On the other hand," Kirk said, "you can put that gun down and take charge of reuniting your people, helping us discover what changes were made in this ship since she left Earth's system. My Chief Engineer is good—but this vessel is just too big—and there's a very good chance he won't be able to bring all those engines back on-line in time. Your people, though—you have the knowledge—and you're head of the Science Council, Dr. Hobie; you know how to use it, and you have the authority. Your people will listen to you, and if your people can do the job, then there's no reason why my people should have to do it—by force or any other way. And what you regain, all of you living here on the *Wanderer,* is your pride in yourselves."

Hobie's expression was troubled as he listened to Kirk's words.

He said, "Kirk—this is all happening so fast—"

Kirk added, "Let me introduce you to someone who may be able to give you some . . . help?" Slowly, he opened his communicator and adjusted the channel. "McCoy. Would you let me speak to Gomez please?"

"Gomez? The *satan?"*

"Hardly," Kirk smiled gently.

The communicator barked abruptly, "Gomez here."

Kirk handed his communicator across to Hobie. "Talk to him."

"This is Dr. Hobie."

"Of the upper levels?"

"Yes."

"You helped save lives, sir. We are grateful."

"Yes. Uh—Gomez—"

"Captain Gomez. I hold the logbook. I am duly elected."

"Uh, Captain Gomez. We need to talk. You and I. Kirk says we must trust each other."

There was a moment's silence. Then, "You can trust Kirk."

"I know that. The question I need answered, Gomez, is this. Can I trust *you?"*

Gomez said, "Can *I* trust *you?"*

"We have the same problem, sir."

Gomez was silent again. Then, he said, "Each of the tribes has a logbook, Dr. Hobie. Each logbook has details of a different set of sabotages carried out against this ship."

Kirk and Spock exchanged a look. Gomez hadn't told them that. Of course, he would have needed something to bargain with—the man was no fool.

Hobie was saying, "If I guarantee your people food—and access to the core-space so you can start farms of your own—will you give me access to your logbook?"

"And knowledge?" asked Gomez. "Teachers? And

access to the ship's library? Including the forbidden tapes? And what about the other tribes? Are they included?"

"I—I can see that this is not going to be easy," Hobie admitted. "There is so much to be done."

Gomez answered, "Sir, we cannot continue to make war on each other forever."

"I know," Hobie said sadly. "In three years, this ship will die. Captain Frost could not read his own instruments, but I can. Captain Gomez, we *must* work together. We have no choice."

"Then Kirk was right."

"About that, yes, but—" Hobie sat down in a chair, putting his pistol down on a nearby console. "—Captain Gomez, hasn't it seemed to you that he and his crew have been mucking around all over the *Wanderer* without accomplishing anything? They just don't know what they're doing. If we combined our energies, do you think we might be able to demonstrate to them a few things about the way a vessel like this *should* be run?"

"I've been wanting to kick him out and take proper charge for some time now."

Kirk grinned at Spock. "Let me have your communicator," he said. Spock handed it over. Kirk opened a channel. "*Enterprise.* We're secure."

Scotty's voice came back. "Aye, Cap'n, but that was a close 'un. We've blown our monitron cells. The main transporter room will be out of commission for a while."

Kirk said, "Sure. Now when I *want* to beam back—"

"We'll be sending the auxiliary bridge crew over by the cargo transporter. We can pick you up then."

"I don't think they're going to be needed, Scotty. The locals seem to have the situation in hand—which is just as it *should* be."

Kirk switched off and turned to Spock. "Now, what's this about six of one and half a dozen of the other?"

Spock shrugged innocently. "It seemed an appropriate answer at the time."

Kirk shook his head. There was a saying in Starfleet: "Ask a Vulcan only what you *don't* want to know." It was more true now than it was the first time he had said it.

44

Riley found Katwen in a dirty room, surrounded by dirty children. She was telling them a story about a child who asked too many questions. The children were giggling nervously, as if still afraid to laugh out loud. And yet, their eyes shone.

"Katwen—?"

She looked up.

"I have to go back to the *Enterprise* now."

Katwen held up one hand to him in a "wait a moment" gesture. She said to the children, "Is must talk. Wait." She stepped outside into the corridor with him. "Is proud to know you, Kevin Riley."

"I don't know when we'll ever see each other again, Katwen."

She took his hands. "Is known that too. Is already miss you." She looked down at the hands she held in her own, then into his face again. She blinked and Riley could see the glisten of tears welling up in the corners of her bright blue eyes.

"Is something perhaps . . . not meant to be . . ." Riley managed to say. His throat was tight and the words just wouldn't come. "Is learned to care about you, Katwen."

"Care—?"

"Is like . . . love. Is beginning of love."

"Love," she repeated softly. "Of all the different things I know, love has not been one of them, Kevin Riley. Until now."

Riley clutched her hands suddenly. "Katwen—I asked Captain Kirk if I could stay here on the *Wanderer* as part of the transition team—so I would not have to leave you."

"Is possible?"

"Is not. Not yet. Perhaps not ever. I'm sorry."

"So am I."

They held each other then, for a long moment. He sniffed the warmth of her hair and she clasped his shoulders tightly.

"Teacher?" piped a shrill childish voice. "Is finish story now?"

Katwen broke away to look down at a dirty face, wide-eyed with curiosity and expectation. "Is finish story now," she smiled. "You go back in."

She turned to Riley and kissed him quickly. "Is always care, Kevin Riley." And then she was gone.

Riley stood in the corridor, listening for a moment, and then he unstrapped his communicator and signaled the *Enterprise* to beam him over.

45

Chekov looked glum. "There's good news, *Keptin,* and there's bad news."

James T. Kirk looked at his navigator warily. "Chekov, you're supposed to be the best. Are you telling me that you've . . . failed?"

Chekov looked insulted. And when he spoke, his accent was more pronounced than ever. *"Eef Meester Scott* had had those engines on-line before the thirteen days were up, I could have saved the *Wanderer* using her own engines entirely. But he didn't and I can't and that's the bad news."

Kirk leaned back in his chair. "Go on—"

"The good news is that I have figured out a way to *cheet."*

"Cheat?"

"Yes." Chekov looked proud. "Instead of trying to turn the *Wanderer* away from Ellison's variable, we're going to aim the ship straight for it."

"Straight for it?"

"Well, not exactly *straight* for it, but close enough. The ship will loop around the star, using its gravity for a slingshot effect. It will come out headed straight for Malcor's Pride. That's the good news."

Kirk smiled broadly. "That *is* good news. There's a colony on that planet already. They've been petitioning Starfleet for new colonists, and Starfleet has been wanting to grant their petition. There just haven't been the ships available. Let's get some subspace messages off. There's going to be some paperwork necessary to make it legal."

"Aye, *Keptin.*"

"Oh, and Chekov—"

"Sir?"

"Good job. Thank you."

"Thank you, sir."

Kirk looked around himself. The bridge of the *Enterprise* felt good then. A good place to be.

Lieutenant Riley stepped up beside him with a report to sign. "The *Wanderer* is secure, sir. Our transition crew is already beamed aboard, and they'll be staying with the ship until Starfleet can get another vessel out here to rendezvous. A full cultural mission is probably necessary."

"You're right, Lieutenant. I've already recommended same."

"Oh. And I thought I was doing pretty good—"

Kirk looked at the slender young man. "Kevin," he said, "you're doing fine. I've just had a little more experience with some of these things. That's all. Someday, I'll tell you the story of a certain Lieutenant Kirk and the—" He stopped himself. "Never mind. Maybe I won't tell you that story. By the way, did you ever catch that last prowler?"

"No, sir. It's transponder seems to have been disconnected. It was sighted this morning though, crossing one of the new farms in the core-space. It was still coeurling."

Kirk nodded. "Well, maybe they were ready for some new mythology on the *Wanderer*. The one about demons on the lower levels wasn't workable anymore."

"Yes, sir."

"Oh, Riley. One more thing—"

"Sir?"

"Did you make your farewells to Katwen yet?"

"Yes, sir."

Kirk looked fatherly. "I know how difficult these partings can be—"

"Uh, sir—while I, uh—liked her a lot—it really wouldn't have worked. She has her career—and I have mine—and, uh—"

"I understand perfectly, Lieutenant."

"Yes, sir. Thank you, sir." Riley stepped back, saluted and left the bridge.

Kirk glanced after him almost affectionately. He turned around to see Spock looking at him oddly. "Mr. Spock? Is something the matter?"

"No, Captain. It's just that—"

"Go on, Spock."

"Captain—I don't think the bridge of a Starfleet vessel is an appropriate place to discuss the mating habits of one's species."

"You're quite possibly right, Mr. Spock." Kirk coolly met the gaze of his Vulcan First Officer. "But that's one of the penalties we pay for being so emotional."

Spock said coolly, "Captain, it is immaterial to me what any human being chooses to do with his or her emotions." And then he added, "As long as you don't do it in the streets and frighten the horses."

"Right," grinned Kirk. "We'll remember that." Behind him, he could hear Lieutenant Uhura stifling her laughter.

Kirk swiveled forward. "Mr. Sulu, have there been any additional sightings of that Klingon ghost?"

"No, sir."

"Hm, maybe he's left the area. Are we secured?"

"Aye, aye, Captain."

"Good. Set a course for deep space station K-7. I could use a rest—"

ABOUT THE AUTHOR

DAVID GERROLD made his television writing debut with the now-classic "The Trouble With Tribbles" episode of the original *Star Trek* TV series. Since 1967, he has story-edited three TV series, edited five anthologies, and written two non-fiction books about television production (both of which have been used as textbooks), and over a dozen novels, three of which have been nominated for the prestigious Hugo and Nebula Awards.

His television credits include multiple episodes of *Star Trek, Tales From the Darkside, Twilight Zone, The Real Ghostbusters, Logan's Run,* and *Land of the Lost.*

His novels include *When H.A.R.L.I.E. Was One, The Man Who Folded Himself, A Matter for Men, A Day for Damnation,* and *A Rage for Revenge.* His short stories have appeared in most of the major science fiction magazines, including *Galaxy, If, Amazing,* and *Twilight Zone.*

Gerrold has also published columns and articles in *Starlog, Profiles, Infoworld, Creative Computing, Galileo, A-Plus,* and other science fiction and computing periodicals. He averages over two dozen lecture appearances per year, and also teaches screenwriting at Pepperdine University.

David Gerrold has completed working on the staff of *Star Trek: The Next Generation,* and is now preparing a new SF TV series for The Arthur Company and Universal Television.